TOGETHER AT LAST

WAR GIRL SERIES

MARION KUMMEROW

Together at Last, War Girl Series, Book 10

Marion Kummerow

ISBN Paperback 978-3-948865-07-8

This is a work of fiction. All characters, names, and places in this book exist only within the author's imagination. Any resemblance to actual persons or locations is purely coincidental.

Cover Design by http://www.StunningBookCovers.com

CONTENTS

READER GROUP

Marion's Reader Group

Sign up for my reader group to receive exclusive background information and be the first one to know when a new book is released.

http://kummerow.info/subscribe

CHAPTER 1: URSULA

Kleindorf, Germany, April 1945

Ursula Hermann picked up Eveline, her one-year-old daughter, and carried her out to the front yard. The sun kissed her cheeks on this beautiful April morning. She decided to enjoy five minutes of idle time with her daughter before she walked over to bring lunch to Aunt Lydia and the farmhands.

She sat down on the swing with Eveline, pushing off with her foot to set the swing in motion. A sigh escaped her throat and Eveline turned her head to look at her mother. The child had inherited Ursula's blonde hair, but the beautiful green eyes of her father, Tom.

"I'm so glad I have you, Evie," Ursula said, pressing a kiss on her daughter's hair. "You're the one bright spot to come out of this war. You and meeting your father." Thoughts of

Tom seeped into her mind and the tormenting worry about him almost knocked her off the swing. She had last seen him before she even knew she was pregnant, had never heard from him again. Not since he'd set foot on the merchant vessel bringing him to neutral Sweden. She only hoped that he'd managed to return to his home in England.

"He'll return after the war and find me. You'll see, Evie. And then we'll be a real family."

Evie cooed as if she understood her mother's words.

"We better bring Lydia and her helpers lunch. What do you think?" Being the only adult in the house all day, taking care of her daughter and her baby nieces Maria and Rosa, she missed conversation. Therefore, she had taken to talking to the children as if they were adults.

Ursula got up from the swing, tying Evie onto her back. She found Rosa, who was only six months older than Evie, still napping. Four-year-old Maria had climbed downstairs and was playing with a hand-me-down doll from her older sisters.

"Maria, come, we're bringing lunch to your mom and your siblings," Ursula said and picked up the heavy soup pot while she handed her niece spoons and bread to carry.

Together they walked the long, dusty road up to the field where Lydia was working. Her four oldest children and several women from Mindelheim, the town next to Aunt Lydia's farm, helped her. The rural areas of Bavaria had escaped the air raids all the bigger German cities had endured. Giving the landscape a cursory glance, Ursula noted it seemed to look the same as always.

Only the schooled eye of a local would notice the fields that should be planted and already sprouting, but hadn't even been tilled yet. There simply weren't enough hands to accomplish the tasks that needed to be done each day, since all men between the ages of thirteen and sixty had been enlisted into the *Volkssturm.*

Ursula scoffed. The last resort of a national militia was made up of boys and ancients. How were they supposed to win the war? Her oldest nephew Jörg, the self-proclaimed man in the house, had avoided enlistment because he'd celebrated his twelfth birthday only last month. Not that the Party hadn't tried to bribe, sweet-talk, and coax him into joining up. Thankfully, he'd taken his duties to run the farm too seriously to jump into such a reckless endeavor.

Herr Keller, the mayor, police chief and party official in Mindelheim was the driving force behind this. But Ursula doubted that he seriously believed in a successful outcome. How could young boys from the Hitlerjugend stave off the Allied soldiers when battle-hardened and experienced Wehrmacht soldiers couldn't? What kind of delusional thinking was that?

The sound of marching boots reached her ear even before she saw a column of Wehrmacht soldiers dressed in *feldgrau* come up over the rise in the road. Ursula stepped off the road onto the field and called to Maria, "Come here. Get away from the street. There are soldiers coming."

The Wehrmacht soldiers didn't present a threat, but she thought it prudent to keep the small girl out of their way.

"Auntie, look. Why are these men so gray?" Maria pulled at Ursula's skirt.

"Because their uniforms..." *are gray,* she wanted to say, but the words stuck in her throat as she saw the haggard, skeletal, exhausted and dejected-looking men. The picture of misery tugged at her heartstrings. About a hundred men, their ashen faces, hair and hands the same *field gray* as their uniforms, drudged past, eyes cast to the ground.

They didn't carry heavy weapons, or have vehicles. Ragged handcarts were their only means to haul the limited supplies.

Ursula had seen many soldiers in the past five years, but never an entire column of such miserable figures. If this was what was left of Hitler's army, then the war truly was lost already. And every passing day was simply delaying the inevitable: the complete collapse of the Reich.

One of the men, no older than her own twenty-four years, looked up and his eyes met hers. Even his eyes were gray. His entire being seemed nothing more than an accumulation of ashes. A human being who'd stopped living a long time ago and only his shell kept on marching. She recoiled from the way he epitomized what a miserable fiasco this war had become.

He broke from the line of marching men and mistaking her recoiling for fear said, "Don't be afraid."

"I'm not afraid," she answered, a pang of guilt entering her heart. The poor man had been tasked with protecting his fatherland, protecting her, and she flinched at his appearance.

His gaze wandered down to Maria and the loaf of bread in her hand. Ursula saw his Adam's apple dance as he swallowed.

"Can... may I have a bite?"

Tears sprung to her eyes at his simple request. Since when had the Wehrmacht stopped feeding her soldiers? She nodded, broke a piece from the bread and handed it to him, asking, "Where are you going?"

"Reinforce the Iller Line." His voice made the rasping sounds of an ancient man.

The Iller River flowed from the Alps in the south all the way up to the city of Ulm in the north, where it emptied into the much bigger Danube River.

He seemed to read her thoughts. "We couldn't hold the Danube Line," he said, dejection transforming into embarrassment. "The Iller line is our very last chance to hold off the Americans." Then he rejoined the marching column and left Ursula to her thoughts.

A small hand grabbed hers and Maria said, "See, Auntie? The man was gray. But why?"

Ursula stepped on the road again, not knowing how she could possibly answer the little girl's question. *His skin is gray because he's dejected and hasn't eaten or washed in a long time. Oh, and by the way, we lost the war, even though it's not official yet.* "We should hurry to bring your mommy the lunch," she said instead.

Maria didn't linger over the unanswered question for long and bounded ahead, wielding the spoons in her hand like a rifle.

A few days later, Ursula was tending to the vegetable garden when the mailman stopped at the house.

"Here's something for you, Fräulein Ursula!" the old man on a rusty bicycle shouted out.

"For me?" She dashed to meet him and glanced at the brown envelope in his hand.

"From Berlin. I believe it's from your mother." In such a small place everyone knew everyone. Since Frau Klausen had often visited before the war and even lived here for a few months, the mailman knew her well.

Ursula grabbed it and eyed the handwriting on the envelope. It was her sister Anna's. She narrowed her eyes, a horrible feeling of foreboding weighing her down. Anna rarely ever wrote letters. She was too busy working double shifts as a nurse at the famous Charité hospital and raising her stepson Jan on her own.

"It's from my sister," she said and almost giggled at the comical expression of disappointment on the mailman's face. Since he made no move to leave she added, "I'll go inside to read it. But I'll make sure to let you know any important news from Berlin."

In the kitchen, she took a knife and carefully opened the envelope. The date stamp read more than a month ago, but mail moved slowly these days, if at all, so getting a letter from Berlin was nothing short of a miracle. With bated breath she read her sister's words.

Dearest Ursula,

I hope you and baby Eveline are doing well. I so want to see you both again and hold her. Let's pray that we will soon be able to travel again.

You're probably wondering why I am writing since Mutter usually does. But I wanted to let you know that Jan and I had to move back in with her. The building I was living in burned out and we had no place else to go.

But don't worry, we are still in the highest spirits, confident that these sacrifices are nothing against the benefits waiting for us after the ultimate victory. We don't grieve over a small material loss, but we celebrate the bravery we show.

Ursula broke out into loud laughter. How on earth did Anna come up with such hilarious lines? She could have simply said nothing, but mocking Hitler with his own words while satisfying the censors was brilliant.

Still, she didn't really expect anything less than brilliance from her sister. Anna was the brightest of the four siblings. Once the war was over, she'd make her way as a truly exceptional researcher in the fields of biology and medicine. Ursula was sure of this.

Things here in Berlin are sometimes not ideal. But you shouldn't believe everything you hear on the radio. We are well and happy... except for having to live with Mutter. I feel like I'm a child all over again. Mutter told me to give you her best regards. She's looking forward to seeing you and her granddaughter again at the soonest possible opportunity.

But I have more exciting news for you. Remember the friend of mine who joined up to become a radio operator with the Wehrmacht?

That would be their little sister Lotte. She was living under the name of Alexandra Wagner and risking her life every day spying for the British while working as Wehrmachtshelferin.

Alexandra is well and in good spirits. She couldn't give me details about her whereabouts, except that she is somewhere in Norway. It's such a relief to have news of her.

Professor Scherer is wonderful as always and I'm grateful that I can work for such a renowned scientist like him. He has stopped all of his research and teaching and for the time being is dedi-

cating his entire manpower to the war effort in helping our wounded soldiers.

I can't tell you about the progress we're making in the fields of bacteriology. It really is an interesting time we live in and I couldn't be happier.

The only complaint I have is that we haven't been able to see each other.

Give Aunt Lydia our love, hug the children, and kiss the baby for us.

Love,

Anna

Ursula shared the letter with her aunt and dreamed about the day when she and the rest of her family would finally be reunited. It couldn't come soon enough for her.

Exactly two weeks later, on April 24th of 1945, American tanks rolled up the road and into Kleindorf. It was almost a non-event when it happened. No fanfare, excitement or even fighting accompanied their taking possession of the small farming village.

"For us, the war is over," Aunt Lydia said to Ursula. "What will become of us now?"

"At least it's not the Ivan coming to occupy us, but the Ami," Ursula answered with a thoughtful glance at her nieces, the oldest one ten years old.

"We should hide inside," Lydia said.

"No, we shouldn't. They'll check all the houses, so better we stay outside where they can see that we present no threat." Ursula ran a hand through her blond hair. Unfortunately, the Nazi Party hadn't given them a protocol on how to behave in case of surrender.

Jörg came running from the house with three white pillowcases and handed them out. "Here, take these!"

"What are you doing?" Lydia asked her son.

Ursula reached for the white linen, wondering when her nephew had grown up so much. Now, he actually filled the shoes of the man of the house and told the adults what to do.

"Making sure the Americans know no one here wants to fight," Jörg answered.

"But, Herr Keller said..." Lydia began in a hushed voice.

"Herr Keller is a fanatic and a fool. Do you really want us to suffer the same fate as those living in Mindelheim?" Ursula couldn't believe her aunt was still clinging to the orders the mayor had issued. *Fight to the last man. Don't surrender. We die rather than capitulate.*

It would be laughable if it weren't so sad. News had come from Mindelheim that a hundred boys aged ten to fifteen had launched into a hopeless fight against the American juggernaut. The catastrophic order to resist had come from Mayor Keller's order, a staunch Nazi and a man for whom Ursula harbored a special sort of hate.

How could the mayor send boys armed with slingshots into combat against tanks and experienced soldiers carrying automatic rifles? According to one of the village women, forty-five of the boys had died in the senseless slaughter. The Americans had ordered to leave their corpses lying in the streets as a deterrent and example to others of what would happen if they didn't surrender.

Mayor Keller, of course, had weathered the onslaught in

the safety of the farm he'd stolen from the Epsteins years ago. Once the battle was over, he had then stoically greeted the Americans, pretending to be their friend. He had made sure they knew he was the man in charge of Mindelheim and the surroundings. Ursula wished someone had put a bullet in his head.

"Are you coming?" Jörg called out, shoving a pillowcase into his mother's hand.

Ursula followed him, Lydia, and the children to the road, holding Evie in one arm. As soon as the first soldiers appeared walking up the path to the farmhouse, she waved the white pillow case with the other arm.

"Hello, ma'am, how many people live here?" one of them asked Lydia.

Lydia, who didn't speak English, exchanged a helpless glance with Ursula. The younger woman felt incredibly grateful that after meeting Tom, she had started to learn English. Despite the Ami's godawful accent, she had understood his question.

"Two adults and seven children," she answered, her voice trembling with nerves.

"Just two women, no men?" he insisted.

"No men. My aunt's husband is fighting in the East and I'm not married." She wouldn't even start explaining to him that Evie's father was a British pilot. Better he believed all seven children were Lydia's.

The soldier smiled at Evie and said something in English that Ursula didn't understand. At the harrumphing of one of his comrades, the moment of friendliness passed and he put on a serious expression again. "We will have to check the house. Please step aside."

Ursula nodded and translated for Lydia and the children. For a moment she feared that Jörg would refuse, because he pressed his lips into a tight line. But rationality prevailed and he stepped back to let the American soldiers search the house. They returned several minutes later, apparently satisfied with the result.

"Thank you, ma'am. You'll be notified when and where you have to report as soon as we have installed some kind of administration."

Since Ursula had no idea what an appropriate answer would be, she simply nodded and smiled. Moments later, the group of soldiers disappeared down the path and out of sight.

"Well, that was swift," Lydia said.

"And it went better than expected."

Before Ursula returned to the house, she hooked the sheet over the porch railing, in plain view for all to see, just in case there were more Americans coming.

Right after the capitulation normal life came to a standstill for several weeks. People wouldn't go to work, shops didn't open, schools were closed. Nobody knew what was going to happen...

CHAPTER 2: TOM

Northolt Airbase, England

Tom Westlake always dreaded the flight over to Germany. Not so much for the fear of being shot down. Because nowadays the crippled Luftwaffe didn't pose much of a threat anymore, and neither did the inadequately manned anti-aircraft flak. No, he hated the sorties, because his missions always consisted of dropping deadly bombs over German cities. His rational mind knew the bombing of civilians was a necessary evil to win the war, but his heart never agreed.

The return flight though was pure bliss. With the way his kite became lighter without the heavy bombs, his own heart grew light and blissful in the skies. He leaned back, taking in the striking blue sky – the RAF didn't bother with stealth night sorties anymore.

He was never happier than up here, in the cockpit, at the controls. He just wished he could show his world to Ursula one day – after the war. His headphones crackled and a new order came in. Landing on a small airstrip near Fallingbostel, he memorized the coordinates and set a new course.

You are to pick up and return liberated POWs.

For a moment the past came rushing back. He'd been on a train to *Dulag Luft,* a prisoner camp for air force members. He wondered how he would have fared there. Well, now he'd see first hand.

Tom talked over the com system to let his crew know about the change in plans. He couldn't say they were incredibly enthusiastic about the delay. The landing strip came in sight. The airfield was tiny and crowded. What the heck did his superiors expect?

"Everyone buckled in?" he spoke into his headset.

"Just get us on the ground in one piece," came the reply.

Tom grinned. "Have I ever let you down, lads?"

"You take us down every day." The gunner chuckled into the com system, but Tom had stopped listening to the banter. He needed all his focus for the landing. Even after hundreds, maybe thousands of sorties, it was still a challenge to land the bird safely, especially on an unknown airfield. Anything could happen, even a rogue Nazi attacking the aircraft as it neared the ground.

But the landing was smooth. Soon after taxiing the craft to the indicated parking position, they climbed out and were greeted by the officer in charge of the makeshift airfield.

"Sir, Squadron Leader Tom Westlake and my crew. We've been tasked with taking ex-POWs back home."

"Good that you're here. Conditions are awful. Jones will

take you to the camp." The captain didn't waste time with formalities.

Twenty minutes later, Tom jumped out of the back of a truck as it stopped in the vast yard of the prisoner camp Stalag 357 in Fallingbostel.

His chest constricted as he watched the surreal scene unfold in front of him. Prisoners jumped up waving, their gaunt faces crazed with delight. They walked and hobbled toward the soldiers jumping off the truck. One man, a skeleton-like emaciated figure with skin stretched over his bones, hugged Tom. He demanded an autograph on his prisoner's uniform, while at the same time babbling incoherent sentences of gratitude and asking questions about the fates of old friends.

Tom choked on his answers, and could only hold the other man in his arms and say, "You're free. It's over. You're free."

He furtively glanced around to see equally moving scenes of prisoners hugging their liberators left and right.

"How long have you been here?" he asked the man who'd finally stopped hugging him.

"Twelve months." He grinned through a tooth gap and Tom noticed the edge in his jaw. *Broken and badly fixed,* he thought, balling his fists. Thankfully, there were no Germans around. If there had been, he would have charged them and beaten them to a pulp. Even Tom himself was surprised at the raw ire he felt at the sight of his abused compatriots.

"Come on." Jones urged them forward.

Tom was too choked with emotions to say anything and wordlessly motioned for his crew to follow him across the yard. They passed what looked like the mess where army cooks delivered dishes full to the brim with food. Potatoes, beef, gravy, bread, carrots, you name it. The starved ex-prisoners were about to launch themselves at the food when a doctor came along and yelled, "Bloody idiots. What are you doing? Take the food away."

"What kind of cruel bastard is this doc?" Tom's gunner growled, ready to pounce. "Can't he see the lads haven't properly eaten in months?"

The doctor must have heard him, because he turned toward the group and said in a voice loud enough for everyone to hear, "Too much food after a prolonged period of starvation will only damage the men. They need to get accustomed to eating slowly. For some of them it might take weeks or even months."

A deadly silence ensued and only the clattering of dishes with food taken from the hungry men could be heard. The heartbreak in each of their faces was too much to bear for Tom and he turned away. "Holy Jesus!"

"Yeah, but wait, it gets worse," Jones said, leading them to one of the barracks.

For the life of him Tom couldn't imagine worse than the gruesome figures sitting at the tables staring at simple food as if it was paradise itself. They entered a barracks and the breath caught in his chest. Involuntarily, he hissed like a locomotive and blinked, praying the image would turn out to be a hallucination.

But it wasn't. Dozens of men were lying on the ground, too weak to get up and celebrate their liberation.

"These are the ones we asked to have flown back urgently." John lowered his voice, "Even back home in a real hospital it's questionable whether they'll make it."

Tom blocked out any emotion, for he wouldn't be able to function otherwise, and said in a matter-of-fact voice, "Alright. How do we carry them into the truck?"

"Old-fashioned piggyback."

Tom groaned. Not because of the burden, since none of the men could weigh more than eighty pounds, but because he feared he'd break their fragile bones with the rough treatment.

"Alright." He turned around to see that other soldiers had followed them and John proceeded to assign each one a former prisoner to carry.

Tom approached his partner and said, "Hello. I'm Squadron Leader Westlake and I'm here to fly you back home."

"Home." The man's voice was hoarse but his eyes lit up at the prospect of returning to Britain.

"What's your name?" Tom asked.

"Private Les Allen, Oxfordshire and Buckinghamshire Light Infantry."

"Wait a minute. Wasn't your unit in Dunkirk?" Tom kneeled down with his back to the man and pushed him onto his shoulders. "Can you hold on to me?"

"Sure can... and yes... Dunkirk."

"Holy shit." Tom cursed and straightened his legs. Les was lighter than a field pack with full equipment.

"Could say that."

"What happened?"

"Our unit was ordered to hold the perimeter line so the

others could escape. Most died. Four of us were captured and sent to Germany."

"Man, you've been in this hellhole for five years?" Tom swayed in his steps. Five years in intolerable conditions. Les was a master of resilience if he had survived this ordeal.

"This one and others... more than I care to count. Forced labor, little to no food, random cruelty, you name it..."

A wave of gratitude flooded Tom as he realized this could have been him, if he hadn't managed to escape. Although the Luftwaffe had the reputation of treating its prisoners according to the Geneva Convention, one could never be too sure with those Nazis. Suddenly he missed Ursula so much, it was like a piece of his soul was lacking. She'd risked everything for him, and while he'd fallen in love with her because of the sweet person she was, he also owed her his life. As soon as the war ended, he'd go to Berlin and search for her.

He reached the truck in the main yard and with the help of another soldier, carefully unloaded Les. Once the truck was full with half-dead men, he jumped in. He sat beside Les, putting Les's head into his lap and feeding him tiny morsels of baked potato, like the doctor had showed them.

"What happened to your feet?" Tom asked. In his horror he hadn't noticed the swollen, red, and blistered feet that wouldn't fit into shoes.

"Bloody clogs..." Les's eyes darkened with unspeakable pain. "Walked in them all the way from Gross Born in East Prussia to Fallingbostel this winter."

Tom had a good idea about the distances from his base in England to most places in Germany, but East Prussia?

That must be at least five hundred miles to the east from here.

"You serious?"

"Dead serious." Les chewed on the potato, but was otherwise too weak to move.

"Bloody hell, man. You're a hero."

"I'm anything but a hero." Les suddenly turned his face away. "I should have escaped."

"That's not true. Not everyone has the chance to escape. You did what you could."

"So what exactly did I do? Nothing to help win this war, that's for sure. I got battered up in Dunkirk, never really fought for my country, weathered the entire war imprisoned and..." Les started sobbing, "... and worst of all... I helped the Nazis with their awful ways."

Tom was stupefied. This poor lad had shown survival skills not many possessed, crossed half of Europe in wooden clogs – in winter no less – and here he was blaming himself for helping the Nazis. "But how? You never..."

"I worked for them. Five years! Five long years they used my strength to build their fucking streets, buildings, and whatever else. I'm a disgrace to my country! I wish I had died along with my comrades back in Dunkirk."

The truck stopped at the airstrip, and more soldiers appeared to help unload the former prisoners and carry them over to the waiting bombers.

Tom was grateful for the interruption, because what could he say to Les? That he hadn't had a choice but to obey his captors? That he was a hero nonetheless? That he had survived and now could help rebuild Britain? The boy wouldn't believe a single word Tom said, because he was eaten up by shame, guilt and self-loathing.

Les would need to live with the knowledge that he'd needed to be liberated. He might never feel like a hero, although in Tom's eyes he was. He had survived the worst the Nazis had thrown at him. That was more than an untold number of people would ever be able to say.

CHAPTER 3: URSULA

"I'm leaving for Mindelheim," Ursula said as she slipped on a dark blue cardigan over her short light blue dress. "Will you be alright watching over Evie?"

Aunt Lydia smiled. "I have six children of my own, so I will definitely know what to do with your Evie."

"Why do I even have to register here? I'm still officially reported as living in Berlin."

Lydia had already gone to the new American administration in the old town house in Mindelheim to register herself and her children. "They want to know how many people are here. I guess it's to distribute ration books – if they ever intend to feed us – and quotas for the refugees pouring in from every corner."

"Shouldn't I take Evie with me? I mean, I have to register her, too." Ursula kissed her baby, reluctant to go without her.

"The Amis didn't even want to see the young children, only the ones of school age."

"Do you think they will open up the schools anytime soon?"

"I really don't know. In fact, I heard they have dismissed all the teachers who were in the Party, and even declared occupational bans for some of them. They call it denazification." Lydia took the baby from Ursula's hands. "Now go, it's just a formality and won't take long."

Ursula pressed another kiss on Evie's chubby cheeks. Lydia was right, the baby was better off with her at the farm, rather than being dragged to stand in a queue at the town house. "I'll see you later, sweetie. Promise you'll be a good girl?"

"Now go." Lydia laughed and pushed Ursula toward the door. "And while you are in Mindelheim, could you go to the hardware store and see if they have opened up again? Jörg says we urgently need spare parts."

"I will. See you later." Ursula left the farmhouse and walked the pathway down to the road that led to Mindelheim. Since she had no means of transport, it would take her more than an hour to reach the town.

She joined the queue in front of the town house and waited for another hour, before she reached the reception desk. The man behind the counter gave her a pencil and a five-page questionnaire in both English and German to fill out.

"And here I thought they merely wanted me to register," she murmured under her breath. Seeing that the waiting benches were already occupied with people scribbling notes onto the questionnaire, she walked back outside and settled on the stairs leading up to the entrance.

It started with her personal information, including her occupation.

Housewife, she wrote truthfully.

Have you ever been a member of the NSDAP? Yes. She had joined after Pfarrer Bernau's death, because it had been the best way to keep herself and Evie away from suspicion.

Then followed a list of questions about positions she'd held in the NSDAP.

Reichsleiter. No. Gauleiter. No. Kreisleiter. No. Ortsgruppenleiter. No. Beamter in der Parteikanzlei. No. And on it went.

The next question made her furrow her brow. *Do you have any close relatives who have occupied any of the positions named above?*

What the heck? And here she'd thought the snitching and ratting out had ended with the fall of Hitler's reign. She wrote a big, bold **NO** on the line, not even considering whether one of her relatives might have held such an office.

Page two of the questionnaire mentioned any and all organizations that had existed in Nazi Germany, and she put a *yes* beside the *Bund Deutscher Mädel.*

Page three demanded she list any and all publications under her name. At least here there was nothing for her to write down. Unlike her brilliant sister Anna, she'd never said or done anything worthy of being published.

"What else do they want?" Ursula mumbled as she scanned the page. Her gaze stopped at the next heading and she groaned.

Dienstverhältnis it said and asked for all jobs she'd had since 1930. First, she mentioned the terms completed as *Arbeitsmaid* in the compulsory labor service. Then she dutifully wrote, *Prison guard at the Women's Prison Charlot-*

tenburg 1941 to 1943, Plötzensee Penitentiary from 1943 to 1944.

The next headline asked for income, and she gave a sigh. If only she had an income. As it was, she lived at Aunt Lydia's farm and received food and clothes in exchange for her cooperation in the house and with the children.

After skipping the questions about military service and international travel she finally came to the last page where she put in *widowed* and *one child under eighteen*.

Finished! Glancing at the clock on the church tower opposite the town house she noticed that it had taken her more than thirty minutes to fill out the questionnaire. She would need to have a word with Lydia, who'd called the process *fast and painless*.

If she wanted to visit the hardware store before returning to the farm, she had to hurry. A few of the town's women passed and she nodded at them. Many had come to Lydia's farm at least once bartering whatever material things they possessed for food.

After the German capitulation all public life had broken down. Shops had closed, transport ceased to exist, food supplies dwindled. People had stopped going to work – for there was no need for wartime production anymore. Even those who worked in desperately needed professions, like bakers, had stopped baking bread, because they'd run out of flour.

It was like the entire area had come to a standstill, awaiting new orders. And while the Americans had taken possession of the administration and started registering people, they had not been able to re-start the economic life.

Every day for the past weeks Ursula had thanked God

for Aunt Lydia's farm. In contrast to everyone else, they still worked from dawn to dusk. Tending the fields, milking the cows, feeding the chickens, and thus they possessed the most coveted commodity in Germany right now: food.

She returned inside and the receptionist told her to wait for her turn in front of one of the offices. There was only one woman waiting and she went in and out of the office in a matter of minutes, her newly stamped identification card in her hands.

With a slight trepidation, Ursula clasped the warm door handle and stepped inside the office, where a young GI sat behind the desk that had previously belonged to the registrar. He had short brown hair and not even the tiniest bit of stubble darkened his boyish jaw.

He motioned for her to take a seat and Ursula handed him her questionnaire as she sat down.

The American soldier looked her form over and grabbed for his stamp, when suddenly his brows went up and he peered at her with darkened eyes. "You are a Nazi!"

Ursula shook her head in shock. "No."

"Eh... you were a party member."

"Everyone was. I joined only in 1944, because I needed to keep my daughter safe." Most everyone had been a party member, so she was confident that he couldn't really hold it against her.

"And you belonged to the BDM," he spat out the words as if they were toxic.

"It was obligatory. I joined because I had to." Ursula cursed Lydia for not having warned her about the pitfalls of this questionnaire.

"And... was it obligatory, too, to work for the SS in the

camps?" He glowered at her and Ursula instinctively recoiled from him, afraid. The man's entire body tightened as if he wanted to jump across the desk to strangle her.

"I… didn't. I never worked in the camps. I wouldn't…" She stammered.

He sneered at her. "You are a liar, Frau Hermann. Here it says, written in your own handwriting, *Prison guard*."

Alternating hot and cold shockwaves traversed her body. The way he'd just pronounced the words *prison guard,* they sounded like a death sentence.

"Both Charlottenburg and Plötzensee were regular prisons, not camps," she insisted.

"Regular prisons? And who were the unfortunate prisoners?" His voice became so agitated that the connecting door to the next office opened and another uniformed soldier appeared. He was older, maybe in his thirties, and wore several stripes on his uniform. "Something wrong?"

"Captain, no. I mean, yes." The young GI jumped up and pointed at Ursula. "This woman, she is SS."

The older man jerked his head, giving her a once-over. Ursula felt her skin burning in the wake of his disapproving glare and she swallowed.

"I'm not SS—"

"Shut up. You only open your mouth to answer my questions, understood?"

Ursula nodded mutely, while the younger man explained that she had worked as a prison guard in the camps and thus belonged to the SS.

His conclusion was riddled with factual errors, but she didn't dare contradict him. She simply perked up her ears to understand their rapid English, while her heart thudded against her ribs.

"We should shoot her, I swear," the young soldier said and she felt a dizzy spell attacking her. What would happen to Evie if she were murdered in cold blood?

"Do you have to say anything in your defense?" the captain addressed her.

She wasn't sure it would make a difference, but she tried anyway. "I never worked in a camp and definitely not for the SS. I was simply a prison guard in a regular prison, where convicted criminal women were held during their sentence."

"During their sentence, you mean until they were murdered by your government?" He sneered at her.

As much as she detested his conclusion, he was right. The so-called trials at the *Volksgerichtshof* had been nothing but a farce. Everyone tried there had been found guilty before the first word of defense. So it was only a matter of issuing the sentence. More often than not the verdict had been the death penalty. She shuddered at the memory of the many courageous women who'd defied the regime, only to end up on death row in Plötzensee.

But contrary to what this American captain believed, the women prisoners had been treated comparatively well. Ursula herself had done everything in her power to alleviate their desperation with the tacit consent of her superior. She'd left the women alone in the room when relatives visited. Other times she had looked away when the thirty minutes' visiting time ended, pretending to be incredibly busy with some important task.

"No answer to this?" the captain reminded her of his presence.

"There was nothing I could do," she said.

"Oh, were you just following orders?"

She sighed. "I was."

"So did you beat, kick or punch the prisoners?"

"Never."

"That's a lie. We know everything about your camps. And we know how the prisoners were treated. Are you going to tell me you were the only SS guard to never use violence?"

"I wasn't SS and I wasn't in the camps."

"More lying. Do you admit that you had a baton?"

She nodded. "I had one, but I never once used it."

"So you were, in fact, the guardian angel ensuring that nothing happened to your charges?" The captain's fist slammed down on the desk and she jumped.

Should she admit that the women prisoners had actually given her the nickname *Blonde Angel,* for the very reason that she'd always treated them like human beings? And should she explain that she'd worked hand in hand with the prison priest Pfarrer Bernau to smuggle people – including Tom – out of Germany?

"Take her to one of the cells," the captain ordered the younger soldier.

Cold horror threatened to strangulate her, but she managed to speak with a trembling voice. "Please. You don't understand. It was nothing like that."

"I'm sure our interrogators will dig up the truth," he said, turning on his heels.

"Please, don't! I have an infant daughter waiting for me," she cried, tears running down her cheeks.

"You should have thought about that before you helped the SS do their atrocious work."

Ursula dragged her feet, even as the young GI took her elbow and shoved her out of the room. "Please, you have to believe me. I even helped the Jews."

The American soldier didn't slow down but dragged her behind him across the hallway and down into the basement where there were two cells. He sneered at her. "Every German I've met so far says they're not a Nazi and have helped the Jews. Do you think we're all stupid? Did we fight this war for nothing?"

Ursula tried again, panic rising in her chest. "No, you're not stupid and there were more than enough Nazis in Germany, but I'm telling the truth."

He opened one of the cells and shoved her inside.

Desperate, she cried out, "It's the truth. I worked for a resistance organization, helping Jews escape from Berlin. I even smuggled a RAF pilot, Flying Officer Tom Westlake, out of the country. Ask the English about this, they can verify my story."

"I'm not talking to the Brits about anything. Give your bullshit sob story to the interrogators." He locked the cell door and left her alone in the basement of the town hall that doubled up as police station.

Ursula settled on the cot, her mind frantic with worry about her daughter. She'd never been away from Evie for more than a few hours and the thought of her little baby alone and screaming for her mommy tore her heart apart.

Although, if she were honest with herself, Evie probably

wouldn't be crying but chortling with delight, playing with her cousins. She was in good hands with Aunt Lydia. In the best hands. Ursula had nothing to worry about... yet she worried. How could a mother not worry?

The hours ticked by and Ursula counted the passing minutes. By now Lydia would wonder about her whereabouts. She might even send Jörg to Mindelheim, to look for her. Or, she might not have noticed yet. Days at the farm were filled with work and nobody had time to question what the others were doing. Lydia might only notice when she returned to the house and nobody had prepared dinner, the hens hadn't been fed and the dirty dishes from breakfast were still sitting in the sink.

She would ask someone to give a phone call to her aunt – if the Americans even remembered her and came down into the bleak hole of the basement. The thought of letting Lydia know her current fate filled her with relief. Then she remembered that the telephone had stopped working weeks ago, probably as a result of cut cables in the last days of battle.

With a loud sigh, she sank onto her back on the hard cot. What irony! To be arrested for working in the job she'd been assigned to against her wishes. Although she'd come to terms with it, because she could actually make a difference in the lives of those accursed women.

Some, very few indeed, had been actual criminals, while the vast majority's only crime had been to oppose Hitler's regime. She remembered Hilde, a gentle brunette, who'd been sentenced to death for typing leaflets for her husband. Ursula's heart broke some more at the memory of Hilde's little son, the cutest boy, who resembled an angel, with his white-blond curls and blue eyes.

Tears pricked at the back of her eyes. She knew her aunt would take care of Evie, but she was shattered at the thought of not being there to see her grow up. To hold her. To console her. To see her take her first steps…

The door opened and the same young GI who'd dragged her down the stairs came inside with a tray of food. He put it on the cot beside her, without even a word. The revulsion for her alleged crimes was evident in his movements, his gaze and his posture.

"Please, you have to believe me. I was never a Nazi. I don't belong in here."

He scoffed. "Like I've never heard that before. Quiet down or else."

A lump formed in her throat, making it impossible to speak, for which she was actually thankful, because she might have cursed the soldier for his unwillingness to listen. When he left the cell and locked the door again, she started screaming with desperation.

The last thing she'd thought might happen when the war ended was to end up in a prison.

CHAPTER 4: TOM

Tom climbed down from his plane and jumped onto the ground.

"Hey, lovesick for your kite?" one of the other pilots shouted as he saw him walking toward the hangar.

"Nah, just making sure she's good to go any time." Tom had been on standby since his last bombing mission several days ago. Grueling weeks and months of almost constant sorties to deliver his deadly cargo over Germany lay behind him. And now he used the time off flying duty to check up on his kite and polish the cockpit until it shone.

"Kinda feels strange to be grounded, right?" the other bloke, called Jeff, asked.

"We're not grounded."

"So what are we then? Nobody's flying right now. All sorties have been canceled."

Tom cocked his head. "Something big's coming. I can feel it in my bones."

"You and your bones." Jeff laughed. "You remind my of

my old grandpa, who used to predict the weather by the aching in his bones."

Sometimes Tom felt like an old man. In fact, he had ever since the Gestapo had done their best to pull him limb from limb. Before that unpleasant experience, he'd always chalked up the weather-feeling bones to superstition and charlatanry. But nowadays the old fractures in his bones ached and pulled whenever something was prone to happen. He couldn't explain it, wouldn't even try with his comrades, or risk being ridiculed, but he still felt it.

Tom looked toward the barracks in the distance, deciding he'd take a nice hot shower first. He might be able to get some news later in the mess hall. He waved at Jeff as they reached the hangar. "Catch up with you later."

"Sure, mate."

Tom walked into the barracks, where he came across his friend and superior, Wing Commander William Huntley, who grinned when he saw where Tom had come from. "You already missing the sorties?"

"Yes." Tom decided to use the opportunity and asked, "I hear we're grounded for the next few days?"

"Are we?"

"Any reason why?" He asked as casually as possible, making it sound like an afterthought, but William gave him an infuriatingly lazy grin.

"Trying to tease classified information out of me? You should know better," William roared and punched Tom's shoulder. "If I have any news worth sharing, everyone will be hearing it."

Tom grinned. "Can't blame me for trying." He passed and went to his room where he grabbed a towel and took off for the ablutions block. Much to his dismay, the shower wasn't hot, but at least it was lukewarm, and he scrubbed off the oily smear from his hands and face.

When he was finished, he headed out for the tarmac where several other men were playing football to pass the time. Tom joined the game, realizing he was going to need another shower by the time it ended. An hour later, he wiped the sweat from his brow just as the siren rang out across the base and an overhead speaker crackled.

A booming voice summoned all flight personnel to the main hangar. Tom wondered at the cause for such an unusual request. In the hangar the Air Commodore himself stood on a makeshift platform, waiting with a serene but happy face for the men to assemble.

"Gentlemen, the war is over," he said without preamble. "Yesterday, Germany surrendered unconditionally."

Tom looked at those standing around him and asked, "Did you all hear the same thing I did?"

His mates nodded and after several seconds of shock-induced rigidity, whoops of excitement rang out all across the base. The men hugged, slapped each other on the back, jumped into the air, raised their fists to the sky, shouted, yelled, and some even cried. Obviously nobody wanted to be caught expressing such an unmanly emotion, and Tom saw more than one fellow furtively wiping his eyes.

Himself, he choked on the emotion. *Ursula,* was his first thought. *I'll go and find her*. He'd left her in Berlin in 1943 and he still loved her with every fiber of his soul. Despite their technically being enemies, despite not having seen or heard from her in such a long time. If it had been up to him, he'd board his kite this very instant and fly across the channel to search for her.

Instead, he celebrated with his fellow pilots. Someone unearthed a bottle of gin that soon made its way around. More bottles followed and the jolly good mood captured the entire base.

"Can't believe it. Thought this day would never come," Jeff remarked.

"I wonder how long before we can go home. I haven't had a furlough since Christmas."

"First thing I'll do is marry my girl," a shy youngster from the ground crew said.

"That's a good plan, lad." Tom looked at him, a wistful dream forming in his brain. He would find Ursula and marry her. And then they'd live happily ever after. With that thought it was Tom's turn to furtively blink a tear from his eyes.

After several minutes the Air Commodore's loud voice filled the hangar again, "I'm sorry to disrupt your celebration. However, I must remind you all that we still have a job to do."

Groans of disbelief and disappointment echoed through the large space.

"While the war is over, our part isn't. I realize that you'd rather go home to see your sweethearts, but there won't be extra leaves for the time being." The Air Commodore gazed at the crowd of gathered men and then continued, "We have been ordered to support the ground troops. We'll be flying supplies into Germany and bringing back our released prisoners of war." His gaze hardened. "Some of them are in pretty bad shape, so time is crucial."

Tom nodded, remembering the lads at Fallingbostel. The term *in pretty bad shape* definitely had applied to them.

Looking around, he saw the faces of his fellow pilots, along with the faces of all those who weren't amongst them anymore. Shot down. Killed. Bailed out. Missing. Imprisoned. If they could rescue even one of them, he – and all of his comrades – would gladly forgo their furloughs for another month, or even a year.

Tom, though, had another reason to be happy about the continued missions. He hoped to be able to go to Berlin and find Ursula.

CHAPTER 5: ANNA

Berlin, June 1945

Anna returned home from a night shift at the Charité hospital. Like the rest of the city, it now was under Soviet administration. Even with the war officially over, nurses were very much in demand, although the horrendous influx of new patients had slowed down.

"Good morning, darling." Peter, her husband, greeted her with a kiss as she opened the door. "We were just about to have breakfast. Do you want to join us?"

"No, thank you. I already ate at the hospital." She said out of habit, even though it was true only about half of the time. Without her mentor and boss, Professor Scherer, it would be true even more rarely. But Peter and his thirteen-year-old son from his first marriage needed the little food the family could get hold of more than she did.

Peter had just returned home from a POW camp and weighed little more than she did. And Jan... she looked at her stepson with a smile. He was growing again, evidenced by the trousers that ended mid-calf and the shirt with the rolled-up sleeves to disguise that it was much too small.

Peter gave her a doubtful gaze, but didn't insist. "Will you at least have a cup of tea with us?"

"I will." She settled at the table with Peter, Jan, Peter's brother Stan, and her mother. Mutter poured her a cup of herbal tea – real tea was a luxury they hadn't tasted in years.

"How was your work?" Mutter asked.

"Like always. Although we finally have fewer new patients coming in. But I hate working for the Soviets; the soldiers at the hospital make my skin crawl."

"Soon the Western Allies will enter Berlin," Stan said.

"I hope so." Anna was too tired to even care. Each and every day was an awful struggle to survive.

"I'll go and queue up for food," Mutter said, finishing her own meager breakfast. Mutter's hair had turned white over the last weeks and she'd become incredibly gaunt. Just like Anna, she gave most of her share of the meals to the men.

"Can I come with you, please?" Jan asked his grandmother. He seemed to be the only person who enjoyed leaving the safe confinement of their apartment and always volunteered to run errands.

Mutter nodded. Anna knew that she liked having the boy around, even though she didn't approve of his techniques to *organize* food and other things.

Beggars can't be choosers. And we are beggars. Anna sighed. If morals had been blurred during the war, it had only become worse now that every person in Berlin literally fought to survive another day.

Jan and Mutter left, and Stan glanced uneasily at Anna. It wasn't his fault, but every time she looked at him, she remembered what had happened, and shuddered. He noticed the shudder and said, "I should fix some holes in the wall of the other room." Then he walked out of the room, filled with guilt and shame.

"He's doing well. You almost don't notice his wooden leg," Peter said.

"Physically he's doing astoundingly, but mentally..."

Peter came over and put his arms around her. "Don't you think we should get properly married, now that it's not illegal anymore?"

"I'd love to." She leaned back against his bony chest. Despite his emaciated figure, he still managed to make her feel protected – and loved. Peter and Stan were Poles, swept from their homelands to Berlin by cruel twists of fate. She and Peter had married in a clandestine, Catholic ceremony last year, but hadn't been able to make it official due to the racial laws.

"Let's go to the administration and find out what we need to get married," he suggested.

"Right now?" The tiredness blew away at the prospect of becoming his legal wife.

"If you insist." He grinned, letting his fingers trail down her back. She shuddered involuntarily. Anna stood up, gathered the dishes into the sink and then turned around to say, "Let's go then."

"Yes. The worst they can say is no, right?"

"They won't. Now that the Nazis are gone, there's no

reason to keep us from finally getting officially married." He took her hand and together they left the apartment, walked down the dilapidated stairs and to the next administrative office two blocks down the road.

They approached the door and a Soviet soldier stepped forward, barring the path. "Identification."

Peter handed over both his and Anna's papers and she glanced nervously at the soldier while he examined their papers. Moments later he handed them back. "What is your purpose here today?"

Peter looked at Anna and then reached for her hand. "We would like to start the proceedings to get married."

The soldier looked at them and Anna believed she saw him smirk, but it must have been an illusion, because he moved aside and even opened the door for them. "Go ahead."

Inside was a reception desk manned by yet another soldier. Anna kept half behind Peter's back and let him do the talking. She hated the Soviet soldiers with a passion and not even Peter's big hand around hers could make her uneasiness go away.

"Excuse me, we would like to apply for a marriage license," Peter said.

The soldier pointed towards the hallway. "Second door on the right."

"Thank you." Anna clung to her man as they made their way to the indicated office and Peter knocked on the door.

"Come in." An elderly man in uniform sat at the desk, not looking overly happy that they'd disturbed whatever he had been doing.

"We would like to apply for a marriage license," Peter said.

The man fumbled in one of the drawers and handed them two sheets of paper, "Fill these out. I'll also need to see your identification papers."

Anna and Peter filled out the paperwork, which she found incredibly simplistic. It didn't ask for a lengthy family history, proof of heritage, health certificates and whatever other red tape the Nazi administration had required. In fact, it asked nothing but her name, birth date and nationality.

She completed the form in a matter of moments and handed it back to the clerk along with her identification. Peter did the same and the Soviet glanced at them, before he took out another official-looking form and transcribed their data. Then he took not one but four of the seals standing on his desk and stamped the form meticulously with each one of them.

"Congratulations. There you go."

Anna looked at the form in the soldier's hand, not really comprehending what had just happened. Peter stepped forward and took the paper from the soldier's hands. "What is this?"

"Your marriage certificate. You said you wanted to get married."

Anna looked at him in shock. "We're married? Just like that? Because you stamped this piece of paper?"

"Yes. Have a good day." The man mustered a smile and then busied himself reading some papers in Cyrillic letters.

Anna stood, stupefied, until a tug on her hand reminded her that Peter stood by her side. Her husband. He still held their marriage certificate in his other hand and the expression on his face mirrored her own shocked one.

Hand in hand, they left the administration building. It wasn't until they had reached the street that they both woke from their shock-induced rigidity and he wrapped her into his arms, twirling her around.

"Congratulations, Frau Zdanek."

"I still can't believe it," she said, pressing a kiss on his mouth. "I thought they'd make us jump through all kinds of hoops and here we are, married after receiving four stamps on a piece of paper." Peter placed her on the ground again, but her brain was still unwilling to process the events. "He didn't even ask me whether I want to become your wife."

"Too bad, because now it's too late to back out. You're stuck with me for the rest of your life." Peter chuckled, some of the old shimmer returning to his ice-blue eyes. After his ordeal at the POW camp, she'd feared he'd never return to his joking and teasing old self.

"I could go in there again, and ask for a divorce," she said, giving him a smirk. "I'm sure it's a matter of two minutes and some more stamps on another piece of paper."

"And do you want to?" His voice had turned serious and she quickly wrapped her arms around his chest. "You should know that I never, ever, want to live a single day without you again."

"Me neither. I love you more than you'll ever comprehend. Only the thought of returning to you kept me alive these past months."

Anna caressed his face, and the scar under his eye that told of his experiences, when she suddenly remembered.

"Oh, my goodness! Mutter will never forgive me for getting married without even telling her."

"We should hurry home to tell her. And Jan." His face clouded over.

Anna knew he was thinking about his first wife, Ludmila, who'd been killed by the Nazis for being a Jew.

CHAPTER 6: URSULA

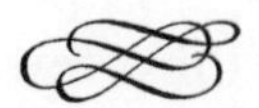

After two days in the cell, Ursula was finally released. They didn't give her a reason, they simply stamped her denazification forms and classified her as *not a war criminal.*

They'd probably made inquiries and found out that the prisons where she'd worked had, indeed, been normal prisons where the convicted had been treated well. On her way out of the town hall, she saw the former mayor and chief of police Herr Keller talking to one of the American officers.

At least the fervent Nazi Keller would now receive his just punishment and be tried for the crimes he'd committed. She still had a bone to pick with him and would gladly turn up at his trial.

Ursula walked back to the farm, her steps bouncing with joy at her regained freedom and the prospect of hugging little Evie again.

"Aunt Lydia! I'm back," she yelled even as she entered the path up to the house. Lydia stood in the backyard, wringing clothes and hanging them on the line. With Ursula gone, Lydia had had to take on the household chores herself instead of working in the fields.

Her aunt dropped the freshly washed white pillowcase and it floated in the air for a few moments, before it slid onto the muddy ground. "Ursula! Whatever happened to you? I was sick with worry."

"The Amis arrested me."

"I sent Jörg to Mindelheim to ask about you, but nobody would tell us anything. It was like you never existed." Lydia moved a strand of her thick, blond hair behind her ears.

"They accused me of having worked for the SS and having committed crimes against humanity."

"Good gracious. They are idiots. They should go after the real criminals, like our former mayor." Lydia had never liked Herr Keller, and she detested having him as the nearest neighbor to the farm, only half a mile up the road. He was a man who'd never physically worked in his entire life and didn't know the first thing about farming.

"I saw him speaking to some of the Ami officers. He'll get what he deserves. The new administration is meticulous like that."

Lydia scoffed. "You don't have the slightest idea. The Amis only prosecute when it's convenient for them. Keller is best friends with this Major Chambers. They made him mayor again."

Ursula groaned at the injustices of life. The rich and powerful would always come out unscathed, while the normal people bore the brunt. It had been like this forever. Things hadn't changed during the war and apparently weren't about to change now, either.

"Where's Evie?"

"Sleeping." Ursula left her aunt standing and rushed into the house, not listening to her aunt's admonishment: "Don't wake her!"

She silently stepped in front of the bed Evie shared with her cousin Rosa, a blessed smile appearing on her lips as she watched her daughter sleep. "I've missed you so much, sweetie. But Mommy is back now." She couldn't resist and reached down to pick up the sleeping baby.

Evie stirred and started crying. As she opened her eyes and recognized her mother, she cried even louder.

"Shush, sweetie. I'm here. All is good. I'm here." Ursula rocked her daughter, who stopped screaming after a while. She turned around and saw Lydia standing in the door-frame. "Did she do fine?"

"She missed her mama, but she did fine," Lydia said, a smile appearing on her lips. "I'm glad you're back. Your mother would have never forgiven me if something happened to you."

The weeks passed and the locals grew accustomed to the presence of the American occupiers. Their worst fears hadn't manifested. Apart from being notoriously grumpy, bordering on hostile, the American soldiers usually behaved well.

Ursula didn't mind either way, as long as they left her alone, which they mostly did. After her unpleasant encounter with the new administration in Mindelheim, none of the soldiers had ever ventured out to Kleindorf and Lydia's farm.

Schools hadn't reopened before summer, but there were rumors the new administration would see to that in the fall – much to the dismay of the school children, who'd enjoyed the absence of schoolwork. Although Lydia's children couldn't complain about the absence of hard work. Fields didn't tend themselves and producing food was the first priority.

Shops still hadn't re-opened either, and Ursula honestly had no idea how people in the big cities like Augsburg or Munich managed to survive. At least the country people all had gardens and could – although forbidden – harvest the fruits of the forests and lakes.

The relative peace didn't last and one day, an American jeep appeared in front of the farmhouse. Ursula was the only person in the house, except for the three smallest children. A shiver ran down her spine as she stepped outside to greet the GI coming toward her.

"Lydia Meier?" he greeted her.

"No, that's my aunt, but she's working in the field up there behind that hill right now. Can I maybe help?" She hoped he'd say no and leave, to search for her aunt.

"Who are you?"

"Ursula Hermann, I'm Frau Meier's niece."

"That'll do. Here." He shoved a piece of paper into her hand. "You are to receive a homeless family in your house."

"What? Why? How?" she stammered, but he'd already turned on his heel and jumped into the jeep that dashed off, leaving a cloud of dust in its trail.

Ursula took the paper, which was printed in both German and English. It announced that tens of thousands of German refugees expelled from their lands in the east were pouring into the American sector. And due to the precarious housing situation, Aunt Lydia was to host a woman with her five children in the farmhouse.

She sighed. Whether she liked it or not, there was no way to oppose the new authority. The Amis ordered and the Germans obeyed. It was that simple. Ursula returned to the farmhouse and took stock of the available rooms. Then she got to work clearing out the servant's room attached to the main house. Before, it had been used to house the foreign workers assigned to work on Lydia's farm.

An hour later she had fitted the room with straw mattresses and blankets they'd hidden away in the attic of the barn during the last days of war. She just hoped the refugees would bring their own ration books. The Amis surely couldn't expect Lydia to feed six extra mouths with the little food they left her. All farmers had been required to sell nearly all of their produce to the administration and could keep only tiny parts for their own usage.

Less than an hour later, the refugees arrived at the farm, looking dreadful. The woman had five children between the ages of seventeen and five with her, but at first glance Ursula assumed she must be the grandmother of the children. Frau Hansen had black-gray hair, a sunken face and hollow eyes.

"Good day, I'm Ursula Hermann, and this is my daughter, Evie," Ursula introduced herself.

"I'm Frau Hansen, and these are my children." She rattled off the names and ages of her children, without showing the slightest trace of emotion.

To Ursula, she appeared to be some kind of lifeless machine, if it weren't for her eyes that showed the abyss of human cruelty.

"I'll show you your room," Ursula said and walked to the servant's quarters. It had its own entrance from the yard, and a small connecting door to the kitchen of the farmhouse. It was only one room, and the only furniture was the mattresses Ursula had put on the ground, but it had a tiny alcove with a washbasin and running water. The outhouse for everyone on the farm was behind the vegetable garden, a ten-yard distance away from the house.

"It's small, but you can use the kitchen and the living room of the big house as well," Ursula said.

"It will do," Frau Hansen said with blank eyes and put down the bag she'd been carrying.

"Is this all your luggage?" Ursula stared at the piece of luggage that seemed to contain the possessions of an entire family of six.

"That, and the clothes we're wearing."

Disbelief settled into Ursula's soul. She couldn't fathom losing everything she owned, and involuntarily grabbed Evie tighter, who protested with a squeal.

The oldest girl, Matilde, looked at Evie and her eyes grew sad. With a barely audible whisper she said, "Our baby sister was the same age. She didn't make it."

Ursula felt as if someone had stabbed a sword through

her heart and she backed away from the family of refugees. "I'll leave you to get settled. Come into the kitchen when you're ready."

Matilde proved to be a chatty one. While her mother and her siblings never said a word about the ordeals they'd endured on their flight from Breslau, Matilde needed to talk.

And she talked. A lot. Whenever her mother wasn't around, she talked to anyone who would listen. And if she didn't find a compassionate human, she would talk to the hens and the cows.

Ursula would rather not know all the gory details, but she couldn't avoid hearing the girl's confessions. It was disturbing. What was happening right now in Poland and Czechoslovakia was worse than anything that had ever happened under the Nazis, at least from what Ursula knew.

"Please stop," she said one day when Matilde indulged again in retelling the most sickening and repulsive details of the crimes committed against the fleeing Germans.

Matilde looked at her, her eyes exposing her wounded soul, and gave a deep sigh. "My mother said to forget, but how can I forget?" Tears pooled in her brown eyes. "If I talk about it often enough, it eases the pain. I hope the horrible memories will one day leave my body together with my words and let me live in peace again."

Ursula couldn't help but put an arm around the girl, who was barely seventeen and had already experienced more evil than anyone should in a lifetime.

"My brother, Richard. The last we know of him is that he was in Poland…" Ursula stopped talking. The raw pain threatened to overwhelm her. Richard had been on a train back to the front when the partisans blew up a tunnel, but his body or dog tags had never been found. What if he was still alive and trying to reach home? What if he'd experienced the same evils that Matilde was recounting in gory detail? She shuddered. "I'll show you how to milk the cows," she said instead.

A routine settled in and despite the cramped quarters Aunt Lydia was quite happy with her new lodgers. Frau Hansen proved to be very efficient around the house and the three older children had taken up working on the fields.

One day towards the middle of June, American soldiers came to the farm and loaded all the adults including Matilde on their truck.

"Where are you taking us?" Ursula demanded to know.

"You'll see." The GI hopped into the driver's seat and dashed away. The truck stopped at every farm on the way to their destination, loading up more and more women, and the odd man.

Almost two hours later they passed through the town of Türkheim and stopped minutes later in front of a labor camp. Türkheim had been a relatively small satellite site to the Dachau concentration camp.

Ursula's first steps inside one of the camps were under the raised firearms of American soldiers – which seemed ironic after having been accused of working for the SS in the camps. Although she'd never seen the horrors with her own eyes, she had a pretty good idea about the deplorable conditions. But now she found that the bits her sisters

Lotte and Anna had told her, paled in comparison to reality.

"Look what your people have done," one of the GIs said as he marched the women across the camp.

They stopped in front of the mass grave where skeletons were piled up several yards high. Despite having prepared herself for ghastly sights, Ursula gagged.

Matilde, though, didn't seem to be the least bit surprised or even appalled. She even smiled and murmured incessantly, "The same. Everywhere it's the same. They did it here. And now they do it there. What we see now is nothing compared to how it was then. It's happening again. Now you have to believe me. I wasn't making things up. It's true."

Ursula looked at the young woman in shock. She'd never seen her so vibrant, so... relieved. Matilde seemed to have lost her mind.

The other women, though, all recoiled in different states of shock. Those who fainted were roughly roused again by the GIs guarding the flock of women.

"That's what you Nazis did. Have a good look," one of them yelled.

Several women cried, "We had no idea. We didn't know what was happening. We were trying to keep our families safe and alive. This wasn't us."

"So you had no idea about these camps? How could you not have noticed these fences and wonder what was happening behind?" the GI said.

"I have never been to this place before. Maybe the people in Türkheim knew, but we didn't. I minded my own business, tending to my farm. I didn't know a thing."

Ursula could only shake her head. Even her twelve-year-old nephew, Jörg, who worked all day and rarely ever left the farm, had heard the rumors. Everyone had relatives or friends who lived nearby a camp. And everyone had heard the stories of the *poor souls* who worked so hard and got so little food. And everyone had told anecdotes of someone throwing bread across the fence and the prisoners fighting for it, or the guards coming and threatening the civilian who threw the food.

Who, in their right minds, could still pretend not to have known?

Yet, the women pleaded ignorance, but Ursula could only shake her head. Either those women were deaf and blind or they were lying. There was no way anyone could have survived the war without at least suspecting what was happening.

"I guess people only see what they want to see," she murmured, shame creeping up her spine. At one time she had believed the propaganda, too. Had thought the strict course had served the betterment of Germany. Had believed everyone had to make sacrifices and the Führer knew best.

The women were put in groups and each group was tasked with digging a grave and putting the skeletons inside, while the American soldiers watched. Left and right, women were groaning, complaining, and gagging, except for one.

Matilde feverishly dug her shovel into the hard earth, attacking it as if it were the devil himself. She unleashed her wrath, cleansing her soul from the abominable things she'd witnessed. Once the graves were filled and covered with earth, Matilde stretched her back and beamed at Ursula. "You know, they're gone! The ghosts that have haunted me for all these months, they are gone. I couldn't help them, but I could at least lay these people to rest. You can't imagine how it feels to be free again."

Ursula could only nod. At least one person would sleep with a happy smile on her face that night.

CHAPTER 7: TOM

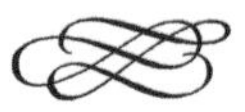

Tom was starting to lose hope. He'd been flying the combined supply and rescue missions for weeks now, but he still hadn't set a foot into Berlin.

Stalin turned out to be the arsehole everyone had known him to be. He broke his part of the bargain and didn't allow the Western Allies access to Berlin as stipulated in the Yalta Conference.

Tom wanted to pull out his hair in desperation. Without a British stronghold in Berlin, there was no chance he could ever get there and find out whether Ursula had survived the war. In his heart, he felt she was still out there, waiting for him to return. Like he'd promised. Like she'd promised.

But right now he couldn't even make inquiries about her whereabouts. How would he even explain his interest in a German woman to the Soviet authorities?

Thankfully, neither Churchill nor Truman seemed willing to sit back and watch Stalin get away with his attempt to keep the coveted capital for himself. It would only be a matter of time until their armies forced their way into Berlin, whether Stalin liked it or not.

He decided to talk to Willie, who was not only his superior, but also his best friend. The two of them went way back to the public school they'd both attended. Later they had absorbed the pilot training together and even managed to fly in the same unit for most of the war.

Willie was the only person he'd ever told the truth about Ursula and how much he loved her. Everyone else knew she and her resistance organization had smuggled him out of Germany. Full stop.

"Hey, Willie. Can I talk to you for a minute?" he said.

Willie gave him a scrutinizing stare. "What's up?"

"Not here."

Willie rolled his eyes. "Alright, let's go to check on our kites. There shouldn't be anyone around right now."

As soon as they reached the airfield with the parked planes, Tom broached the delicate subject. "You remember Ursula?"

"You still pining for her?"

"It's more than that. I love her. And now that the war is over, I want to find and marry her."

Willie's mouth hung agape. "You can't be serious old chap!"

"I am." Tom ran his hand through his cropped dark hair.

"Even if the bloody Soviets finally let us take possession of our sector in Berlin, you can't just go looking for her, much less marry her."

"I know." Tom grew ever more despondent.

"You're in deep shit. The bosses are not joking about the

anti-fraternizing rules. Haven't you listened to the Air Commodore's speech last week?"

Tom had, and he recited the rules that applied in interactions with all Germans. "In streets, houses, cafes, cinemas etcetera, you must keep clear of Germans, man, woman, and child, unless you meet them in the course of your duty. You must not walk out with them, or shake hands, or visit their homes, or make them gifts, or take gifts from them. You must not play games with them or share any social event with them. In short, you must not fraternize with Germans at all."

"If you're caught, that could mean the end of your military career and possibly even prison time."

"But men break the rules all the time and the commanding officers turn a blind eye."

"Yeah… right… the bosses know our men have needs. But a secret hanky-panky with a German Fräulein is entirely different to a bloke crazy enough to plan on marrying a German. They would not be amused."

"First, I have to find her, but how?"

"Have you tried the Red Cross?" Willie suggested.

"I thought about it, but wouldn't it look suspicious and get me into hot water with the Old Man?"

"Probably." Willie slapped him on the shoulder. "The way I see it, you're driving yourself crazy thinking about her non-stop. Go and find yourself a nice girl from London."

"You don't understand. I don't want just any girl. I want her. Only her."

"Then you must wait until you can ask to be transferred to Berlin. I'll sign your request, if that helps."

"Thanks, old chap. I appreciate it." A sliver of hope remained in Tom's heart. As soon as the British arrived in Berlin he'd hand in his transfer request and with Willie's signature, how could the Air Commodore not approve?

Then he'd go after the woman who owned his heart. There was nothing or nobody who could stop him. He owed it to her to never stop trying to find her.

CHAPTER 8: URSULA

July 1945

Ursula hadn't heard from Anna and Mutter since April and had grown increasingly worried with every passing day.

"I wish I could go to Berlin and see them for myself," Ursula complained to her aunt.

"You know that's not possible, my dear."

"But why won't they send us at least a letter?"

"Maybe they have and the mail is not delivered?" Lydia looked up from her needlework and gazed at her niece. "They'll write as soon as they can. You'll see. There's no use in worrying."

Ursula wished she possessed the same stoic calm as her aunt. "Are you never worried about Peter?" Lydia's husband had been fighting first in France and then in the East, and they hadn't heard from him since last fall.

"I miss him, yes, but since there's nothing my worry will

accomplish, I don't worry. I do pray for him every night and send him my love." Lydia peered down at her needlework again. "The children are growing so fast..."

Ursula wondered whether the two youngest ones, Rosa and Maria, would even remember their father. She and Lydia sat in silence, mending worn-out clothes for another season of wear, until Lydia spoke again several minutes later.

"Have you tried the Red Cross? You could file a missing persons report. Maybe they have a way of communicating with those living inside Berlin?"

Ursula considered her aunt's suggestion and nodded. "That's a good idea." A shudder racked her body, because the closest Red Cross office was in Mindelheim. She still reeled from her experience during the denazification process and preferred not to go into town.

"Jörg and Matilde can go with you. I have a full list of errands to run in town."

She might as well get it over with. "You're right. We'll go tomorrow. If we go first thing in the morning, we'll be back by lunch time and still work half a day in the fields."

Lydia gave a tired wave. "Sometimes the fields have to take a second place to the people we love."

"Thank you, Aunt Lydia." Ursula felt warmth spreading through her heart. Lydia didn't express her emotions very often, so this was a precious moment of love between the two women.

In the absence of her mother, Lydia was the closest confidante Ursula had. However, she still hadn't told her about Evie's father. During the war it had been too dangerous and now... Ursula sighed, afraid she might never see him again. How should she even begin searching for him?

The next morning, Ursula, Jörg and Matilde set off for Mindelheim. As promised, Aunt Lydia had given them a long list of errands to run in addition to filing a missing persons report.

Just as they were about to reach the town, Jörg recognized a girl who'd worked on Lydia's farm as *Arbeitsmaid* the previous summer.

"Hello, Helene, how are you?" he greeted her.

Helene stopped for a moment, smiled and then said, "They found one of the Nazis' food storage locations and are handing out oil. It's about four miles from here."

Ursula's mind raced. Oil was a hard-to-come-by source of fat for cooking and they had run out of it weeks earlier.

Usually when someone *found* a storage location, they broke them open and left them to be raided by the hungry citizens. It worked strictly on a first come, first served basis, as urgency was mandatory. As soon as the Amis found out they'd stop the illegal distribution of foodstuff – if the supply hadn't dwindled already.

"Matilde, you go with Helene and get some oil for us. Jörg and I will meet you at the town square in Mindelheim after running our errands."

Matilde pouted. Chasing after the rumor that somewhere some food might be obtained wasn't nearly as exciting as going to town. But she obeyed and took off with Helene, leaving Jörg and Ursula to walk into town.

"Do you think she'll get some?" Jörg asked.

"I don't know, but it's worth a try." Aunt Lydia had often scolded Helene for being a no-good who wasn't adept at *organizing* stuff – organizing being an euphemistic expression for obtaining things that you couldn't get a hold of through normal channels.

Jörg set off for the hardware store and Ursula paused a moment in front of the newly opened Red Cross office next to the town hall. A tremble ran through her body. She steeled her spine and stepped inside, finding an elderly woman sitting behind the only table in the room. The woman had her dark hair tied into a bun at the nape of her neck and smiled.

"How can I help you?" the woman asked, even though she must know that everyone walking through the door wanted the same thing: to know whether relatives and friends were well and alive.

"I come to inquire about my mother and sister. They live in Berlin."

"Berlin?" The woman's face fell. "I'm afraid we have received no lists from Berlin. Working with the Soviet administration is rather… challenging."

"So… is there anything you can do?" Ursula asked in a feeble voice.

The woman handed her a form. "Fill this out and leave it with me. You will receive a letter as soon as we have records about them."

Ursula did as requested and filled in the names, birthdates, and last known locations of Anna and Mutter. Then she handed the form back to the woman, who glanced it over and put it on a stack of other completed forms. Each sheet representing one person, loved and missed by someone.

"Anything else I can do for you?"

"In fact, yes, I have a friend, Alexandra Wagner. She was last deployed to Stavanger, Norway as Wehrmachtshelferin." Alexandra was her sister Lotte's new identity.

The woman's face lit up. "We have much better records about Wehrmacht employees than we do about civilians. Let me check for you."

Ursula filled out another form and the woman walked to the back of the room, where several filing cabinets stood.

"Here it is," she murmured and returned with a list. "All Wehrmachtshelferinnen from Stavanger were evacuated via Denmark in May." She frowned. "I wonder what took them so long." Her finger trailed down the sheet of paper. "That's strange."

A lump formed in Ursula's throat, making it difficult to breathe, and she prepared herself for the worst. "What is it?"

"All the women arrived in a transit camp except for two, who are noted as missing."

"Missing?" Ursula's own high-pitched voice echoed in her head.

"Yes, Alexandra Wagner and Gerlinde Weiler have gone missing somewhere in Denmark."

Ursula slumped into the chair, all the blood draining from her face. Gerlinde was Lotte's best friend. What did it mean that both of them had gone missing? It couldn't be anything good.

She knew her father was a POW in Russia, had been for close to three years. So she inquired about her brother Richard, who'd gone missing a year ago somewhere in Poland.

"I'm sorry. He's still registered as missing in action," the

Red Cross helper said and busied herself returning the lists to the filing cabinet.

Ursula stared after her, unable to get up from her chair. It would have been better had she refrained from inquiring, because she wasn't any wiser, but only more anxious.

The older woman seemed to sense her state of despair and said, "You cannot lose hope. We get new records every day. As long as your loved ones are not confirmed dead, you're better off than most persons who come here."

"Thank you," Ursula uttered and left the suddenly oppressive room. As she stepped onto the town square the blazing sunlight blinded her. On any other day, she would have enjoyed the beautiful old fountain in the center of the square.

Someone had taken the trouble of planting pansies and forget-me-nots in the stone flower boxes attached to the fountain. But even this uplifting sight couldn't brighten Ursula's mood. Too heavy weighed the burden of uncertainty.

With a sigh, she took out the list from her bag and began working off point after point on the list. Two hours later she was finished and found Jörg skipping stones on the water of the river lazily flowing through town.

"Hey, Jörg, did you get everything?" she called out.

"Not even half of it." He made a concerned face. "I bargained some spare parts for the plow in exchange for part of the potato harvest, but that's about it."

"Let's go to the town square, I'll buy us a treat," she offered.

"Ice cream?" His eyes became dreamy and he ran a dirty hand through his slightly too long blond hair.

"I'm afraid not. But I saw fruit gum in the grocer's." The fruit gum probably was made without sugar, but it was still a treat and Jörg eagerly agreed. As they reached the town square they saw Matilde walking up the hill, hands empty.

"You should have sent me, I'm much better at organizing stuff," Jörg said.

"We needed the spare parts more than we need the oil, that's why I put you onto the more important task."

Jörg beamed at the compliment. Despite considering himself the man of the house, he still was a boy – although a boy who'd had to mature much too early.

Matilde trudged into the square and washed her sweaty face at the fountain. "I'm sorry, but we arrived too late and none of the oil was left."

"Don't worry about it. It was worth a try," Ursula said.

They walked back to Kleindorf and as Ursula had predicted, Aunt Lydia cherished the spare parts more than she mourned the lack of cooking oil. The tractor had long stopped working because there was no fuel to be had, but at least they still had the ox and the cows to yoke to the equipment.

The Americans, in contrast to the French and Russians in their sectors, hadn't requisitioned any and all machinery the civilian population still possessed. Apparently, they were wise enough to realize that the farmers relied on equipment if they were to produce enough food to feed the population come winter.

But the farmers still lacked manpower and all around Aunt Lydia's farm lay fields ready for harvest, but there weren't enough people to do the work. Wheat, barley, oats, all were rotting on the ground. Potatoes had to be harvested and vegetables picked. Only the cherries and plums on the trees had found their way straight into the mouths of climbing children.

Lower Bavaria might have been spared from the devastating destruction the bigger cities all across German had endured. But its men had been drafted into the Wehrmacht years ago and were yet to return. With only women and children left – and devoid of powered machinery – there was only so much they could do. The lack of manpower had become even direr after the capitulation, because the foreign prisoners of war and forced laborers had been released. They were dearly missed in the farms.

"It looks like rain. We urgently need to bring in the crops. Maybe we could ask for extra workers in Mindelheim..." Lydia started to suggest and then she stopped herself. "Never mind."

The next few days Aunt Lydia's family, including Ursula and Frau Hansen, harvested from sunup to sundown. The only persons exempt were the three youngest children Evie, Rosa and Maria.

In the evening they got word that the entire town of Mindelheim was puking their souls out. Soon someone had found out that the cooking oil had indeed been diesel oil.

Lydia remarked dryly, "We sure could have used the oil for our tractor."

CHAPTER 9: RICHARD

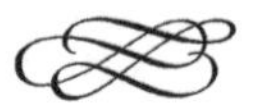

Richard stepped from the train that had taken them as far as Mindelheim and helped Katrina down onto the platform. "From here on we have to walk. It's less than ten kilometers to Kleindorf."

"After walking several hundred kilometers across half of Europe, I'm sure I can manage another ten." Katrina smiled and once again he thought how lucky he was to have found her. He couldn't have wished for a better partner.

"What's your aunt's last name?" Katrina asked, wringing her hands.

"Why?" He glanced at her, taking in her frail body, the headscarf that covered her short brown hair, and her beautiful brown eyes. It had been her eyes that had first captivated him.

"To address her, of course." A sliver of irritation flashed across her face. "I can't well greet her with 'Aunt Lydia', now can I?"

He stopped short and gave her a bewildered look. "I never really thought about that."

"Of course not, you simply assume everyone will welcome me with open arms."

"They will. Don't you worry so much." He pressed a kiss on her nose. "Lydia's last name is Meier. You'll see; she can't do anything but love you."

"How can you be so sure? The German people have been indoctrinated to hate the Slavs for more than fifteen years. Why do you think your aunt will accept a Polish woman into her family?"

"Because I love you. And she loves me," Richard said, not really understanding why she worried so much.

"Shouldn't we at least find a pay phone and give her a warning that we are coming?"

Richard laughed out loud and pointed at the railway building lying in rubble. "Suit yourself. The chances of finding a working pay phone are less than slim."

She looked around and nodded.

"Come on, sweetheart. It'll all be fine. You'll see." He took her hand into his and gently pulled her forward down the road leading away from the small town of Mindelheim.

Already deep into summer, the sun burned down on them. She stopped and wiped sweat from her forehead. Cocking her head, she gazed at the ripe ears of wheat in a field and said, "The harvest hasn't been brought in."

"What do you mean? It's not yet time." Richard frowned.

She laughed at him, because clearly one year living on her farm hadn't made a farmer out of him. "Back home we'd begin harvesting right now, but here we're hundreds of miles further south and these crops look overly ripe." She closed her hand around one of the ears and pulled, the grains staying in her hand. "See?"

Richard reached for some and shoved them into his mouth. "They're still good."

"But only until it rains the next time. If they aren't harvested by then, all the produce will rot in the fields. What a shame." With millions of people suffering from hunger it was akin to a crime not to harvest the fields.

"Not enough hands I guess," Richard said and picked up the journey down the road. They walked in silence for a time until he pulled on her hand, hopping up and down like a small boy with a look of pure joy on his face.

"There is the farm. We have arrived!" He started forward, but she pulled him back.

"What if your aunt doesn't like me? What if she doesn't want me on the farm?" Her voice came across as a feeble whisper.

Richard hugged her close for a moment. "Stop worrying, sweetheart. Aunt Lydia is going to adore you. I promise." He released her, took her hand and continued walking towards the main house. "Let's see if anyone remains home."

"No other way to find out than go and knock on the door."

He held his breath as he knocked, but no one came to greet them. His heart crumbled at the possible meaning and he almost didn't notice her hand squeezing his.

"They… they'll probably be working in the fields. You know, a farmer is never sitting idly at home."

Richard cast her a gaze full of doubt, but walked around the house into the vegetable garden. He froze as soon as he recognized the young woman hanging laundry up on the clothesline, and Katrina bumped into him.

"Ursula?" He quietly said her name.

His sister looked up. After several moments of incredulous amazement Ursula's face lit up with recognition and she dropped the white shirt to the ground. Richard held out his arms and she flew into them.

"Richard! Oh, God. Richard! You're alive!" Tears streamed down Ursula's face as she hugged him again and again. "We thought we'd never see you again."

"You look good," he finally said, holding her at arm's length.

Ursula was so overwhelmed with the joy of seeing her only brother that she still hadn't noticed Katrina.

"Where's Aunt Lydia?" he asked.

"She's out in the fields with the older children. Oh, I have to go get her…"

"Wait. I want you to meet my fiancée." Richard reached for Katrina's hand and pulled her forward. "Ursula, this is Katrina Zdanek. Katrina, my sister, Ursula."

Before Katrina could extend her hand, the cry of a child echoed from the house and Ursula hurried inside.

"Your sister hates me," Katrina whispered to Richard, the discomfort evident on her visage.

"No, she's just overwhelmed."

Ursula returned a few minutes later with a teary-eyed infant in her arms. "This is my daughter, Eveline."

"Your daughter? How old is she?" Richard bent down to look at the infant. He hadn't even known his sister was pregnant.

"Evie is just over a year old." Meanwhile two dirty-faced

girls about two and three years old came around the corner of the house and, upon seeing the two strangers, clung to Ursula's skirts.

"Are they yours, too?" Richard said with amazement in his voice.

"No," Ursula laughed. "They are Lydia's youngest. Maria and Rosa." Then she said to the older one of the two girls, "Maria, quick, go and get your mother and the others. Tell them Richard is here."

The little girl took off for the fields with feet flying.

"Come inside. Where have you been? How did you get here? You must be hungry. Have you heard from Mutter?" Ursula interlaced her arm with Richard's, and showered him with questions, not giving him the time to answer even one of them. "I can't believe you're back," she uttered time and again.

They'd barely settled around the huge kitchen table when a voice cried from the back door of the house. "Richard! Good gracious!"

"Aunt Lydia. It's been such a long time. You can't imagine how happy I am to see you." Richard hugged the older woman, almost choking on his emotions. She wasn't his mother but seeing her and Ursula filled him with joy. Then he shook hands with each of the six children lined up behind her.

"You have grown a lot, Jörg," he said, barely recognizing his oldest cousin.

"He's twelve now and has done most of the work

running the farm," Lydia explained, before her glance fell upon Katrina. "And who's this young lady?"

Richard could feel Katrina tense up and hurried to say, "She's my fiancée, Katrina Zdanek."

Lydia clasped Katrina's hand and then smiled warmly at her. "You must be hungry. Ursula, help me get them some food."

Once everyone was seated with a bowl of steaming soup in front of them, they caught up on each other's struggles during the war. Richard glanced at Katrina, noting that the hot soup and the chitchat was easing her tension. She seemed content to listen to the conversation although she never said a word.

"Why aren't the people working in the fields?" Richard asked.

Lydia's face turned into a grimace. "No workers. All the men are dead, away or imprisoned… and since the war is over, we don't even have the foreign workers to help."

"We do what we can, but without diesel oil for the tractor a day's work isn't nearly sufficient. Furthermore, we have only the children and some women from town to help." Jörg nodded at his smaller siblings, obviously counting himself as the only adult man on the farm.

"We'll help," Katrina offered, speaking up for the first time.

Lydia shook her head. "No, you just arrived here and must be exhausted from your journey."

"Katrina is right. Her family owns a farm near Lodz and she's well-versed in the ins and outs of farm work. She even taught me," Richard said.

"You?" Aunt Lydia laughed. "The boy who wasn't

anywhere to be found whenever there was work to be done?"

Richard felt his ears heating with embarrassment. It was true. When his family had spent summer vacation with Aunt Lydia, he'd preferred to hide with a book in his hands in the barn while everyone else helped with the harvest.

To deflect attention from the misdeeds of his youth, he said, "Katrina not only knows about farm work, but she works miracles with her knowledge of medicinal herbs as well."

"You do?" Ursula asked, visibly delighted. "There's no medicine to be found even on the black market and the old doctor died last year."

"My parents were healers and they taught me everything they know about using plants and herbs to treat many ailments. With the proper equipment I can make ointments, dressings and syrups. Ask Richard," she said with a nervous little laugh. "I fed him with wild plants, berries and mushrooms for most of our escape through Poland and Czechoslovakia."

A pensive expression came over Ursula's face and then she asked, "Why did you even come here, if your family owns a farm in Poland? You're obviously a Pole."

Richard's heart stopped beating for a moment, but the building tension quickly dissolved when Aunt Lydia took the lead.

"Isn't it obvious, Ursula? Richard and Katrina are clearly in love."

CHAPTER 10: TOM

"Hey, Westlake. The Air Commodore wants to see you," Ed Bronson, one of the other pilots, called out into the barracks with a smirk. "Got yourself into trouble?"

"None of your business," Tom answered. He'd never particularly liked the petty man. For some reason Tom had yet to understand, Bronson had taken a dislike to Tom and never missed an opportunity to show it.

"You wanted to see me, sir?" Tom said, after knocking on the open office door.

"Yes. Come in." The Air Commodore was a man in his forties with reddish-blond hair, freckles and a mustache. Despite his age he still looked like a mischievous boy and the men liked him, for he was always fair and knew when to turn a blind eye. "You're aware that the 284 Field Squadron finally arrived at Gatow?"

Tom nodded. It was a rhetorical question. Everyone knew that the RAF regiment had to fly into Magdeburg and reach Gatow airport in Berlin by land. Simply because the bloody Soviets hadn't allowed British aircraft into Berlin air space. The poor RAF lads had been received with extreme hostility by the superior-in-numbers Soviet troops.

They claimed the squadron had arrived too early and even attempted to put them behind barbed wire fences. Tom could only imagine how Churchill had reacted to *that* news. Germany's unconditional surrender had happened less than two months earlier, and already the former allies were mangling each other.

Due to the constant activity occasioned by the presence of unfriendly troops, most men had changed their opinion about Royal Air Force Station Gatow. Most preferred other locations for their tour of duty. Hamburg being on top of the list.

"Your request to be transferred to Berlin has been approved."

Tom was surprised and elated, but kept his voice calm. "Thank you, sir. I look forward to being part of the Gatow team."

"Don't thank me just yet," the Air Commodore said. "RAF Gatow is receiving the delegates of the Potsdam Conference starting next week. Therefore, you are due to leave tomorrow morning and there won't be any days off until the conference is over."

"That's no problem, sir," Tom answered, while he inwardly groaned. He'd be stationed in Berlin – finally – and yet he still couldn't go looking for Ursula.

"Wing Commander Huntley will give you the details of your tour of duty. Good luck! Oh, and one more thing, Ed Bronson has been transferred, too."

Tom swallowed hard. Of all the pilots on base they had

to send petty Bronson with him. He left the Air Commodore's office and rushed to his barracks to pack up his belongings. He cursed himself because he hadn't had the foresight to ask for a photograph of Ursula back then. Because, while he still remembered the silky softness of her skin and the sound of her silvery voice, he couldn't for the life of him conjure up her face. The only image that came to his mind was her blond, wavy hair and her long, slender hands. He hated his own brain for letting him forget her face.

He arrived at Gatow the next morning. As the Air Commodore had promised, the RAF station resembled a beehive with aircraft humming in and out. They delivered delegates, supplies and whatever else was needed for the success of the Potsdam Conference.

His new superior Group Captain Moore didn't lose time with giving Tom time to get his bearings. Instead, he sent him on his first sortie back to Britain even before Tom could inspect his quarters and unpack. The next days passed in a flurry of flights back and forth, transporting goods and people to the conference.

On his fifth day, activities finally slowed down and he had time to take a breath. With several hours' off-time on their hands, a few of his new comrades persuaded him to down a beer or two in a nearby bar with them.

"Come on, we deserve some fun after all the work," Corporal Ken Blake, a short but burly man, urged him. Despite being one of the MPs on base he was a jolly lad – in his off hours – and Tom had become friendly with him.

Ken had a wife and two darling little girls, whose pictures he never failed to show off, back home. He was one of the few lads who actually cherished his marriage vows. Tom suspected Ken was a romantic at heart, although the other man did his best to appear stern and curt, just like any good MP would.

The bar bustled with men in uniform, mostly British and American, but a few French were amongst them. They ordered beer at the bar. When they went in search of a table, he accidentally bumped into a hunk of a man with pitch-black hair.

The man turned and growled at him, "Watch where you're going!"

"Holy shit! Is that really you, Mitch?" Tom stared into the familiar gum-chewing face of the American pilot. They'd both been stationed on an airbase in Italy, flying airdrops for the Polish Home Army during the Warsaw Uprising. He hadn't thought about the fun-loving, outgoing fellow since returning to England.

"No kidding, Tom!" Mitch lost the growl and gave Tom a shoulder-slap before he clunked his beer bottle with him. "Never thought I'd see you again. You in Gatow?"

Tom nodded.

"I heard about the warm welcome the Soviets gave you guys," Mitch chuckled. "Were you there?"

"No, I just arrived five days ago for the Potsdam Conference."

"Oh, yeah. It's been quite busy, right? We do nothing but fly back and forth for our delegation."

Tom smiled. That sounded a lot like what had been happening at the British airbase. "You're at Tempelhof I take it?"

Mitch gave a nod while gulping down the rest of his

beer. "I arrived here with the first lot on July 2nd. After the disaster with your fellows, the Soviets didn't bicker and left the airfield early." Mitch stared at Tom's half empty beer bottle. "Another one?"

"Not yet."

"Back in a moment. Don't leave." Mitch disappeared into the crowd to get himself another beer.

"Who the hell is that uneducated Yank?" Bronson said with a snobbish smile on his face.

A man who's worth a million times more than you, weasel. Tom didn't speak his thoughts out loud and only shrugged. "American pilot."

When Mitch returned, the two men searched for a quiet place in the bar to catch up on things. Lacking such a place, they finally stepped outside onto the semi-dark street.

"Have you done some sightseeing?" Mitch asked him after a while. "Not that there's much to see."

"No, tonight's my first few hours off duty. But the boss promised generous leave after the conference is over. What about you?"

Mitch chuckled. "I can say with confidence that I know all the bars in the American sector and have now ventured to *reconnoiter* those in the British sector."

"I wouldn't have expected anything less of you." Tom grinned. They might not agree in lifestyle, but Mitch had proved a great friend back in Italy and Tom actually looked forward to seeing more of him.

"Despite the damage Berlin is great. The Fräuleins are…" he pursed his lips and made a kissing sound, "…first class. They'll do about anything for chocolate, cigarettes or nylons. I can't understand their obsession for nylons. I much prefer them without." Mitch chuckled again.

"Isn't fraternization forbidden?" Tom asked.

"Pahh." Mitch made a dismissive gesture. "That doesn't apply to *nightly* encounters. Do you actually believe there's one man in my unit who doesn't have a tryst every now and then?"

"Definitely not you."

"Exactly. My girl is tucked away safely on the other side of the pond. She won't mind me indulging in all the willing Fräuleins happy to be with an American pilot. We do have quite the good reputation with them, if I say so myself."

"Well, I'm not interested in finding me a nightly companion, but I'd love to see something of Berlin," Tom said with the idea in mind of finding Ursula. He knew the flat where she lived was in the American sector, but he couldn't be sure he'd find his way without help.

"After the conference our boss promised leave, so why don't we go meet up and I'll show you the American sector? And if you change your mind about the Fräuleins, I'm sure we can find one for you, too."

"Thanks. Sounds great. Let's get in touch after the conference."

CHAPTER 11: ANNA

Berlin, August 1945

Anna and Peter watched his brother Stan hug his nephew Jan, and then it was their turn to say goodbye.

"Are you sure this is what you want to do?" Peter asked one last time.

Stan nodded. "This is what I need to do. I don't belong in Berlin. At home in Lodz I'll figure out a life for myself."

"We'll miss you," Anna said, hugging him tight and whispering in his ear. "Thanks for saving my life."

Stan nodded and squeezed her one last time before releasing her. Anna stepped back, proud of the fact that she'd been able to hug Stan without having a panic attack.

All three of them stayed on the platform and watched Stan climb into the train. The train set into motion and slowly drove out of the station, leaving many waving friends and relatives behind.

"He'll be fine," Anna said when they left the remains of the Anhalter Bahnhof. "He's a grown man and can take care of himself."

"I know that, but he's still my younger brother. I'll always worry about him."

Anna smiled and then she glanced at the clock adorning the station, "If you don't hurry, you're going to be late for your job interview with the British administration."

Peter squeezed her hand and then left for the British sector. He'd applied to work for the newly installed British administration a week earlier. Since he'd been a combatant with the Polish Home Army before becoming a POW, he was granted an interview without problems. Several hours later, he strode into the apartment with a huge grin upon his face.

Anna had never doubted he'd get the job. "You got the job."

"I did." He picked her up and twirled her around the living room. "And you know what's the best?"

"What?"

He set her down again. "I can eat at their canteen on workdays."

"Wow!" That was a huge benefit. A job that would not only bring in money but also much needed food was akin to winning the lottery, since food was almost impossible to get in occupied Berlin. The rations were notoriously low, because the Allies simply couldn't bring in enough supplies to feed the population. Not with the devastated infrastructure and the reluctance of the Soviets to allow free transit through their zone.

"I'll still get my ration cards... and I want you to use my rations from now on."

"We can't possibly..." Anna started, but Peter stopped her with a shake of his head.

"I know that you've been lying to me all this time when you claimed you had already eaten at the hospital."

Anna's eyes widened. "Not always, sometimes we really got something to eat. If you knew, why didn't you say so?"

He smiled. "Would it have changed anything?"

She felt herself blush. "Probably not."

"Certainly not. You'd have fought me tooth and nail and not eaten anyway. So I decided to keep quiet. But I have noticed... and before you argue with me, this time I'm digging in my heels. You, Jan and your mother will eat my rations and that's my last word about it."

She bit her lip, a warm feeling spreading through her. "How have I deserved such a wonderful man like you?"

Peter's face lit up with raw joy at her words. "I love you, sweetie. And I wish I could bring some food home to you. But my new boss already warned me that anyone caught smuggling food will immediately be fired and sent to prison."

"Just having your rations is more than enough," she quickly said, intent on wiping away the guilt clouding his beautiful ice-blue eyes. The situation in Berlin had been going downhill for many months prior to the end of the war. But since the Soviets had arrived, things had gone from bad to dire.

Apart from the lack of food – unarguably the biggest problem for all Berliners – the telephone service still hadn't been repaired, mail wasn't being sent or received and even the electricity only worked intermittently.

Sometimes it felt like living on a remote island, cut off from the rest of the world. Anna thought of her sisters. Lotte was somewhere in Norway with the Wehrmacht and Ursula with Aunt Lydia in Lower Bavaria. She hoped both of them lived in better conditions than hers. Still, she worried about them and she knew that both of them would be frantic with worry about her and Mutter.

Over the next days she rarely ever saw Peter, since she worked night shifts and he during the day. As much as she missed seeing him, it also relieved her, because it gave her time to come to terms with her fear of being intimate with him.

After what had happened while he was imprisoned, she still shrunk away from him every time he wanted more than a casual kiss on the cheek. They'd finally gotten legally married and they slept in the same bed since his return, but that was it. She loved him with all her heart, but she simply couldn't.

But while he never complained she knew he was getting weary of her minimal responses, up to the point that he was blaming himself for not having been there to protect her. The lack of a physical relationship was hard not only on him, but also on her. She missed the closeness of lying in his arms and making love. Anna wanted that again.

Sighing, she made a deliberate decision. She couldn't let what had happened define her future. She couldn't risk losing the most wonderful man in the world – and his son – just because she wasn't able to overcome her fears.

Several days later she started working dayshifts again

and in the evening she took the initiative. After putting Jan to bed – he slept with Mutter in the other bedroom – they retreated to their bedroom. Peter looked at her longingly, but didn't make a move. He was waiting for her to come to him in her own time.

Anna almost choked on her own courage, but she opened the buttons of her blouse with deliberate intent, watching him watching her. His eyes became big and dark, but he still didn't move. Only the twitching of his Adam's apple betrayed his emotions. Not giving in to the slight panic creeping up her back, she opened her skirt and let it drop to the floor.

"Anna, darling," he groaned. "Are you sure?"

She met his gaze and nodded shyly. "As sure as I can be. I miss you so much."

"I miss you too." He closed the distance and wrapped his arms around her.

A slight shudder ran through her, but she decided to ignore it and whispered in his ear, "Make love to me."

Peter blew out the breath he'd been holding and swooped her into his arms, carrying her over to the bed, where he carefully set her down. Then he shed his own clothes and crawled in beside her, pulling her atop of him. She appreciated the fact that he didn't attempt to roll her beneath him, and decided to focus entirely on the love she felt for him. Nothing else.

CHAPTER 12: URSULA

Ursula was sitting in the garden with Evie and the other younger children when a shadow fell over her. She looked up and then quickly got to her feet. "Herr Keller."

"Frau Hermann."

"Did you need something?" Ursula asked, shocked to see him after what he'd pulled when the Allied Forces had arrived.

"I just stopped by to see your aunt. She's out in the fields?"

That lying snake. He never paid social visits, he always wanted something. She forced a honeyed smile. "Yes, bringing in the harvest."

"Well, please let her know I stopped by. As the mayor it is my duty to check up on all the families in the area."

"Is it?" Ursula asked in dismay. She'd gritted her teeth at the fact he'd gotten away without punishment. But now she yearned to scratch out his eyes and strangle the vile monster with her bare hands.

He smirked. "Well, yes. Will you please let your aunt know I wish to talk to her?"

"I'll tell her you stopped by," Ursula said, still wondering how the man wasn't rotting in a prison.

"You do that. Since she's having difficulties tending to her farm properly, I might be able to help," Herr Keller said with an appalling air of self-importance. "Have a good day."

Repulsive snake! Ursula's mind flashed back to the day when she'd arrived home to the news that her sister Lotte had gone missing. Herr Keller personally had sent her to a concentration camp for the crime of hiding four Jewish children in Lydia's barn.

She strained her brain to remember what had happened to the children. Oh, yes, Lotte's friend, Rachel Epstein, and her baby sister, Mindel, had been caught and deported to Bergen-Belsen. The two boys, though – she didn't remember their names – had made it to the convent in Kaufbeuren, which was only twenty miles from Kleindorf.

In the evening Ursula asked Katrina if she could take care of the young children, so she could take a trip to the convent. Now that she remembered the Epstein boys, she wanted to find out whether they had survived the war.

Jörg provided her with the boy's names. They were both only slightly younger than he was. "Israel is the older one, and Aaron the younger."

The next day she took the old bicycle and pedaled to Kaufbeuren. It was a hot and sunny August day and she actually enjoyed the trip, in spite of the many hills where she had to jump off the bicycle and push.

With a thundering heart she arrived at the convent, which showed no trace of war damages, and knocked on the door. She waited for quite a time and was about to leave, when the door opened with a creak and an old nun in her black habit stepped outside. "How may I help you?"

"Sister, I'm looking for two young boys, Israel and Aaron."

"I'm sorry. We don't have boys with those names." The nun gave her an empathetic smile and went to shut the door.

"Wait. Please." She now remembered that the boys had been given false papers with Aryan names. "They're Jewish. Twelve and nine years old. I believe they came here under different names."

The nun raised a brow. "I wouldn't know anything about this." Ursula's heart sank. "But the Mother Superior would. Follow me."

Ursula followed the nun through the dark and quiet corridors of the ancient convent dating back to the Middle Ages. Despite the oppressive August heat, a chill permeated the air and she shivered.

The nun stopped at an open door into a courtyard that was filled with light – and noise. Dozens of children of all ages played in the yard and Ursula's heart hurt, thinking that all of them had in one way or another lost their parents.

"They are in recess after lunch." With a wave of her hand, the nun excused the noisy behavior, obviously expecting a much more subdued one from the children.

They crossed the courtyard and entered another dark corridor on the other side. Ursula admired the beautiful dancing lights in different colors on the floor, caused by rays of sunshine entering through the stained glass windows. It was a gleeful beauty and stood in stark contrast to the serenity of the dark, chilly corridor.

The nun stopped in front of a door and knocked, then opened the door and announced Ursula. "Mother Superior, this woman is looking for two Jewish boys living here under false names."

"Thank you, Sister Agnes, you can return to your duties," the Mother Superior said and invited Ursula to take a seat in her office. "Can you tell me more, please? Are you a relative?"

Ursula clasped her hands together, her nerves suddenly getting the best of her. "I'm not. I… don't even know them. My sister Charlotte Klausen brought them here about two years ago."

The Mother Superior furrowed an eyebrow, seemingly not recognizing Lotte's name.

"She… she lived here for a while, too." Then it dawned on Ursula and she added. "You may know her by the name of Alexandra Wagner."

Finally the old woman showed a reaction. Her lips pursed into the tiniest of smiles. "I well remember Alexandra. She was a very headstrong thing, and frankly, we were quite relieved when she left us again."

Ursula could only imagine how her wild tomboy sister had stirred the strict daily routine at the convent and said in a low tone, "Yes, that would be her."

"Has your sister survived the war?"

Ursula gave a deep sigh. "We don't know. She's still missing somewhere in Denmark."

"I will pray for her safe return," Mother Superior said.

"Knowing your sister, I'm confident she will make her way home.

"The two boys you're looking for are still with us. They have papers identifying them as Peter and Klaus Müller. Are you here to take them with you?"

Ursula flinched. "I... I'm afraid not. Neither their parents nor their older sister Rachel have returned. I just wanted to make sure they are still alive."

"Come with me." Mother Superior got up and led Ursula to the courtyard again. She whispered a few words with one of the younger nuns and then explained, "Sister Margarete will fetch the boys for you. As you can see we have too many children here and more are brought here every day. If you could find a home for the two boys, we would be very grateful."

Israel and Aaron were adorable boys, but Ursula could hardly take them with her. Aunt Lydia had her hands full with her own six children, the refugee family living with them, Ursula and Evie and now Richard and Katrina. There simply wasn't more space in the farmhouse to host additional people.

"I'm sorry. The only thing I can do is try and find their family. I'll go and file a missing persons report with the Red Cross in Mindelheim. Maybe we'll get lucky."

"God willing, you'll receive positive news."

Ursula smiled. "I'll return with news when I can. I wish I could do more."

"Your sister saved them; that's more than enough. I will pray for all of you," Sister Margarete said as Ursula took her leave.

Ursula rode back to the farm, her mind in turmoil. The

two boys were well and alive, and now she yearned to hear about Rachel's and Mindel's fates. With all the excitement about finding them alive, she'd almost forgotten her sorrow about Tom and her need to get to Berlin. Maybe there she could find out his whereabouts.

CHAPTER 13: RICHARD

The peak season for harvesting crops passed, and everyone on the farm took a break from working from dawn to dusk in a race against the weather. Finally, they found the time to attend to less pressing, but equally important matters.

"Have you, by any chance, registered at the mayor's office in Mindelheim?" Lydia asked him.

Richard grimaced. He should have gone to register himself and Katrina as soon as they arrived in Kleindorf, but with all the work he'd completely forgotten about the issue. "Sorry, no. What papers do we need?"

"I guess your identification will do. At least for Ursula and me they didn't ask for anything else," Lydia said.

"Aaarg. That's what I don't have. The only thing I own is this travel permit and Wehrmacht discharge papers expedited at the border checkpoint."

"What about your *Soldbuch*?" Ursula asked about the booklet every Wehrmacht soldier had to carry with him.

"Destroyed." He slumped his shoulders at the prospect of the volumes of red tape he would have to wade through to prove his identity.

"Wait." Aunt Lydia disappeared to her room and returned with a sheet of paper in her hands. "This is a certified copy of your birth certificate."

Richard opened his mouth in surprise. "How… did you get this?"

Aunt Lydia smiled. "Your mother and I exchanged copies of all important documents in case one of us lost the papers for our family."

"That was quite farsighted," Ursula said. She knew her mother had kept suitcases with the bare necessities, some money and copies of their papers with several friends in Berlin. It was a thing most Berliners did in case they should be bombed out. "I had no idea she sent birth certificates to you."

"It was Frida's idea. She's always been very resourceful," Lydia said.

"Frida is my mother's first name," Richard explained to Katrina.

The next day he and Katrina walked into town and presented themselves to the American soldier at the registration office.

"Your papers," the man demanded with an outstretched hand.

"My identification was lost, but I have a certified copy of my birth certificate," Richard said, handing over the document.

The soldier looked at them. "*Soldbuch*?"

"Sorry, but I lost that when the Russians attacked our

farm." It was not entirely true, but close enough.

A glint of suspicion entered the GI's eyes. "Where were you when you heard about the German capitulation?"

"In Breslau," he answered without thinking.

"Breslau? Eh? Where's that?" The American unfolded a map on his desk and prompted Richard to point to the location. Even before he put his finger on the Polish city that was now called Wroclaw, he felt Katrina's elbow in his back and knew he'd made a mistake.

"Poland? That would make you a prisoner of the Russians. We'll have to return you to their sector."

"What?" Richard almost choked on the reply. He hadn't endured unspeakable horrors during their escape through half of Europe to be sent to a Russian POW camp.

"I'm afraid so." The young GI seemed to be truly empathetic as he explained, "We signed an agreement with the Soviets stipulating that all German soldiers found west of the American stop line by one minute after midnight on May 9 would become American prisoners. In exchange those found east of that line would be Soviet prisoners. Under this agreement we are to return any German soldier caught infiltrating American lines after that deadline to the Soviets."

The room began swimming before Richard's eyes and his brain stopped working for a moment. Thankfully, Katrina wasn't fazed in the least and she stepped up and pulled some more papers from her bag.

"Please have a look. Herr Klausen has a proper travel permit and Wehrmacht discharge papers signed by the American Colonel Sinclair at the border checkpoint in Pilsen."

The GI took the papers and studied them carefully, including the colonel's personal note about the invaluable service Richard had delivered to the Americans in Pilsen. The young soldier rubbed his chin. "I'm afraid that's above my paygrade. I'll have to get Major Chambers to have a look at these. You wait here." He glanced around the room. "You're not going to run, are you? Or I'll have to lock you up meanwhile."

"We won't. I promise." Richard said, suppressing a smile. Even if he wanted to run, how far would he get without valid papers when the entire area teemed with American soldiers?

The young soldier left with Richard's documents in hand. Ten minutes later he returned with a man in his forties with graying hair and a broad chin.

"Major Chambers." He introduced himself and then addressed Richard, "I hear you prefer staying with us over the Soviets."

"That's right, sir," Richard answered, relief sweeping through his body, because the major seemed to be a friendly man. "Colonel Sinclair was kind enough to expedite—"

The major silenced him with a motion of his hand. "I've seen the documents. The colonel seems quite fond of you. Why did you stop working for him?"

"Because his unit was pulled out of Czechoslovakia and he didn't have further use for me. And… I wanted to find my family. My aunt and my sister live less than ten miles from here on a farm in Kleindorf."

"You're a farmer?" the major asked.

"Yes, sir. We're both working at my aunt's farm." Richard had an idea. Major Chambers surely was aware of the dire situation in regard to the food supply for the population. "Since there's a shortage of farmhands, she was delighted to have two extra pairs of hands to bring in the harvest. This is also the reason why we didn't register earlier as we should have. We've been working sixteen hours a day on the fields."

"Can't send a farmer away, now can I?" The major grinned and signed a form, ordering his subordinate to expedite proper papers for Richard. Then his gaze caught Katrina. "What about her? Is she your wife?"

"No, sir. We haven't been able to marry because of my lack of papers," Richard said and handed over Katrina's identification.

The major's jaw fell and he stared at her with a blank expression. "You're a Pole, for God's sake. Why would you even want to stay in Germany of all places?"

"Because I love this man and never want to be separated from him ever again. And since he won't be able to live with me in Poland, I decided to live with him in Germany."

"Sir, the new policy..." the soldier interjected.

"I know all about the policy," Major Chambers said and explained, "Since we're flooded with displaced persons, the policy is to return everyone to their place of origin, so for Miss Zdanek this would be Poland."

"Please, can't she stay here?" Richard pleaded with him.

"For now, yes, but I can't guarantee this will be true forever."

CHAPTER 14: TOM

After several weeks in Berlin Tom finally found the opportunity to explore the city on his own. He jumped off the recently repaired tram and walked with determined steps down the street toward the location of Ursula's apartment house.

The area looked only faintly familiar. It had been damaged two years earlier, but the destruction he and his bomber pilot colleagues had caused in the two final war-years was staggering. It looked a hundred times worse than in London. Some buildings were only empty shells, a wall or two rising into the air, a dark charcoaled shadow against the bright blue summer sky. His pulse ratcheted up and he started running, afraid of what he might find.

He reached the five-story building where he'd spent several days in hiding and glanced up. It appeared to be holding together only by the inertia of masses and patches of mortar. Unprecedented emotions hit him. Fear combined with joy. Hope, desperation, love, and agony, all lumped into one stabbing pain making him immobile. He bent over to catch his breath – and his bearings. For a split-second he considered walking away. Too overwhelming was the fear of receiving bad news about Ursula.

He shook his head, gathering his courage around him. Either way, he had to find out the truth. He hadn't waited, yearned, and worried for her for two long years to give up moments before possibly finding her. Although it was unimaginable how people could live in this building.

Back in his barracks he'd struggled for the longest time whether to shed his uniform and wear civilian clothes during this illicit visit with a German family. He'd finally decided on staying in uniform because it facilitated easier travel between the British and American zone. Otherwise, he might have been picked up by patrols and asked endless questions. Now, lingering in front of the building, he wished he were wearing something more inconspicuous.

"It is as it is," he said to himself and walked in through the empty doorframe and up the stairs. He remembered Ursula's flat was located on an upper floor, but wasn't exactly sure which one. But thanks to German neatness, while the building itself was in shambles, the name plates on the doors were not. He quickly found the plate reading "Klausen / Hermann / Zdanek" on the fourth floor.

His hand half lifted as if to knock, but nerves and the danger surrounding his visit caused him to pause and sent him on a quick trip down memory lane. He exhaled deeply and then tapped on the door, shifting nervously from foot to foot.

The sound of footsteps approached from the other side and then the door slowly opened. Tom could only stand there and stare at the beautiful woman on the other side. She was just as beautiful as he remembered, and yet, something didn't seem right.

"How can I help you?" she asked, eyeing his uniform with a weary expression on her face.

Her voice was definitely wrong. That wasn't his Ursula. Speechless, he searched his brain, until he remembered. That must be her sister, Anna.

"Sir? Why did you come here?" she asked with a slight irritation in her voice at the British airman knocking at her door and then standing there like a dumbstruck fool.

He cleared his throat. "I'm Tom Westlake and I came in search of your sister Ursula."

The young woman gasped and then quickly looked up and down the hallway. "Come in before anyone sees you." She pulled him inside and shut the door. "How in the world did you get here?"

He grinned, happiness flooding his system. "I'm stationed at RAF Gatow, flying supply runs for our British sector. Is Ursula… is she…?" Suddenly, the air escaped his lungs as he hoped against hope Anna wouldn't give him bad news.

"She's alive." These two words took a load equivalent to a tank off his mind. "But she isn't here. She's in Bavaria with…" Anna hesitated and then said, "… with our aunt."

"In Bavaria?" The jubilation left his heart and his legs threatened to give out beneath him.

"Yes, it was the best for her and… to leave the city. Thanks to you and your colleagues showering us from above." The cool tone of her voice stabbed at his heart and she looked at him with barely concealed disgust.

"I'm sorry." There was nothing else he could say.

"Why are you here?" Anna asked, as they still stood in the small hallway of the flat.

"Isn't it obvious? I came to find Ursula."

Her eyes narrowed into tiny slits. "Fraternization is forbidden."

"I know that, but I don't care. I want to see her, need to see her." She didn't seem convinced. "Look, Anna, I don't expect you to understand, but I love your sister. Two long years I've waited for this day and I'll do everything within my power to see her again."

"Come in," she finally said and he followed her into the kitchen he vaguely remembered. "I can't offer you anything but water."

"I'm fine. Thank you." He looked at her. She was rail-thin, skeletal even, and it squeezed his heart thinking that his Ursula was equally starved. He cursed himself for not having had the foresight to bring some food with him. It would have been the obvious thing to do, but he'd been too nervous to think straight. "Will you tell me where she is, please?"

Anna sighed. "She's in Kleindorf. That's a tiny village near Mindelheim."

In the American sector, Tom thought. That wasn't ideal, but a million times better than if she'd been in the Soviet sector. It would have been next to impossible for him to travel there without causing major suspicions.

He heard the door open and moments later a deep voice called out, "I'm home, sweetie."

"In the kitchen," Anna called back.

Moment later a big, yet emaciated, man entered the

kitchen and stopped in his tracks when he saw Tom. Giving him a hard look he asked Anna, "What's he want?"

Anna gave a theatrical sigh and said, "This is Tom Westlake, the British pilot my sister has been pining for all this time."

Tom almost jumped up in delight. *So Ursula still is in love with me.*

"No shit." Peter flopped on the chair and gave Tom a once-over. "You have balls, that's for sure. Walking in here in your uniform and asking for Ursula. I'm Peter Zdanek by the way, Anna's husband."

"Nice to meet you," Tom shook Peter's hand, doing his best not to recoil from the touch of the skeletal hand. "Where have you been?"

"Germans took me POW in the Warsaw Uprising."

"You fought there? We heard great stories about you lads. Sorry for the lack of support you received."

"You could say that." Peter's jaw tightened.

"For what it's worth, I was one of the pilots flying in from Italy dropping supplies. Wish we could have done more, but the higher-ups didn't want to enrage Stalin."

"Let's not talk about this," Anna interjected, as she gazed at the darkening expression on her husband's face.

Tom nodded. "You're right. It's over now. What can I do to help you?"

Anna shook her head. "You can't return here. Ever. You'll only get yourself into trouble."

Despite the truth of her words, they didn't make him feel any less shoddy. The least he could do was return with a bag full of food. Peter seemed to read his thoughts, because he said, "Look, man, if there's anything you want to give Anna and her family, the two of us could meet casually in a bar."

"How?" Tom didn't quite follow his train of thought.

"I'm not a German and I even work for the British administration. So, no rule keeps us from downing a beer together," Peter's ice-blue eyes shone brightly as he chuckled. "That is, if you pay."

"Grand idea. I'll get in touch with you." They exchanged contact information and Tom promised to arrange for a meeting as soon as he had another day off. But the next time he'd come prepared with a bag full of food.

With that promise, he left Anna and Peter and returned to his barracks. His heart was light with the knowledge that Ursula was alive, but hurting that she was out of his reach.

Somehow he needed to find a way to travel to Kleindorf.

CHAPTER 15: URSULA

Ursula noticed that Katrina was not her usual upbeat self. The news about her looming repatriation to Poland had put a damper on Katrina's spirits. Since her brother didn't possess the good sense to do the one thing to keep Katrina by his side, Ursula decided to take the matter into her own hands.

She waited for Evie to take her nap and then sought out Katrina. She found her in the herb garden – a new addition to the vegetable garden that provided all kinds of medicinal plants for Katrina to make her medicines.

"You have done fantastic work with this," Ursula said.

"It's only the beginning. There's so much more I want to do next year..." Katrina's voice trailed off and worry entered her eyes.

Ursula grabbed the opportunity with both hands and didn't beat about the bush. "About that. Why don't you and Richard get married? Wouldn't that solve the problem?" *And the other 'problem' you're hiding from us,* she thought with a glance at Katrina's rounded belly.

Katrina cast her eyes downward and murmured something Ursula couldn't hear.

"What did you say?"

"We aren't getting married because he hasn't asked me."

Ursula frowned. That was typical of her withdrawn bookworm of a brother, although she had gotten the impression that he'd changed during his time away from home. "I'll talk to him."

"Please, don't," Katrina whispered.

"No worries. I won't tell him we had a chat. Leave that up to me, will you?"

Katrina sighed and nodded. And Ursula remembered how she'd waited for her deceased husband's proposal. She'd been walking on eggshells for weeks.

Ursula returned to the house to find her brother on the side of the barn chopping wood for the stove. "Richard?"

"What's up?" He swiped the sweat from his forehead and Ursula couldn't help but notice how much her younger brother had matured these past years. When he'd left for the front, he'd still looked like the schoolboy he was, but now the war had turned him into a man. His face had lost the softness; harsh life wisdom was etched into it. His shoulders had broadened and he'd grown considerably, towering more than a head above her.

"Can I talk to you for a moment?"

He eyed her suspiciously, but nodded and swung the axe into the log, leaving it stuck there, before he turned around and said with a grin, "Am I in trouble?"

"Perhaps." Ursula returned his grin. Back in their childhood she, as the oldest child, had always been the one to help her mother keep the others in line. Ursula herself had never once been in trouble, never done anything inappropriate or against the wishes of her mother. Which couldn't be said about her three younger siblings. Most notably wildcat Lotte, who'd never once been *out* of trouble, and bookworm Richard, whose main talent had been to disappear from sight when he smelled work.

She considered for a moment how to best break this delicate matter to him. Unfortunately, she didn't find a diplomatic or subtle way, so she went straight to the point. "Do you love Katrina?"

"What kind of question is that?"

"Do you?"

"You know I do." He pursed his lips and she could see his patience was hanging by a thin thread.

"Then why haven't you asked her to marry you?"

"What...? That's none of your business, Ursula." He turned and yanked the axe from the log. He looked like a medieval warrior, smeared face and grim expression included.

She had to suppress a laugh and stepped between him and the log. "It's just... I'm worried about her." His expression softened. "Wouldn't getting married get rid of the looming threat of her repatriation to Poland?"

"I guess it would, but..." He sighed, weighing the axe in his hands. A frown wrinkled his forehead as he continued, "I asked her, almost a year ago, but we couldn't marry for my lack of papers."

"You have papers now."

"Hmm... right. But I don't want to pressure her. She

wants her brothers present at the wedding, but we don't even know whether they survived the war, let alone where they are."

"You're daft. If you don't ask her again right now, you may not get the chance to. Apply some common sense. Marry now; celebrate later."

"Won't she be horribly disappointed?" Richard asked.

Ursula thought back to her own wedding. It had been the most peculiar ceremony, with a tin helmet taking the place of the groom. But she would have been more disappointed never to have been married to Andreas. "Trust me. She won't. Not if she loves you."

A beautiful smile lit up his entire face, bringing back some of the boyish gleam as he handed her the axe and said, "I'll ask her right now. How do I look?"

"Deeply in love," she answered, disregarding his sweaty, dirty and smelly appearance. Katrina wouldn't mind.

As he dashed off, she had to think of Tom. She still had no news of him. Didn't even know if he had survived the war and had no idea how to make investigations. A deep sadness settled over her soul and though she pasted a smile upon her face when others were around, every day that passed threatened to push her into depression.

CHAPTER 16: RICHARD

Richard rushed into the herb garden where Katrina was tending to the plants. She gazed up at him with her warm brown eyes and it stabbed at his heart. He'd been a daft idiot. How could he let his worry about her disappointment keep him from doing the one thing that would keep her safe by his side?

Since he hadn't had time to plan for this moment, he took his sweet time wrapping her in his arms and kissing her. But despite, or because of, her enthralling nearness, his mind drew a blank. Where were the masterfully crafted words when he needed them?

"I don't want to leave," she murmured.

"You won't." He took a step back and went down on one knee. "I asked you sixteen months ago, but I'm asking you again today. Do you still want to marry me?"

"Of course I do," she said. "I never wanted anyone else but you."

"I love you more than life itself. And the only reason I

didn't suggest getting married right now was because I knew you wanted one of your brothers to give you away."

A soft smile spread across her face. "I did. But that's secondary. What I want to be most of all is your wife."

"I promise. We'll make up for it and have a big celebration sometime in the future. It will be the biggest and happiest wedding celebration the world has seen in years."

Katrina took his hand and pulled him up with a smile. "I could do with a white dress."

His face fell. "You know that getting a bridal gown right now is next to impossible…"

She kissed him. "Not now, but maybe next year when we celebrate. When do you want to go to the town hall?"

"What about today?" His heart was overflowing with joy and now that she'd said yes again, he didn't want to wait another minute.

"Isn't that a bit early? And I'd at least want to have a good wash before getting married," she teased him.

Richard hadn't noticed, but Katrina was covered in dust from head to toe, probably the same way he looked after a day's work. "What about tomorrow then?"

"Tomorrow will work." Her eyes twinkled with delight. "I love you, Richard."

"I love you, too."

During supper they announced their plans to get married the next day.

"I was wondering what kept you so long," Aunt Lydia said, walking into the pantry and coming out with an entire bar of chocolate to celebrate. She broke it into ten pieces and everyone except Evie, who looked quite disappointed, received one.

The next morning, Richard and Katrina set off early. Ursula and Evie formed their wedding party. Ursula had loaned her finest summer dress to Katrina, and to Richard his bride looked like a queen. He didn't care that none of them had a single Pfennig to their names, because everything that he wanted was right there with him: Katrina and the baby she carried. Aunt Lydia had stayed behind, arguing that someone had to take care of the farm in their absence.

At the registry office in the town hall, they were both asked to show their papers and fill out a one-page form. Then, the soldier in uniform led them to another room, empty save for a few chairs and a speaker's desk. An old man in civilian clothes stood at the desk. Richard recognized him as a local from town. Apparently he worked for the Americans now.

"I'm the registrar," he said and looked at the four people present. "Are you the witness?" he asked Ursula.

"Yes, I'm the groom's sister."

"Very well, let's begin." The registrar didn't dawdle, and took a small black book from a drawer, reading a short paragraph about the institution of matrimony and then asked, "Will you, Richard Klausen, take this woman, Katrina Zdanek, to be your lawful wife? Will you love, honor and provide for her your entire life?"

Richard looked into Katrina's eyes and smiled. "I will."

"Katrina Zdanek, will you take this man, Richard Klausen, to be your lawful husband? Will you love, honor and obey him your entire life?"

He saw the glint of discomfort flash through her eyes, but she dutifully answered, "I will."

"I herewith declare you husband and wife. Congratulations." The registrar closed his little black book and bid them a good day.

Richard was stupefied. He'd definitely thought his wedding would be a bit more romantic. Gratefully, Ursula saved the situation as she put Evie on the floor and hugged bride and groom ferociously, all the while trying to keep her flowing tears hidden. "I wish you so much happiness. May you always be happy. I'm so delighted," she repeated again and again, until Richard wordlessly handed her a kerchief and picked up Evie.

Evie chortled with delight as he threw her into the air, but started complaining when he showered her with kisses to her chubby cheeks.

"She doesn't like your beard," Katrina giggled.

With a sliver of guilt he let go of the baby, and then asked, "What about you?"

"I love your beard," she lowered her voice to a murmur, "especially how it tickles on my thighs."

Richard felt a hot flush of passion rush through him and cast a side-glance at Ursula, hoping she hadn't noticed. Then he kissed his wife until she wriggled breathlessly in his arms and she pushed him away, whispering, "Not here."

He whispered back, "Haven't you just promised to obey me for the rest of our lives?"

"About that... I didn't really mean the obeying part." She cast him a most cheeky smile and if it hadn't been for his sister and niece present, he'd have consummated the marriage right there in the office.

"Too late, sweetheart. Now you're mine forever and have to cater to my every wish." He gave her the grin that he knew she found irresistible and added, "Just wait until we're alone tonight."

Ursula cleared her throat. "We should leave. I'm sure there are other couples waiting to get married."

"I'll bet they can't wait to experience the most romantic wedding ceremony ever," Richard replied with a sarcastic grin, but dutifully followed his sister out of the room.

"You haven't been at my wedding, or you wouldn't say that," Ursula said and both Richard and Katrina stared at her.

Katrina scrunched her nose. "I thought you were…" She was too polite to finish her sentence.

"Andreas died before…" Ursula sighed. "And Evie is not his child."

"So who's the father?" Richard didn't have the same qualms Katrina had.

"I can't say."

"What do you mean? You don't know?" His mind immediately filled with some of the most disgusting images he'd seen in his years as Wehrmacht soldier.

The horror must have shown on his face, because Ursula hurried to clarify. "Nothing bad happened. And of course I know the father, I just can't reveal his identity."

That explanation didn't do much to ease his worries, but judging by Ursula's thinned lips that was her last word about the topic. He wondered whether Anna knew. She and Ursula had always been close and despite their different characters had shared all their small and not so small secrets with each other.

Unfortunately, there was no way to ask Anna, so he'd have to live with his curiosity, but he was determined to find out the big secret. Sooner or later. For now though, he decided to seize the day and enjoy life with his new wife.

"... so when are you going to tell us?" Ursula's voice interrupted his reminiscing.

He stopped in his tracks, caught unawares, and stared at her inquiring face. "Tell you what?"

"That Katrina is expecting."

His jaw fell to the floor. How on earth had she even found out?

Thankfully, Katrina came to his rescue and said, "We wanted to announce the big news as soon as I had permission to stay here, so today would be a great opportunity, right, Richard?"

Unable to do more than nod, he continued to walk toward Kleindorf, shaking his head at the ways of the women in his life. As they arrived at the farm, he didn't see anyone around, not even the little children, and it stabbed at his heart. He hadn't expected any huge festivities, but after the drab ceremony at the town hall he had at least hoped for a word of congratulations.

He sensed the same disappointment in Katrina and squeezed her hand, trying to convince himself that he was overreacting. Aunt Lydia had a farm to run, and they had postponed the reception to the future when – hopefully – Katrina's brothers could attend.

A mumbled noise caught his attention and he jerked up his head, instantly ready to fight against whatever evil waited behind the closed door.

"Wait here," he told Katrina and Ursula before he sneaked up to the kitchen door and slammed it open. He froze in place, chills rushing down his spine as he peered into the expectant faces of Aunt Lydia, Frau Hansen and eleven children.

As soon as they saw him, Lydia cried out, "Congratulations to the freshly married couple," and then everyone started to sing, *"Eine Hochzeit, die ist lustig, eine Hochzeit, die ist schön."* A wedding is jolly; a wedding is nice.

Katrina sidled up to him and he saw that she had tears in her eyes. It might not be the most unromantic wedding after all. Hugs and kisses were shared and all the children wanted to touch the bride.

Aunt Lydia ushered them into the kitchen where she had set the table for everyone. In the middle stood a wedding cake with real cream on top.

Richard's mouth watered and he licked his lips. He couldn't remember the last time he'd eaten whipped cream. "Aunt Lydia, there was no need for this…" he feebly protested, but she waved his remark away.

"I'm not about to stand for letting my only nephew get married without so much as a wedding cake. Not on my farm!"

"Thank you, Lydia. That's so generous of you." Tears of joy spilled down Katrina's cheeks.

"We all have come to love you and I'm sure you'll be a good wife to Richard."

Katrina nodded, having difficulties voicing a word. The next moment, one of the children asked, "Can we now eat the cake?"

Everyone in the room laughed and settled around the table for the feast. Frau Hansen served homemade cherry juice for the children and coffee, albeit not the real kind, for the adults. Then Lydia distributed the cake: one piece for each person, the biggest ones for Katrina and Richard.

After some chatting, Richard clinked his spoon against a glass. "Thank you so much for this wonderful surprise." He looked around the table. "While the ceremony itself in the town hall was less than memorable, this," he encompassed the kitchen with a gesture, "... celebration made our special day truly wonderful. We're both incredibly happy and moved by the efforts you've gone to. And..." he paused for a moment, "... we have another announcement to make."

He could see the knowing glance on not only Ursula's but also Aunt Lydia's face and wondered why'd they never said a word. "My lovely wife is expecting a baby."

More congratulations followed and happiness filled the room.

Ursula stood. "In absence of our parents it's probably my duty as Richard's oldest sister to say a few words." She smiled. "Welcome to our family, Katrina. I must confess I wasn't overly pleased in the beginning. But you have proven to be the best woman Richard could wish for, and a good friend for all of us." She leaned over to pick up a box from the kitchen counter. "We didn't have much time, but thanks to Aunt Lydia, I made this for you." Then she handed the box to Katrina and said with a wink, "Sorry, but I don't have anything for you, dearest brother."

Katrina opened the box and took out a simple, caramel-colored dress with lace at the hem. She held it up and Richard noticed that it was loose enough to fit until the baby was born.

"It's beautiful. But I can't possibly accept this." Katrina fingered the fabric, her hands caressing the fine material.

"You can and you should, or you'll soon have nothing to wear," Ursula said with a wink.

Richard took a closer look at the dress and a faint memory came up from times before the war. His aunt would set the table in the living room with the fine china and a silky linen tablecloth – caramel-colored with lace on the edges.

"Put it on," one of the older girls urged Katrina. She smiled and left the room. A few minutes later, she returned in the dress, positively glowing. The caramel color enhanced her suntan and made her brown eyes shine. As far as Richard was concerned, she was the most beautiful woman on earth.

"You look stunning," he whispered against her ear as everyone cheered them both.

Much later, when the children had been put to bed, they bid their goodnights to Ursula and Aunt Lydia. When they climbed the stairs to the attic, he turned to Katrina with a mischievous grin, "I haven't forgotten about your promise to love, pleasure and obey me for the rest of our lives."

"Hey… the registrar said nothing about pleasuring you…" she protested, but he'd already swept her up in his arms and carried her across the threshold and put her on her feet in front of the bed.

His hand skimmed over the soft material of her loose dress and he couldn't wait to see how she'd look when her swollen belly filled it out. But for now he'd show her how much he adored and worshipped her.

CHAPTER 17: TOM

Tom had been mulling over a plan on how to get to Kleindorf and look for Ursula. Since the Potsdam Conference was over, he received regular leave days and most of his colleagues used them to either visit family back home or explore Germany. Despite its dilapidated condition, the country still had beautiful places to go, especially in summer and at the coast. But Tom wasn't interested in exploring. He needed to find Ursula.

One Friday night he sat in a bar with his American friend Mitch, who talked about his latest trip to the Alps. That's when it hit him between the eyes. Mitch would be his ticket to Kleindorf.

"Another beer?" Tom asked and, upon the other man's nod, gestured for the bartender to bring another round.

"Say, when are you flying into Munich again?"

Mitch glanced up, a big grin spreading across his face. "Next week. Got me a beautiful Fräulein there. Can't leave her alone for too long."

"Did you cut ties with Irene?" Irene was the Berlin girl Mitch had been laying.

"No need. They both know I'm just in it for the sex. I'm simply not a one-woman guy."

Tom shook his head. He definitely *was* a monogamous guy, hadn't even looked at another girl since he'd met Ursula. "And they're okay with that?"

"Sure. It's not that they don't enjoy it. But I suspect they're more interested in the presents I bring them." Nylons, cigarettes, chocolate, even a loaf of bread were coveted items in occupied Germany and young, pretty girls would often lower their moral standards for those who could provide them. Tom didn't judge them, but he felt a twinge of sadness that the girls felt the need to do so.

"About Munich." Tom returned the conversation to the topic burning on his tongue. "Could you take a passenger along?"

Mitch gave him a questioning look and asked, "You have a burning desire to see Munich?"

"Hmm." Tom took a long drink of his beer.

"You really have to come up with a better explanation if you expect me to take you."

Tom nodded and then lowered his voice, "It's about a woman."

"Ah, so you changed your mind about the Fräuleins. But why Munich? Aren't there enough peachy dolls around here?"

"It's not just any woman." Whether Tom wanted to or not, he had to bite the bullet and tell his friend the truth. "It's the one who smuggled me out of the country two years ago."

Mitch put his beer bottle onto the bar with a loud thud. "Holy shit! You kidding me?" Since Tom offered no answer except for a shake of his head Mitch took a while to process the information. "I can't believe this. That's nuts. Downright nuts. You a lovesick puppy still pining for that girl… do you even know whether she's still alive?"

Tom looked around to make sure nobody was within earshot and said in a low voice, "I went to her flat and her sister told me where to find her."

Mitch's face froze into a mask of incredulity and he downed the rest of his beer, ordering another one. "Man, you know what this is? Fraternization. This isn't a bit of hanky-panky the higher-ups will turn a blind eye to. You're in deep shit."

"I know."

"Man, I really shouldn't take you to Munich." Mitch ran a hand through his cropped hair.

"Please. I must see her."

Mitch stared into Tom's eyes, still shaking his had. "You're nuts. Crazy nuts."

"Come on. Nobody will be the wiser. And even if someone finds out, you can always say I didn't confide in you." Tom waited with bated breath for Mitch's answer.

"Okay. Give me a few weeks. I'll make the arrangements. But no word about the why to a living soul, you hear me? Tell everyone you're going hiking in the Alps."

"Thanks, mate. I owe you one."

~

Two weeks later he walked up to the Tempelhof airfield used by the USAAF. Mitch was already waiting for him at the main gate and nodded in greeting, "Morning, Mitch."

"Right back at you. You have your identification?" Mitch asked.

"Always."

"Good. Just follow my lead. And remember you want to go hiking." Mitch led them into the guardhouse where he handed over his military identification and signed the logbook. "Hey, John. This is my passenger, Squadron Leader Tom Westlake from the British Royal Air Force."

The NCO on duty took Tom's identification, transcribed his name and rank into the record book and then showed Tom where to sign his name.

"Have a good flight," the NCO said as he handed back the ID card.

Mitch lifted a hand in greeting and then strode toward the aircraft parked at the edge of the airfield. Tom matched him stride for stride. "The guy seemed quite friendly."

"Yeah, if he wants to be. But he's also a stickler for the rules. You definitely don't want him getting wind of this woman."

"Got it."

Mitch stopped at the first hangar and talked to one of the mechanics. Addressing Tom again, he said, "We have to wait. They just finished loading the cargo. But we're cleared to take off in an hour. Wanna grab a bite?"

Tom nodded and they headed to the officers' mess, where they chose pancakes with syrup and a cup of real coffee.

"Man, you've got the good stuff here. We still live on the fake coffee."

Mitch grinned, stuffing a big piece of pancake into his mouth. "Pays to come from the right side of the big pond. You're welcome to stop by anytime you want."

Tom glanced around. The mess looked similar to their own, except for the different uniforms and the annoying chewing-gum-like accent.

"Is the Red Army still giving you trouble?" Mitch asked.

"All the time. There's constant activity from those bastards and just last week one of them made an emergency landing, pretending not to be able to reach their airfield in Staaken."

"Isn't that just a few miles north?"

"Damn well it is. Just a ruse to spy on us."

"Stalin wouldn't dare do this here. We'd shoot them sons of bitches down," Mitch said.

Although Tom wasn't convinced the Americans would indeed risk a severe diplomatic falling-out over an emergency landing, he liked the idea. The Soviet presence right next to RAF Gatow was annoying as hell. The Ivans seemed to forget on a daily basis that the area had been ceded to the British in exchange for a much bigger area in Spandau.

"Nobody wants to start another war," Tom said.

"Like hell we don't. But Stalin sure is asking for it. The ink on the Potsdam Protocol hasn't dried yet and already he's doing his best to ratchet up tensions." Mitch looked at his wristwatch. "We'd better get going. We'll have to sign you in with the squadron and at the hangar."

Tom grinned. "Same procedure everywhere."

"Yep, wouldn't want some crazy Nazi sneaking onto the

aircraft with you." Mitch completed the security protocol and soon enough they were sitting in the cargo plane headed for Munich.

"Where exactly are you going?" Mitch asked as they both leaned back and admired the dark blue sky. Flying had become so much more pleasurable again since Tom didn't have to drop bombs on civilians anymore. He occasionally suffered nightmares from his actions, despite his best efforts to block out the results of his sorties.

"It's a tiny village about seventy miles west of Munich."

"That's a long ways, and all for a woman."

Tom smiled. Ursula wasn't just any woman.

Mitch turned to look at Tom's face. "Shit. You're smitten. I've never seen a fella with such a cheesy smile."

Tom didn't reply. Mitch might be a good man and good friend, but he had no idea about true love. At least not yet. "When are you flying back?"

"I managed to get twenty-four hours off and stay overnight. Return flight is scheduled for tomorrow evening. Be punctual, because I won't be able to wait." Mitch chuckled.

"I'll do my best. I'm back on duty the day after tomorrow."

"So you meet her and then what?"

"I haven't thought that far ahead. I mean… first I have to find her, right? Then I'll take it from there." Tom scratched his head; he suddenly wasn't so convinced about his plan anymore. He couldn't very well take her with him to Berlin, or even promise any kind of serious relationship. They'd have to hide from both her people and his, and he wasn't so sure she'd be willing to be his *secret flirtation*. Heck, he himself wasn't sure he wanted to have an illicit affair with the woman who owned his heart.

His gaze roamed across the landscape below them and he tried to conjure up her sweet face, searching for words to say to explain the depth of his feelings. He shook his head. The nearer the aircraft approached its destination, the harder his heart thundered in his throat.

What if she didn't feel the same? What if she'd found herself another man? The knot in his stomach tightened and he had the urge to vomit.

Once they landed at the Riem airport in Munich, Mitch secured a ride for Tom all the way to Mindelheim. "Good luck, man, and I'll see you here tomorrow at five p.m."

"Sure."

Tom hopped onto the military vehicle at once eager and reluctant to arrive in Kleindorf. The driver dropped him off at a crossing and pointed his thumb to the left. "That way. Shouldn't be too far. If you want a ride back come to the town hall in Mindelheim tomorrow before noon."

"Thanks, mate." Tom nodded and trotted off. As soon as he reached the village of Kleindorf, he took out a sheet of paper from his breast pocket with Anna's drawn directions to her aunt's farm.

His pace slowed down with every step, as if an invisible force dragged him backward. The sensible thing to do would be to forget about her. Seeing her again would only lead to heartbreak – for either one or both of them.

They simply weren't meant to be together. Not in this world. Not when their countries officially hated each other.

CHAPTER 18: LOTTE

Berlin, August 1945

Lotte returned home on a sunny day in August. The shock at the deplorable condition of Berlin in general, and the building where her family used to live in particular, struck a chord in her soul, impeding any movement.

She stood frozen to the cobblestones on the street, a car honking at the obstacle she presented, her eyes widening by the moment. A barely standing structure with gaping bomb holes in walls peppered with bullet holes, and smashed windowpanes, confronted her.

Please God, let them be alive and here, Lotte prayed, as she slipped through the entrance door that hung off its hinges. She rushed up the damaged stairs, taking three steps at once, when a young boy dashed down, brushing past her without a word as he darted on outside into the street and disappeared.

Lotte's heart nearly stopped. He hadn't recognized her, but despite his having grown so much in the past year she recognized him immediately. If her nephew Jan was here, the rest of the family must be, too. With newfound energy she bounded up to the fourth floor and stood on the landing, heart thumping and palms sweating.

She banged on the door with both fists, not caring whether she alerted the entire neighborhood. Her brother-in-law Peter opened the door, scowling angrily. The last time she'd seen him in Warsaw he was an impressive, fear-inspiring, burly man. Now she stared in shock at his hollow face and skeletal frame. Riddled with shock, she couldn't utter a single word.

"You want to break a door that's already hanging on its last hinges? We have no money, nor anything else. Go away." He attempted to slam the door in her face, but she was faster and pushed a foot between door and frame.

"Peter, it's—"

In that moment she heard her sister Anna's voice calling out, "Who is it at the door?"

Tears spilled from Lotte's eyes and before Peter could say a word, she screamed, "Anna. It's me, Lotte."

Moments later she was staring at her sister, who had an expression of total disbelief in her eyes.

"Lotte, honey, you made it home." Anna pushed her husband aside and wrapped her arms around her sister, both women bawling like babies right there in the door-frame, until Peter finally pulled them inside.

"Oh, Anna..." Lotte had yearned such a long time to reunite with her family that now the words slipped from her brain. Moments later she found herself on a dilapidated sofa, holding a glass of water in her hands, tears spilling down her cheeks.

"Goodness, Lotte, they told us that you'd gone missing…" Anna hugged her so hard she thought her ribs would crack. "I'm so glad you're here."

"Where's Mutter? And Ursula?"

"Ursula moved to Aunt Lydia's with the baby and Mutter is running errands."

"Thank God…" Lotte barely dared to ask her next question. "What about Richard? And our father?"

Anna shook her head. "We haven't heard from them."

"Which is a good thing," Peter said. "If they had been killed, your mother would have been informed." It was a small solace.

"I saw Jan dashing down the stairs, but he didn't recognize me."

Peter chuckled. "I didn't recognize you, either. Thought you were a vagrant coming to beg."

Moments later the door opened, and her mother entered the apartment.

"What's…" Mutter dropped her shopping bag, and a dozen potatoes for which she'd probably been queuing for hours tumbled to the floor. Lotte jumped into her mother's opened arms. "Lotte, my baby. God… darling… you're here… my baby is here."

Lotte had never been one to remain idle. She jumped with both feet into activities and became a *Trümmerfrau,* working nine hours a day cleaning up the city. And cleaning up had nothing to do with mopping, sweeping or brushing.

No, Lotte and her coworkers did the backbreaking work of removing rubble, taking down unstable buildings, hammering mortar off the bricks or handing buckets full of debris down the line into a waiting container.

She didn't especially like the work – because who in their right mind would – but she got paid 72 *Reichspfennig* per hour, which was actually a misery, and extra rations. As *Schwerstarbeiter,* the highest category of hard labor, she received twice the fat rations than a *Hausfrau* did. This amounted to four hundred grams of fat per month, plus one hundred grams of meat and half a kilo of bread per day and helped to feed the family.

The devastation in the city was hard to look at and her heart grew dreary every time she walked through the streets to her workplace at some construction area. But she also saw the small signs of improvement, when an unstable building had been cleared away and the heavy machinery arrived to build a new one in its place. With time and plenty of hard work, her beloved Berlin would one day shine in its former glory again.

One day she returned home in the evening, her hands full of red and oozing blisters from shoveling debris all day. She stretched out her shoulders, arms, and neck, before she fell on the dilapidated sofa in the living room.

"Want some peppermint water?" Jan asked from the kitchen. Since school hadn't opened up, he spent most of his time wandering around, organizing whatever might be usable.

"Yes, please. Although a fat piece of bread with butter

and ham to accompany it would be even better." She could already smell and taste the fatty butter on her tongue and had to laugh when Jan replied.

"Coming." The little butter they were given was never wasted by spreading it onto bread.

She closed her eyes and dozed off until Jan woke her with a glass of fresh and minty-smelling water.

"Here." He handed her a thick slice of bread with barely visible traces of a whitish spread.

"What's that?" she asked, biting into the bread. The taste wasn't familiar.

"Kefir," Jan said, sitting next to her on the sofa.

Lotte had long given up asking him how and where he got the stuff he brought home. Some things were better left in the dark.

Minutes later her sister Anna returned from her work. She glanced with a hungry expression at the bread in Lotte's hand.

"Want a bite?" Lotte asked, but Anna shook her head.

"I already ate at the hospital."

"Liar," Lotte said. "You know, it won't do us any good if you starve yourself to death just so we can eat more."

Her sister gave a deep sigh and changed the topic. "What happened to your hands?" Before Lotte could hide them, Anna took one of her hands and scrutinized it with her nurse-gaze. "They're cankerous. Wait here and I'll get my kit."

Anna returned with a small bag and frowned. "Don't they even give you gloves?"

"Gloves? We're lucky when they give us tools."

Lotte gritted her teeth as Anna cleaned and disinfected the wounds and then dressed them.

"Good as new." Anna stored her utensils in the small bag and fumbled for a roll of American army-standard tape in a matte olive color. "The American soldiers call it duct tape and it keeps anything in place," Anna explained. "Before going to work tomorrow, paste it over the dressings on your hands. It should help avoid more blisters."

"You sure that's state-of-the art medicinal advice?" Lotte giggled at her sister's unorthodox treatment.

"Don't tell Professor Scherer, will you?" Anna smiled.

"My lips are sealed," Lotte promised and leaned back, her eyes falling shut after another hard day of work. She must have dozed off, because when she woke, it was already getting dark outside and she heard voices from the kitchen. Mutter must be preparing dinner and Anna's husband Peter had arrived home from work.

Jan came to announce that dinner was ready and Lotte moved her tired bones from the sofa into the kitchen. She fell like a stone on the next best chair and then stared speechless at the apparatus on the workbench. "What's that?"

"You worked as a radio operator and have never seen a radio before?" Peter teased her.

"Of course I know a radio, but how did it get here? And why?" The Soviets had requisitioned – stolen was a more appropriate word – all radios in Berlin when they first arrived, along with wristwatches, alcohol and anything of value.

"Peter brought it," Anna said, not giving any more explanations. "And he has some great news. Apparently the

Western Allies have installed a mail service between Berlin and their occupation zones as of today."

"Wow." That was indeed great news.

"They said it will take some time to work through the backlog, but mail will be entering and leaving the city daily now," Peter said.

"Mutter and I have written a letter to Ursula already. Do you want to add something?" Anna asked, handing her a sheet of paper and a pen.

Lotte skimmed the letter, summarizing what had happened to the family in Berlin and letting their loved ones know they were well and alive.

"Does Aunt Lydia even know I'm not dead?" Lotte asked.

"Ursula will explain it to her, when she receives the letter." Mutter took the pot from the stove and placed it on a trivet on the table.

Nodding, Lotte wrote, *Love you and hope to see you soon, Lotte,* beneath Anna's writing. It felt strange to sign with her real name again.

Mutter glanced at the sheet of paper and remarked, "Did you visit the administration to get things with your real identity sorted out?"

"No," Lotte sighed. "When would I even have time for that?"

"You really should start the process as quickly as you can, since it might take a while."

"Yes, Mutter."

CHAPTER 19: URSULA

A loud knock on the front door startled Ursula. The only ones who knocked were the American soldiers. Usually they drove recklessly in their shiny jeeps and she could hear them from miles away. But today she hadn't heard a vehicle come down the road.

She dried her hands on her apron and walked over to open the front door. The knock came again, softer this time, and she wondered who it could be. The visitor certainly didn't follow the pattern of the occupiers, but who else would knock on their door?

Not the neighbors, who came in through the backyard. Definitely not the people who lived on the farm. Her heart sped up. Maybe Lydia's husband Peter had returned from captivity. It was a possibility. Her feet rushed to open the door and for a moment she froze in shock.

The man standing outside wore a uniform, but it wasn't the familiar khaki-green one of the Americans, nor a Wehrmacht uniform in *feldgrau*. It was RAF-blue.

The moment she locked eyes with him, her knees gave out beneath her. Thanks to his quick reflexes, he caught her in his arms, preventing her from crashing to the floor.

"Ursula, are you alright?" he whispered, pressing her against his chest.

Tears spilled from her cheeks and she couldn't utter a single word if her life depended on it. She regained control over her legs and snuggled against him, her tears wetting his uniform jacket.

After what seemed to be an eternity, she looked up at the face she'd dreamed about every single day for two long years and traced a finger down his cheek. Finally she found her voice again. "Tom. You're here."

"I'm here." His green eyes shone bright, making her heart sing.

"I'm not dreaming, am I?"

"Definitely not. You can't imagine how much I missed you." His voice was deep, slightly choked with emotion, and incredibly soft. His words transcended the gap of time, and she felt as if mere days had passed since their last encounter, not two years.

"How did you find me?" she whispered. Her eyes riveted to his, she forgot about anything except her love for him.

"I'm stationed in Berlin and Anna told me."

"Anna... so she's fine?"

"She, her husband, your mother, your nephew."

"Oh, my God. I still can't believe you found me." More tears spilled down her face. His eyes became impossibly soft and he leaned down to kiss her.

Ursula closed her eyes as sensation rushed through her body. She wrapped her arms tightly around his neck, clinging onto him, returning the kiss, while laughing and crying all at once.

"What in the hell is going on here?" Richard's angry voice interrupted their happy reunion.

She broke the kiss, the heated flush on her cheeks turning into embarrassment. Kissing a man in public, the way she'd done, wasn't the way a decent woman behaved.

"Get away from her," Richard demanded, taking a menacing step towards Tom.

The perplexed look in Tom's eyes showed confusion, hurt… and fear. "Is he… your…?"

"Brother. I'm her brother and you have no business kissing her." Richard stepped between Ursula and Tom and scrutinized Tom's blue uniform. "You don't even have business being here, since you obviously are a Tommy."

"Richard. Please… it's not what it looks like."

"It isn't? I could see quite well how you threw yourself at this man. What did he promise you in return?" Ursula had never seen her brother so livid and she feared he'd strangle Tom with his bare hands.

"Nothing but my undying love." Tom had found his voice again and sidestepped Richard to put an arm around Ursula's shoulders, while sending a threatening stare toward her brother. She felt like a zookeeper in the cage with two growling lions about to tear each other apart.

"Here you are, can you…?" Katrina came round the corner from the herbal garden and stopped mid-sentence. She quickly assessed the explosive situation and put her arm around Richard's waist.

At least now we're two zookeepers with the lions, Ursula thought, sending her sister-in-law a relieved glance before she explained. "This is Flying Officer Tom Westlake. He's the man I fell in love with two years ago. And this is my brother Richard Klausen and his wife Katrina."

Richard squinted his eyes. "Flying Officer, eh? A Tommy pilot?"

"Actually it's Squadron Leader," Tom said with an apologetic grin toward Ursula. "I've been promoted since returning to England."

"Doesn't change the fact that you're an enemy soldier," Richard stubbornly insisted.

"Look who's talking," Katrina said. "The man who fell in love with a woman from an inferior race and abandoned his army because he hated what they were doing."

"That's different." Richard pouted. Although the tension was slowly leaving his body, Ursula sensed that he wasn't convinced yet. "This man in his ritzy RAF uniform is only here to take advantage of my sister."

"You can't know that. In fact, I believe he wouldn't have made the long journey from the British sector all the way here if he didn't have true feelings for Ursula." After Katrina's wise words, Ursula wanted to kiss her for her mediation.

She decided to take off the edge by changing the topic. "Tom brought news from Berlin. He's visited Anna and Mutter and they're alive and well."

Richard gave a growl, but didn't say a word.

"Would you like to come inside and have something to drink?" Katrina asked.

"I'd love to, thank you." Tom glanced around, making sure there weren't any people around who might see him, and followed them inside. He greedily drank a glass of water in the kitchen and then unpacked several things from his kitbag that Ursula hadn't seen in months. A full kilo of sugar, a bar of chocolate and real tea.

She gave him another – modest – kiss on his cheek, in spite of Richard's dark stare, when suddenly a nagging fear crawled into her bones. She smiled it away and helped Katrina set the table for four.

Lydia had taken the older children to the nearby forest searching for mushrooms and wouldn't return until dusk. The younger children swept the barn under Matilde's supervision. Ursula deliberately focused her attention on the here and now, the tension between the two men still resembling a tinderbox waiting to explode.

Katrina managed to distract them with chit-chat and questions about Berlin. Soon, Richard relaxed, but still eyed his sister's improper suitor with suspicion. Ursula couldn't even blame him for it, because she knew everything about how inappropriate, impossible, and illegal her love for Tom was.

Because of the Nazis' ban on any and all relations between Aryan women and foreigners it had been illegal when she fell in love with him. And it had stayed illegal even after the tides had turned, because the new powers had installed anti-fraternization policies.

So deep was her concentration that she didn't hear the patter of small feet. Moments later the door opened and Matilde peeked her head inside, a deliciously dirty Evie in her tow.

"Mami!" Evie rushed toward Ursula, a frightened-to-death frog in her hand.

"I'm sorry, she..." Matilde swallowed at the sight of the

uniformed soldier in the kitchen and backed out immediately, leaving Evie behind.

Ursula wished for the earth to swallow her whole. She'd sought for a less daunting way to introduce Tom to his daughter.

"You... have a daughter?" Tom stammered.

Ursula wanted to explain, but since no words left her mouth, she simply nodded. An uncomfortable silence ensued and only Evie wasn't fazed in the least at the drama unfolding in the sunlit kitchen. The frog had escaped the captivity of her hands and she chased him across the room, giggling and yelling in the process. Since she'd only taken her first steps several weeks ago, the frog was immensely better suited for the race, which she didn't seem to mind in the least.

"I'd better go. Thank you for your hospitality." Tom jumped up as if stung by an adder and grabbed his kitbag lying in the corner.

"Wait!" Ursula yelled. "Please..." He turned around and the bottomless hurt in his green eyes slashed her heart into pieces. The time for breaking the news gently and privately had passed and the only thing that might mend the situation was blurting out the truth. "She's your daughter."

"What?" three voices said in unison and Ursula felt the stares of three pairs of eyes on her.

"No wonder you didn't tell anyone who the father was," Richard said. "This is—"

"Don't," Katrina silenced him. From the corner of her eyes Ursula noticed how her sister-in-law pushed Richard in the direction of the hallway, picking up Evie on her way.

When they were alone, she gave Tom a pleading look. He

sunk back on his chair and asked with a trembling lip, "Is it true? I have a daughter?"

She couldn't hold his disbelief against him; it was a lot to cope with after just having met her again. Ursula sat down beside him and took his trembling hand into hers. "Can't you see it? She has your eyes."

"But how?"

"Don't you remember the night before you left Germany?" She smiled, although his words had wounded her soul deep within. How could he not remember, when she'd been reliving those precious few hours over and over again?

"Of course, how could I ever forget, but… we did it only that one time. I never expected…" He choked on the emotion.

"Neither did I." She swallowed. "You can't imagine how scared I was."

"And rightly so. If anyone had found out…" A frown wrinkled his forehead. "You couldn't even tell your family, you poor thing." He reached out to caress her cheeks. "My poor darling, I'm so sorry. I wish I could have been there for you."

"Anna is the only person who knew – and now Richard and Katrina."

"Anna didn't tell me a word."

Ursula bit her bottom lip and then giggled, as the tension left her body. "What did you expect? She was sworn to secrecy and she'd catch hell if she'd be the one to deliver the message."

"Can I? I mean can I talk to her?"

"I'd love for you to get to know her." Ursula had

dreamed of this moment, but now she wasn't sure how to best handle it. In her fantasies interfering regulations and laws had never been featured. "Although, maybe... maybe we shouldn't tell her just yet."

His face fell and she put a hand on his arm. "It would make everything more difficult for all of us if the wrong people got wind of it." She in particular thought about some of the turned ex-Nazis who'd delight in ratting her and Tom out to the authorities just to gather some goodwill for themselves.

Tom nodded with a stern expression that showed just how much he hated the secretiveness. "What's her name?"

"Eveline, but we call her Evie. I wanted a name that sounds well both in English and in German." Her cheeks heated up, but her anxiety was unfounded, since Tom beamed like a floodlight and finally kissed her again.

"I love you and I'm sure I'll love our daughter," he whispered into her ear.

Ursula's heart melted the same way her body melted into his arms. After a minute she broke away and said, "Let's go and find Evie." They found their daughter playing in the yard with her cousins.

"Evie, come here!" Ursula called out and when the little one came rushing toward her, her heart warmed the way it always did when watching her daughter. But this time it was even better, because for the first time since the child was born, her father was standing by Ursula's side. "This is Tom. He's... a good friend. Can you say hello to him?"

Evie nodded and waved with her little hands, not too pleased that she'd been interrupted in her play. But when Tom lifted her into his arms and threw her into the air, she squealed with delight. The cautious mother in Ursula wanted to step in and tell him this was too dangerous for a one-year-old, but seeing the happiness on both faces, she bit her tongue and stood by – although not without watching with an eagle's eyes and preparing herself to jump forward in case he let the child drop.

Tom didn't drop his daughter and during the next hour the two of them became best friends. Ursula's heart dropped into her shoes when she saw Aunt Lydia and the older children walking down the road toward the farm.

Caught up in Tom's return she'd totally forgotten her chores and hadn't even prepared supper for the family. She rushed into the kitchen where she bumped into her sister-in-law setting the table.

"No need to worry; I've got you covered," Katrina said. And for the second time that day Ursula wanted to kiss the other woman. She'd never forget what Katrina had done for her.

With mixed feelings, she stepped out into the yard where the rest of the family had just arrived. Tom had been wiser this time around and she saw him walking out of sight with Evie in his arms. That would give her some much-needed time to prepare her aunt for the news.

"Look what we found," Aunt Lydia proudly showed off their porcini harvest.

"So many?" Ursula eyed the baskets full with the precious mushrooms. "We can dry some and keep them for winter."

"Exactly my thoughts," Lydia replied.

When she wanted to step inside the house, Ursula held her back. "Can I speak to you for a minute?"

Lydia raised an eyebrow, but nodded and handed her basket over to one of her children. "Get that inside, will you?" Then she turned toward Ursula again, her face suddenly tense as if she knew what was coming.

"It… I never told you…" Ursula had no idea how to break the news.

"Are you in… trouble… again?"

"Oh no," Ursula hurried to say. "But… Evie's father is here."

Aunt Lydia's head jerked up.

"But you can't tell anyone."

"Why not?"

"Please. Promise you'll keep your composure—"

"Why would I have a fit? Is he some kind of criminal or lunatic?" Lydia pursed her lips, looking at her niece with that strict stare she used to shut her children up.

"He's…" Ursula writhed like a trapped snake "He's a British pilot."

"Good lord! And he's here? On my farm?"

"Yes. Please, will you not report him?"

Aunt Lydia shook her head in disgust. "You don't actually expect me to go to the Amis and tell on him? How could you think such a thing? Does your mother know?"

"No."

"So where is this soldier of yours?" Lydia seemed to take the news surprisingly well. Maybe because she herself had left home at sixteen to run away with her now-husband, the son of a farmer – and a suitor her parents didn't approve of.

"Follow me," Ursula said and walked around the corner where Tom was playing with Evie in the grass. "Tom, this is my aunt, Lydia Meier."

Tom stood and dusted off his uniform before he said almost without an accent, "Tom Westlake. It's a pleasure to meet you, Frau Meier, and I'm sorry if I am inconveniencing you."

Aunt Lydia smiled and extended her hand. "Herr Westlake. I see you already made friends with your daughter."

"Isn't she adorable?" Tom beamed with pride.

"She definitely is. But you shouldn't be seen here with that uniform of yours. Better come inside." She frowned and then added, "We have a refugee family living with us, and we can't be sure how they will react. Neither can we trust the children to keep a secret, so I'll introduce you as an acquaintance of my husband from before the war."

Ursula sat on tenterhooks throughout the supper, trying her best not to glance in Tom's direction, for fear she'd betray her feelings for him. With the Hansen family sharing supper with them she really couldn't afford to raise suspicions.

As they finished eating, Tom winked at Ursula and said, "I should take my leave; many thanks for your hospitality, Frau Meier." He walked over to the corner and picked up his kitbag.

"Wait, Herr Westlake, I'll show you to the main street," Ursula said and hurried after him. On her way out she almost tripped over Katrina, who'd gotten up as well and whispered into her ear, "Take your time. I'll take care of Evie."

That woman really had earned Ursula's undying gratitude today. Slipping into her shoes, Ursula caught Tom staring at her with unabated hunger. His desperation to be alone with her undeniable in his gaze.

They walked down the path, careful not to touch each other as long as they were within sight of anyone looking from the house. Just before they reached the fork in the road that lead to the barn, Ursula grabbed his hand and pulled him behind her.

"Where are we going?" he asked with a chuckle.

"To a place where we can talk. In private," she replied, although talking wasn't foremost in her mind. She closed the doors of the barn behind them and led him up the stairs to the hayloft.

Tom dropped backward into the hay, taking her with him. She struggled for a few moments, but he wouldn't let her go, pressing hot kisses on her mouth. "I missed you so much. I wasn't sure I'd ever see you again," he whispered between crushing her lips with his.

They were frantic for each other and Tom wasted no time in showing her everything they had missed by being apart. He made love to her. It wasn't a soft, gentle coming together, but hard and quick and filled with so much emotion, they were both left panting for breath afterwards.

"I have to go. I should find a place in town for the night," Tom said as they snuggled against each other.

"Please, don't go. We have so much to catch up on," she begged.

"If anyone sees me here…" She could tell he was wavering in his determination.

"We'll sneak into the house after dark."

"I have to return to Munich in the morning and catch my flight back to Berlin."

"You flew here?" Up until now she hadn't given thought to how he'd managed to come all the way down to the south.

Tom chuckled and nudged her nose. "What did you think? That I came on foot? I'm a pilot."

"So you came with your own plane?" She had never traveled by air and wondered whether he might take her one day. A day in the future when their love wouldn't be illegal anymore.

"Of course not." He caressed her naked shoulder. "I'm not allowed to fly into the American zone, but I have a pilot friend from over there. He offered me a ride."

"You caught a ride on a military aircraft, like normal people do on a bus?"

He surprised her with his full belly laugh. "I like the way you laugh," she said. In the short time they'd been together two years ago they'd both been under constant pressure and this was the first time she heard his laughter. It endeared him even more to her.

"You... what?" He shook his head.

"Yes. It's so refreshing, as if you didn't have a care in the world."

"I don't. Not when I'm with you."

Ursula wanted to be as carefree as he was, but she couldn't shake off the worries attacking her. It squeezed her heart not to know.

Night fell and hand in hand they snuck into the house, tip-toeing upstairs into the room she shared with Evie. The child was fast asleep and once again Ursula was reminded that she was deeply indebted to her sister-in-law. She kissed Evie's cheek and Tom followed suit.

"She's so beautiful," he said. "I still can't quite believe that I found not only you, but also a daughter I didn't even know existed."

In the wee hours of the morning, after making love throughout the night, she finally asked the question she'd been avoiding, "When will I see you again?"

Tom smoothed her hair back. "I don't know."

Ursula sighed. Her brain understood, but that didn't make it any easier. To lose him again, after one short day, seemed unbearable.

"I'll keep in touch. Your sister's husband, he works for us. I can give him a letter for you."

"A letter?" The idea of holding something that belonged to him in her hands brightened her spirits. "Can you send me a photograph, too?"

"That wouldn't be a good idea." He kissed her. "I'll find a way to see you again. I promise."

Dawn sent the first streams of light through the window and with great reluctance she pushed him away. "You have to leave."

"I know." Tom didn't move, not until they heard steps on the stairs.

"That'll be Aunt Lydia heating the stove. In less than half an hour everyone will be up."

"I love you, sweetheart." With the tender words he sneaked out of her room.

Moments later she watched his dark silhouette walk down the road toward the main street until it vanished from her sight. It shredded her heart to pieces.

CHAPTER 20: ANNA

Berlin, September 1945

"Do you have a moment, Frau Zdanek?" Professor Scherer asked as he strode into the nurse's room. Her mentor had adapted surprisingly well to the changes after the war. Sometimes she believed he'd completely forgotten everything that had happened before "the zero hour" as he called it.

"Of course, Professor, what do you need?"

"Please accompany me to my office." It was a rather unusual request. The Soviets had assigned him an office in the basement after they'd taken over the hospital. The professor, though, usually didn't use it for talks with his employees. He much preferred the more spacious and better lit upper floors.

"One moment, please." Anna finished writing the

patient report she'd been working on and then followed the Professor down to the basement. She hated going down there since the Soviets were running the hospital. And she hated working for them, but no work meant no food. Thus, she gritted her teeth and tended to her patients.

Professor Scherer closed the door behind her and locked it. A feeling of déjà vu caused her neck hair to stand on end.

"Please sit," he said with a pleasant smile.

Anna obeyed. She knew that smile. It was the one he used when he was about to execute a clever maneuver and his counterpart unsuspectingly fell into the trap. So far, she'd always been on his side of the game. Although she wondered whether he held a grudge against her for marrying the man who'd spied on him for years.

"Frau Zdanek. I must warn you that what I'm about to say is confidential and should never be revealed to the Soviets." His eyes fixed upon her and she noticed just how much he'd aged in the past year. The salt-and-pepper hair that had enhanced his attractiveness had turned almost completely white and the deep wrinkles etched around his eyes spoke of many sorrows.

"They won't hear anything from me," she said. Even if she didn't hate the Soviets, she'd never be disloyal to Professor Scherer. He might not be the perfect human being she wanted him to be, but he was well-connected. It would certainly serve her better to be on his side rather than against him.

"Good. The Charité has lost its luster and, to be frank, the scientific opportunities with the Soviets are far inferior to those the Western Allies can provide. I know, these are dreams of the future, but right now is the best time to lay the groundwork."

Anna didn't quite follow his train of thought, but she nodded nonetheless.

"I have put out my feelers and there's a definite need for highly skilled medical research personnel."

"But… aren't the Allies bringing in their own people?" Anna asked, since she'd heard that before.

"They are, but the wiser ones know they can't do without us Germans in the long run. And… I have found a few very powerful intercessors among the Americans." He leaned back in his chair, a self-indulgent smile crossing his face.

Anna remembered his strategy of doling out favors to those who might benefit him in the last days of the war. Once again, she was surprised at how well he knew the human psyche. His strategy apparently had worked like a charm. The new authorities held him in high esteem and no one seemed to remember that he'd been working for the Nazi regime and had even, whenever it benefited him, claimed to be one.

"The Americans have offered me a position as chief physician in one of their hospitals. And…" he gazed at her, "… I have negotiated with them to bring a confidante. My head nurse."

Her eyes went round. "You mean me?"

"Yes. Who would be better qualified than you?"

"That is… unexpected." Anna's considered the implications.

"Unexpected maybe, but not unwelcome. The Americans have offered generous pay and meals at the hospital." He smiled as he noticed her licking her lips. Even for a man in his position food was hard to come by, and she'd often suspected that he worried about her as she got thinner by the week.

"I'm incredibly grateful that you would think of me."

"You accept." It wasn't a question, but a statement.

"Of course I accept."

"Then you only need to sign the new contract and start working with me at the new hospital tomorrow." He handed her a one-sheet work contract. "I have taken the liberty of handing in your resignation to our Soviet employers."

Anna took the paper and signed it. She should be angry about the way he made decisions for her, but how could she not accept a job offer like this one? Head nurse with food benefits. As far as she was concerned, not having to enter the Russian sector every single day would have been reason enough already.

She loved working at the new hospital, because everything was so much easier than working with the Soviets. Much to her appreciation her new bosses made sure their employees received proper meals during their shifts.

But despite her delight about the food, she could barely eat a bite during her first days at the new workplace. Such was her guilt, thinking of her mother, Lotte and Jan, who had to scrape by on almost nothing. It was especially hard on Jan, an active twelve-year-old boy who needed to grow. But she'd been warned that it was forbidden to take any food home to their families.

Now she understood how Peter had felt all this time since taking up work with the British administration. It seemed the Allies would rather throw food away than give it to the starving Germans. She didn't understand how they could be so appalled at the Nazis' treatment of people and then turn around and do the very same thing, just calling it a different name.

Anna was still pondering how to best smuggle out food to her family when she witnessed something that changed her mind. Two of the nurses, each one the sole provider for several children, raided the garbage cans for food. She fell in line behind them as they exited the hospital after their shift.

"Open your bag please," one of the sentries asked and the first one dutifully opened her purse. He took a cursory glance and waved her through the gate. The second one, though, got nervous and as she opened her bag, a half-eaten sandwich, wrapped in a piece of paper, fell out of her sleeve.

"Stop!" the sentry yelled and within a split-second several soldiers materialized out of thin air, training their rifles at the nurses standing in line. Anna felt her blood turn into icicles and she dropped her purse to the floor, slowly raising her arms.

Every single woman in the hallway had to turn her handbag inside out, take off her coat and undergo a personal search. In spite of knowing that she didn't carry forbidden goods, Anna held her breath, fearing for the worst.

She was waved through the gate, but the nurse caught first and another one weren't so lucky. They were taken to the hospital director and the next day Anna learned they'd been fired immediately. It was a stark reminder not to question the rules of the Amis if she wanted to keep her job – and her ration cards.

From then on, Anna ate every single bite she could get her hands on, because she'd rather nurture herself than let the Americans trash the food. But she made it a habit to give her weekend rations to her family, because when she ate enough at work, she didn't need to eat while at home.

CHAPTER 21: TOM

Tom entered the bar that teemed with mostly British and American soldiers, with a few civilians sprinkled here and there. He scanned the room but didn't see Peter, Ursula's brother-in-law, anywhere. A slight inquietude upset his stomach. He'd surprised Peter with the invitation to go out for a beer. The other man had accepted, but Tom had seen the glint of reluctance.

Surely, Peter must think it wasn't appropriate for him to hang out with Tom in a bar, while his wife waited for him at home. Tom also had mixed feelings about going out with his pals. While he enjoyed the relaxation of an after-hour beer, the conversation inevitably turned to the topic of conquests and German Fräuleins. A topic he wished not to discuss.

Some of his comrades secretly whispered about him and suspiciously eyed his every move, because he didn't have a girl back home – and wasn't interested in a sexual affair over here. But how could he even pretend to be looking for someone else if Ursula owned his heart and soul? Now that he'd seen her and reignited the flames of passion, she captivated him more than ever.

Mitch – helpful but insensitive in affairs of the heart – had advised him to go out with one or two Fräuleins for cover and to ward off any unwanted scrutiny. A healthy man simply didn't go without a woman for too long. Tom shrugged off the unpleasant thought.

"Tom?"

He turned around and stared into Peter's ice-blue eyes. Relieved to be drawn out of his sorry thoughts, he got up and half-hugged Peter, slapping his shoulder. A bit too friendly, judging by the confused expression on the other man's face.

"I really don't think I should be here," Peter said, scanning the bar with the meticulous inspection of a longtime combatant.

"One beer. My treat." Tom gestured to the bartender. "Get my friend here whatever he wants."

Peter relaxed a little and took the barstool beside Tom "I'll have a beer."

The bartender, a skinny but curvy blonde, nodded and put a bottle of beer in front of Peter. Tom couldn't help but notice the way she checked out both of them. "Cheers." Tom clinked bottles with Peter and glanced around before he spoke. "I saw Ursula."

Peter pitched forward, spilling his bear. "Should I even ask how you pulled this off?"

Tom chuckled. "Yank pilot gave me a ride on his craft."

"How is she?"

"Well and alive. They're doing much better down there in the country than you blokes up here."

Peter nodded. It wasn't a secret that Berliners had drawn the shortest straw. "What about… the family?"

"You mean my daughter?"

"So she told you?" Peter took a big gulp from his beer bottle.

"She did. It was quite a shock to meet Evie, in more ways than one." Tom paused, unsure how much he should tell the other man. But the secrecy lay heavy on his chest. Peter was almost family, and after what Ursula had revealed about Peter's clandestine relationship with Anna, Tom was sure he'd understand his inner turmoil. He might even be able to offer advice – or at least consolation. "Did you know?"

Peter shook his head. "Not until after you visited us."

"It's killing me. We decided to keep it secret, because you know… she's a…" Tom couldn't bring himself to say the word *bastard*. But that was exactly what his daughter was in the eyes of everyone. She'd be shamed, mocked and derided should anyone get wind of her descent. "I can't acknowledge her, or even visit her regularly."

Peter's face took on a tortured look and he put his hand on Tom's arm, as if comforting a child. "Man, I'm sorry. I didn't see my own son for five years, had been told he was dead."

"The war is over and yet nothing has changed. I still can't be with Ursula." Tom stared at Peter's hand on his arm, compassion emanating from the other man. He already felt lighter. The old proverb really was true; a trouble shared was a trouble halved.

"You have to maintain hope and believe that in time things will change."

Tom sighed. "You know we all kept that same hope alive

during the war. I guess I was expecting we could just get back to living our lives once it was all over."

Peter chuckled. "Good luck with that. The entire world blames Germany for Hitler and his war and the Allies are determined to make everyone with German blood moving through their veins pay for it."

Tom didn't respond to that. In general, he was onboard with making the Nazis pay for the destruction they had caused, but he also recognized that good people like Ursula existed. People like her had risked their own lives to help those persecuted. It was a very confusing time. Tom finished his beer and shook himself out of his miserable thoughts. "Actually I came here to give you some good news, but thanks for commiserating."

"Good news? I'm dying to hear some of that." Peter grinned.

"Tell Anna that her brother Richard is alive."

Peter's jaw dropped to the floor. "What?"

"He arrived at the Meier farm several weeks ago."

"Did… has… is… there a woman with him?"

"Yes, he's married to a beautiful brunette called Katrina." Tom suddenly felt himself in a tight embrace and lifted up from his stool.

"Katrina? She's alive and well? God, I love you!"

Tom found the sudden emotional outburst of the other man awkward. He wriggled to get out of Peter's grip until another hand slapped him on his back and a familiar voice said, "You're disgusting, Westlake. Having it off with a Jerry!"

Tom turned and saw his nemesis, Ed Bronson. He

inwardly groaned. Leave it to that hotheaded jerk to stir up trouble. "I beg your pardon?"

"The Jerry, there. You're pansying around with this bastard. Shame on you!" Bronson raised his voice and spit on the floor, garnering the attention of the entire bar. "You're both disgusting."

"Bronson, mind your own business." Tom awkwardly stepped away from Peter, who looked as stricken as Tom felt.

Bronson's face grew red. "This is my business. That damn Jerry there is stinking up my bar and I want him gone. In fact, I want you both gone. Maybe a little time in jail would remind you where your loyalties lie."

Tom noticed Peter's tightening jaw and he was afraid the man would do something rash. Friendly nation or not, it wouldn't do him any good if he lost his patience and slapped a British airman in uniform. Tom stepped between the two men, forcing his voice to remain calm. "Bronson, this is all a misunderstanding. This man here is not German..."

Tom didn't get to finish his explanation because Bronson's fist flew into his face. The impact sent him rocking backwards, hitting the back of his head on the bar before he toppled to the ground. He'd experienced worse. Fighting against the red dots blurring his vision he jumped up, fists high and ready to engage.

Peter stepped between the two men and Bronson's next hook landed on Peter's jaw, making him wince. But to give Peter credit, he didn't punch back, very aware of his fragile standing amongst the mostly British soldiers frequenting the bar.

Tom, though, didn't have the same scruples and unleashed the rage and misery he'd been feeling for much too long into his punch against Bronson's stomach. It was only thanks to some man's quick action in holding him back that he didn't rip that bastard to pieces.

"You two. Break it up," came the cold-as-steel voice of an MP. Tom's body slumped and he didn't put up any resistance as the MP pulled his arms behind his back. Moments later the MP slapped cuffs on his wrists while his partner did the same to a swearing, kicking and punching Bronson.

"I'm so sorry, man," Peter said with a guilty face.

Tom shook his head. "This isn't your fault. It's his. Bronson's a loose cannon and he needs to learn to mind his own business."

"You having a drink with a Jerry is my business," Bronson tossed back angrily.

The MPs stood them a short distance from one another and then one approached Peter. "Papers, please."

"Of course." Peter nodded and withdrew his identification paperwork and his worker card for the British administration. The MP looked it over and handed it back saying, "Thank you."

He turned to Bronson and gave him a scathing look. "You're an arsehole. The guy is Polish and works in the administration building."

Tom smirked but knew better than to gloat in revenge.

"He's lying. He's a Jerry. Just look at him." Bronson was like a dog with a bone.

"His papers are in order and you are going to have to explain to the commander why you started a fight with a fellow officer. I would hate to be you," the MP told him as both men were escorted outside.

After presenting the case to the commander and spending a night in a cell, Tom was let go with a stern warning. Bronson, though, got a blot to his personnel record.

Tom almost felt sorry for his comrade, but an inner voice warned him that this incident would only intensify the grudge Bronson held against him. He was sure this wouldn't be the last trouble the man caused him.

CHAPTER 22: ANNA

Anna paced the apartment, a deep worry wrinkle on her forehead. It wasn't at all like Peter to return home late. He should have arrived hours ago.

"Anna, darling, you'll wear a hole in the floorboards if you don't stop," Mutter said and Anna stopped pacing with a sigh. But only for a moment.

"Where is he?" She circled the sofa in the living room.

"Peter is a grown man. He might have had to work overtime."

"He's never worked overtime before. The administration office always closes on time, no matter how long the queues still are."

"Sit and drink," her mother demanded and brought her a glass of hot water with a few leaves of lemon balm soaking in it.

"I need something stronger to calm me down," Anna said with a laugh, but sipped on the infusion.

Several minutes later Peter walked in the door. She

stumbled up, barely keeping the hot liquid from spilling over. "Thank God, you're home!"

Peter chuckled and took the glass from her hands, setting it on the sideboard before wrapping her up in his arms. She kissed him on the mouth and recoiled. Firing angry glares at her good-for-nothing husband she said with an icy tone, "You were out drinking? I've been pacing the floor, imagining all sorts of horrible things happening to you, and you went to a bar?"

Peter held up his hands, trying to soothe her. "I can explain, if you'll give me the chance."

She turned away, crossing her arms over her chest. "How do you explain making me worry like this? And for a beer? A beer we can't afford?"

He clasped her shoulders and turned her around to face him. His bemused smile irked her and she was just about to give him a piece of her mind when he put a finger over her lips. "I promise you'll be on your knees begging me for forgiveness when I tell you my news."

She rolled her eyes at him. "I don't see how you plan to achieve that but go ahead. Give it a try."

"Tom Westlake came to my office and insisted I go out for a beer with him. He paid, so you can stop worrying about money." Peter's ice-blue eyes brightened with delight and she had to focus hard on her determination to be angry with him.

"So you went out with Tom. That doesn't excuse making me worry."

"Ah, sweetheart. You should be more accepting of your husband or I won't tell you the big… grand… fantastic news."

Anna would have laughed at his antics, but she couldn't well give in just yet. First she had to let him stew in his own juices a while longer. Although she couldn't shake off the feeling that he indeed enjoyed the situation and it was she who was left stewing. "Alright then, what's your big news?"

"Wouldn't you like to know?" he teased her and tapped a finger on his cheek. "What about giving your husband the greeting he deserves after a long day of work?"

"God, I hate you," she said. Once again he'd flipped the tables on her. He knew exactly that she was dying to hear the news – and his lips would remain sealed until she surrendered to his demands.

"You love me."

"Maybe a tiny little bit." She pecked his cheek and found herself in his grip, a pair of passionate, beer-smelling lips devouring her mouth. She couldn't stay angry any longer, and when they came up for breath she asked, "So what's the great news?"

"Tom went to Aunt Lydia's farm to visit Ursula."

"He… he saw Ursula? And the baby?" Her legs gave out and it was a good thing that Peter was still holding her in his embrace.

"He did. And he's enamored with both of them."

Anna nodded.

"But there's more good news… he saw Richard."

"Richard? As in my brother Richard?" Suddenly she felt like hovering in the air. "Where? How? Why?"

"It seems that Richard arrived on the farm several weeks ago after an adventurous escape from Poland."

"Oh, wow!" Anna's brain stopped working. All she could think of was the solemn face of her younger brother the last time she'd seen him shipped off to the front. She kissed Peter again.

Her mother walked into the room giving her daughter a stern look. "Tsk. You can do this in your room."

Anna flushed. Her mother was very traditional and didn't like public demonstrations of affection, not even between husband and wife.

"Excuse us, Frida, but we have wonderful news to share," Peter said.

"Oh no, you are not... expecting?"

"No, Mutter." Anna knew that while her mother would love to have another grandchild, she was worried about the circumstances and feared they'd not have enough food to feed another mouth. "It's much better. Richard is with Aunt Lydia."

"Richard?" her mother asked hesitantly. "You have news from Richard?"

"Yes, Tom..." Anna shut her mouth. They hadn't told Mutter about Tom's visit and Anna sure as hell didn't want to be the bearer of *that* news.

Peter came to her aid. "A colleague at the administration found out that Richard was discharged from the Wehrmacht and has married my sister Katrina."

"He did?" Anna beamed with pure joy. "You are forgiven for coming home late. This is such good news. Both of them made it and are well and alive."

Mutter dabbed at her eyes and turned away. The door opened again and Lotte arrived together with Jan. "What's wrong? Who died?" she squealed, seeing her mother in tears.

"Nobody," Peter said.

"Then why is she crying?" Lotte asked. Anna could understand her shock, because their mother never cried. Anna had seen her mother cry only once – followed by a nervous breakdown. Jan put his arms around his grandmother's waist, murmuring, "It'll be alright."

Anna glanced at Peter and could see his heart swell with pride for his son. Frida Klausen and Jan weren't related by blood, but they shared a bond that was much stronger than even with her own children.

"Why do my children keep getting married without me there?" Frau Klausen asked no one in particular.

Anna stared at her mother and shared a look with Lotte, who shrugged and said, "Who got married?"

"Richard."

"You've gotta be kidding me." Lotte flopped onto the sofa, kicking off her shoes. "Is anyone going to fill me in?"

Peter took to the task. "A colleague found out that Richard and Katrina made it safely to Aunt Lydia's farm and got married not long ago."

Lotte gazed from Peter to Anna, to her sobbing mother, and a beaming Jan, who was jumping up and down with glee. "Who is Katrina?"

"My sister," Peter said.

"They got married without me, just like the two of you," Mutter complained.

"Why on earth did I have to be born into this family, where nobody wants to adhere to traditions?" Lotte lamented.

"You're the one to complain," Anna laughed. "When have you ever valued rules and traditions?"

"That's not the point here." Lotte theatrically rolled her

eyes. "The point is... nobody properly informs the family about important events."

"Peter just found out today..." Anna stopped talking as guilt crept into her bones. There were quite a few secrets Lotte didn't know about. One of them was the existence of Tom and that he was Evie's father. She gave her sister a smirk. "Well, it'll be on you to be the first of us four to have a proper wedding then."

"Don't tell me you're planning to get married, too?" Mutter said, boring her eyes into Lotte.

"Definitely not. I'd need a man for that, wouldn't I?"

Anna was immediately sorry for her remark, because she knew how much her sister suffered because she hadn't had news from her boyfriend. Not since he'd been captured by the Red Army in January.

CHAPTER 23: LOTTE

"The Soviets refuse to expedite travel permits with temporary papers." Anna tossed four stamped travel permits and one rejection onto the kitchen table.

Since Mutter knew that Richard and his new bride lived with Aunt Lydia, she itched to travel down there and visit the son she hadn't seen in years. But that meant they had to cross the Soviet zone. And with the tension between the former allies running higher by the day, bureaucratic nitpicking aimed at Berliners was a common occurrence.

"So now what?" Lotte asked, picking up the temporary papers she'd had expedited at the Danish-German border.

"You need to apply for papers under your real name," Anna said.

"Which you should have done weeks ago," Mutter reminded her and walked over to the sideboard, from where she took a sheet of paper. "Here's your birth certificate; that should help."

"Alright." Lotte gave a deep sigh. "I'll ask for time off at work and go to the administration first thing in the morning.

~

The queues at the registry office were long, even longer than those in front of the empty grocery stores and she waited for hours, before it finally was her turn.

"What is your request?" the American soldier manning the registry office asked her. He was in his mid-twenties with fair hair, blue eyes and an amazing smile that even his wartime experiences hadn't been able to wipe away. A handsome chap.

"I need to get permanent papers."

"Do you have proof of your identity?"

"Yes, my birth certificate." She handed him the paper, aware that he was appreciatively eyeing her.

"It shouldn't take long, I'll just check our files." He gave her a bright smile, and despite her reluctance to encourage him, she smiled back. He walked to the filing cabinets in the back of the room and searched for her name. He took out a list, mumbled something and returned, a puzzled expression on his face. "Here it says you're dead."

"Do I look dead to you?"

He ignored her remark. "Died of typhus in December 1943."

She hadn't expected them to have such meticulous records. Her request had just become a whole lot more complicated; resurrecting the dead probably wasn't something this GI did on a daily basis. For a short moment she considered asking for permanent papers under her fake identity. But that would mean she had to live for the rest of her life as Alexandra Wagner – a notion that caused a queasy feeling in her stomach. And the young soldier would be suspicious should she ask him to look for her under a different name.

"I can explain," Lotte said.

"How can you explain your own death? I believe you're an impostor, maybe a war criminal." His handsome face shifted into a grimace and she feared he'd jump up and have her arrested.

Flirt with him, that's what Anna would advise her to do in such a tricky situation. *Whatever you do, don't oppose him, because he has the upper hand.* Lotte hated to pretend, but she gritted her teeth and flashed him a smile.

"Please, Mr. Spark," she read the name on his name tag, "hear me out first, will you?" She gave him another dashing smile, the type she had reserved for Johann, the man she loved. A twinge of conscience attacked her, but she pushed it away. She did it for a good cause.

"It's Terry," his voice softened along with his facial expression.

Thanks, Anna! "I had to fake my own death to escape a Nazi camp. Since then I've been living under the name of Alexandra Wagner." She handed him her temporary papers, a staying permit for the city of Berlin and her worker's ID as *Trümmerfrau.*

His eyes scanned the papers and when he read her current occupation he glanced up, his eyes filled with awe. "Is this true?"

Lotte showed him her calloused, red, and raw hands.

"That's quite some hard work for a peachy Fräulein like you."

She smiled at him again. "It is, but I want to help rebuild my country. You can't imagine how much I yearned for the war to be over."

"You did?"

"Yes, because I expected that after a German capitulation law and order would be restored and I wouldn't have to fear being murdered for my opinions. And… I could resume my true identity again." She ran a hand through her short hair, wishing it had grown longer already.

"Why didn't you come here earlier? I see you registered as Alexandra Wagner a month ago."

Yes, why? Working all day to get food into her mouth. Reluctance to go through the red tape. No. If she was honest with herself it had been apprehension at facing the past. She had been – still was – terrified at the prospect of having to recount in gruesome detail the months in her life she never wanted to think about again.

"Alexandra?" His deep voice startled her. "You've been far away."

"I'm sorry, Mr. Spark, ahem, Terry. It happens when I have to think about the awful time in the camp. And that's probably the answer why I didn't come here earlier. I wasn't brave enough to confront my memories." Her voice turned softer. "But now… the brother I believed dead has shown up in Lower Bavaria and the entire family is planning for a visit during Christmas. But the Soviets," she made a face, leaving no doubt what she thought about them, "won't allow me to transit their zone without permanent papers."

"Nothing but nitpicking!" Terry burst out. "Damned Soviets are making our lives so much more difficult."

"They are."

"Will you go out with me?"

"Uhm." Lotte stared at him aghast. "Wouldn't that be against the fraternization rules?"

He looked crestfallen. "I'll have to take your case to my superior. Please wait here." He left the room, leaving her alone with contradictory emotions boiling inside of her.

Several minutes later he returned with a much older, much more senior officer. Lotte sat more upright.

"I'm Colonel Carpenter. Fräulein… Klausen, it is?" the officer asked.

"Yes. Charlotte Alexandra Klausen." She didn't dare smile at him.

"Private Spark has briefed me on your case. It's quite… unusual," he said. "I'm afraid this is going to take us some time to sort out. We can't issue permanent papers for you just now."

She nodded, a deep frown on her forehead.

"Do you have any proof for the claim that Charlotte Klausen isn't deceased?"

Lotte almost burst out laughing. *I'm sitting here. Is this proof enough I'm not dead?* "My mother and my sister both live in Berlin and could testify for me…"

Colonel Carpenter looked at her and then nodded his head. "This might help. What are their names?"

Lotte gave the requested information and Terry Spark searched for her family's names in the filing cabinets. The colonel scanned them and nodded. "Make an appointment with Private Spark for a hearing next week. Tell the witnesses to bring their own identification and any kind of proof such as photographs."

"Thank you, sir." Lotte sank back into her chair. It sounded intimidating but not impossible. The colonel left the room and Terry grinned at her. "Looks like we'll see each other again."

She forced herself to smile. "Yes. When would a meeting be convenient for you?"

CHAPTER 24: URSULA

Every single day Ursula peered out of the window. Her eyes trained upon where the road merged with the horizon, hoping, yearning, and praying for Tom to appear walking down to the farmhouse.

He never did.

More than a month had passed and she'd had no news of him, except for a letter from Anna that *a friend* had visited them. In the same letter Anna suggested the entire family visit Aunt Lydia's for Christmas.

"I think it's a fantastic idea," Aunt Lydia said. "We haven't been all together since before the war."

Ursula didn't want to rub salt in the wound by reminding her aunt that neither Uncle Peter nor Ursula's father would be present. Both of them were still in captivity.

"It would be very crowded here." Richard stopped when Ursula laughed.

"So, we'll all get close. Like we used to when we were

young. It'll be fun. And if the food situation in Berlin is as bad as the rumors, they need to be fattened up."

Aunt Lydia laughed. "Reminds me of the goose. We'll have to capture one and fatten it up for Christmas."

"I'll write a letter immediately," Ursula suggested. "They'll have to get interzone travel permits and we don't know how long that takes."

Dearest Anna,

Thank you so much for your last letter.

Aunt Lydia thinks a family reunion is a fantastic idea and she's already planning the Christmas dinner.

Richard and Katrina are dying to see all of you and so am I. It will be crowded here, but the more the merrier... we used to say that, before the war. You remember?

Christmas would the perfect time to get the entire family together and to be thankful that the war is over and so many of us have survived.

Please let us know when you'll be arriving.

All our love,

Ursula

The impending visit, though, had given her an idea. If she returned to Berlin, then she and Tom would find ways to see each other regularly. The next day she walked the eight miles to Mindelheim. She entered the town hall and made her way to the registry office.

"I'd like to request a permit to move to Berlin," she said to the soldier in charge.

"What is your reason?"

Reason? She couldn't well tell him about Tom, so she said, "I want to reunite with my family."

He looked up at her, frowning. "How old are you?"

"Twenty-four," she answered, wondering why on earth he would want to know her age.

"I'm sorry. Family reunion is a valid reason only for underage people."

Her shoulders sagged in dejection and he must have noticed her despair because he said in a less formal tone. "Except if you have a husband, a fiancé or a minor child in Berlin."

"No. Just my mother and sisters."

"Then I really can't do anything for you. You may request a permit to visit them, for example for Christmas, but you won't be allowed to stay in Berlin."

"Thank you." She left his office, her heart heavy. The walk back seemed endless and her steps became heavier with every passing minute. Even this morning she'd been hopeful, happy even, and now this.

The damn Americans wouldn't let her leave this place. She'd be condemned to live here for the rest of her life. A tear ran down her cheek as she wallowed in self-pity.

Richard was plowing the field near the road and spotted her walking along. "Hey, Ursula!" he yelled at her.

She straightened her back, attempting to wipe the desolation off her face. "Hello, Richard."

"Where've you been?"

"Mindelheim."

He cocked his head, his blue eyes piercing hers. "Care to tell my why the long face?"

"I requested a permit to move to Berlin, but the Amis said no. I don't have a valid reason." She pursed her lips in disgust.

"Sorry for that. The Allies are trying to control the movement of people. There are so many displaced persons wandering around the countryside and it is posing problems with their rebuilding efforts. I guess Berlin is still in dire straits and they're especially reluctant to let people in."

"I have to find a way. Somehow."

Ursula was determined to not give up that easily.

CHAPTER 25: TOM

Northolt Airbase, West London

Tom walked across the tarmac, happy to be on British soil once again. It had been almost a month since he'd been home and he was looking forward to seeing his parents and catching up before going back to Germany.

"Westlake, I want to talk to you," an angry voice called out behind him.

Tom sighed and turned around so that he could wait while Bronson caught up with him. This awful man seemed to follow him wherever he went. The base commander at Gatow had decided it would be a good opportunity for the two pilots to mend their rift when on home leave together. The commander seemed to believe their personal tension was a result of the general stress presented by the Soviet presence in Gatow.

"What do you want, Bronson?" Tom kept his voice professional, even though the deep-rooted hatred in the other man's eyes made it difficult. Bronson hadn't forgotten their altercation at the bar.

"That little stunt you pulled at the bar gave me a black mark on my personnel record, while you got off scot-free, thank you very much. What kind of strings did you pull for that?" Bronson made an obscene gesture.

Tom felt the vein in his temple pulsating fiercely as he stared at the rotten piece of garbage! "Look, Bronson, I got off without any disciplinary action because you started the fight, not I. And now bugger off."

Wanker.

"Like hell I will. While you're out there fraternizing with the enemy..."

"Peter is Polish, you idiot. You saw the MP check his papers just like everyone else in the bar did that night. Let it go."

Tom turned his back and headed for the flight hangar, anxious to fill out his paperwork and then get off the base. His leave officially started in the morning and he was planning to head straight to his parents' place.

"Hey, what's up? How's life in Berlin?" Willie, his friend and former boss, asked when he saw him returning to the barracks.

"Great." Tom gave him a friendly punch on the shoulder and grinned. "I saw her."

"Seriously? Tell me details." Willie gave a juicy grin.

"She's living in a tiny village near Munich."

"Munich? That's not exactly next to Berlin." Willie

looked at his wristwatch. "I have a meeting with the boss. Beer at five? And you can fill me in on your misdeeds."

"Alright." Tom nodded. He'd gone out less and less with his comrades, because all they talked about were their amorous conquests. Many of them had German mistresses in Berlin and took great pride in boasting about them. But Tom had no interest in finding a Berlin girlfriend and refused to join the men when they were heading to the social clubs in search of willing women.

And he sure as hell didn't want to talk about Ursula, for she wasn't a fling that provided sexual release, but a serious relationship. She was the woman he wanted to marry – as impossible as that seemed at the moment.

He finished his paperwork, took a shower and then went to their favorite watering hole, waiting for Willie to arrive. He was actually looking forward to confiding in his best friend, since it was taking a toll on him keeping all his problems bottled up inside.

"Hey, Tom. You back from Berlin?" one of his fellow pilots asked.

"Nah… on leave for a week. Going to visit my parents in the morning," Tom replied.

"Are the German Fräuleins as willing as they say?"

"It's still forbidden to fraternize," Tom said, taking a sip from his beer.

"Don't believe a word he says, boys." Bronson had entered the bar and overheard the last comment.

Tom scowled at the newcomer and shook his head. "Looks like it's time for me to get going. The mouth has arrived."

"Can't take the truth, Westlake?" Bronson asked with a sneer as he stopped at the end of the table.

"And what truth would that be?" Tom asked, running out of patience with this guy.

"The truth is, chaps, he can't tell you about the girls because he's batting for the other team. He's openly paraded his Polish lover through the bars of Berlin."

A hissing went through the room and Tom could only see Bronson's smirking face, intent on ruining Tom's reputation. Something snapped, and before Tom knew what was happening, his fist took on a life of its own. It connected with Bronson's jaw, sending the man flying backwards into a nearby table.

Moments later Tom felt two strong arms holding him back and Willie's stern voice commanding, "You cool it right now. Both of you. Or I'll call the MPs."

"He attacked me out of the blue," Bronson whined.

Tom wanted to lunge at him, but Willie increased the pressure on his shoulders and Tom raised his hands in defeat. "I'm calm. Promise. Not going to ruin my career for this vile piece of shit. I'm out of here."

Willie let go of him, and Tom made his way to the exit. He headed back to the barracks where his friend later caught up with him.

"You have to be more careful, man. I heard about the brawl in Berlin and you're lucky you got off lightly, but make no mistake, you're under observation."

"No idea what Bronson has against me, but he shows up everywhere I go, doing his best to make my life miserable."

"I could have you transferred back here," Willie suggested.

"No!"

Willie chuckled. "Now tell me everything about your girl."

Tom nodded and recounted how he'd found Ursula's sister in Berlin, convinced Mitch to give him a ride to Munich, how Ursula was even more beautiful than he remembered her, the initial hostility of her brother. Then he took a deep breath and said, "I have a daughter."

"What?" Willie almost fell off the bunk he was sitting on.

"Evie is the cutest thing I've seen in my life. She's adorable. I could kiss her chubby face all day long." Tom smiled at the vivid image of his daughter forming in his mind.

"Man, you sure?" Willie wasn't half as excited as Tom was.

"Very sure."

"Bloody hell. You can't tell anyone. They'll immediately post you away from Germany."

"I know." The elation left Tom's body and he suddenly felt like a filthy criminal. "You're the first one to know. Ursula hasn't even told her family, although after my showing up on the farm they must have put two and two together."

"That's quite the mess you've got yourself into. I don't envy you. But if you ever need my help…"

"Thanks."

The next morning, Tom took a bus to Maidstone in Kent, where his parents lived. They owned a beautiful country house about one hour away from the capital, where they'd relocated after their flat in the city had been bombed out.

"Tom. We're so glad you're home. Come inside," his dad said, shaking his hand.

"Where's Mother?"

"Making tea." His father grinned.

Tom entered the house where he'd spent many summer holidays but had never actually lived. His mother had much preferred the hustle and bustle of London and the flat with its modern amenities.

She came out of the kitchen. "Look at you!"

He half expected her to say, "You have grown," and took a step forward to hug her. He towered over her by almost two heads. She was thinner than he remembered. A result of years of rationing. "It's good to see you, Mother."

Teresa, the housekeeper set a platter of sandwiches on the table and greeted him, before she vanished into the kitchen again.

"Are you safe in Germany?" Mother asked him.

"Very safe, Mother. The war is over; we're not fighting anymore." *Except for the odd saber-rattling with the Soviets and fisticuffs with an obnoxious colleague.*

They settled around the table. "Do they give you enough to eat?" his mother asked.

"Yes, Mother. No need to worry about me. How are you?"

They told him about the smaller problems in the village and the general ones in the country, carefully keeping up a chipper face, until his mother casually said, "I have invited Lina over for supper."

Tom's head snapped around. Lina was the neighbor's

daughter, two years younger than him and since his adolescence his mother had pointed out what an adorable, and suitable young girl she was. He groaned inwardly at her continued attempts to make a match between him and Lina.

It wasn't that he disliked Lina. She was a charming, well-educated, intelligent girl, but his heart belonged to another woman. He'd been debating whether to tell his parents about Ursula, but now his mother had forced his hand.

He swallowed and then wiped his mouth with a napkin before he quietly said, "About that. I'm in love with another girl."

"Oh, that is wonderful. When will you introduce her to us?" By the glitter of joy in her eyes he could see she was already planning his wedding and counting the grandchildren.

"Umm. She might not be able to visit, at least for a while."

His father gave him a suspicious glance. "She's not in the army, is she?"

"No, sir. She is German."

His father slammed his hand down on the table. "A Jerry? Haven't we fought those bastards for six long years? And now you want to bring one of them into our house? Over my dead body!"

Tom ran a hand through his hair. This was clearly not the reaction he'd anticipated. He turned his gaze to his mother, who pressed her lips into a thin line.

"How could you?" she hissed.

"I'm sorry. I didn't want to cause you distress." Tom shook his head and decided to keep quiet about the fact that they had a half-German granddaughter. "Mother, your garden looks stunning."

His mother cast him a gaze like a wounded doe, but leaped at the buoy he'd thrown her to keep up pretenses and move the conversation onto safe ground once more. Neither he nor his parents would mention the *German girl* for the rest of his leave. He knew they hoped his infatuation with an unattainable woman would soon die a natural death.

CHAPTER 26: LOTTE

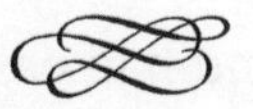

Berlin, December 1945

Two months had passed since her first visit to the American administration, and many more had followed. Terry had not given up flirting with her. While she needed his goodwill to wade through the meters of red tape required to get her permanent papers, she always politely declined his advances.

"Why don't you go out with him?" Renate, one of her coworkers, asked after Lotte returned from yet another visit to the administration office.

Lotte glared at her, taking up her spot in the line of women hammering mortar from bricks that had been collected from a destroyed building. "Because I'm in love with Johann."

"Nobody says you have to jump into bed with the GI, but

he seems nice enough and a harmless date won't hurt anyone."

"Well, if he's so nice, you can have him." Lotte hammered at the mortar, careful not to destroy the brick. Nobody seemed to understand her. Even the authorities had finally realized that it was futile to try to keep Allied soldiers away from German civilians and had eased the ban on fraternization. Since it was no longer prohibited to interact on a social level, frequenting the same bars had become commonplace. Intimate relationships were still strictly forbidden, but most of the servicemen didn't give a toss. It was tolerated as long as both parties adhered to the pretense of keeping it clandestine.

"Believe me, I would take him in a heartbeat." Renate laughed and placed her clean brick into a rusty bucket. "He's young, handsome, nice and…American. He can get you all kinds of things otherwise not available in Berlin. Have you seen Erika? Her Ami soldier showers her with nylons, chocolate and all sorts of food."

Lotte pursed her lips. "I'm not interested. And I don't believe for one second Terry will be content with a harmless date. They all want to be *paid* for their favors."

"And what's so bad about it? Do you want to keep doing this backbreaking work? I'd rather have a nice job as secretary, have a handsome soldier take me out to bars and dancing… and have some fun at night."

"Not me." Lotte focused her attention on the work at hand, indicating the conversation was over. She hadn't heard from Johann in almost a year, had no idea where he even was. But despite most everyone urging her to move on, this wasn't a valid reason to go out with another man.

Johann would return to her side. Wasn't that what the crazy witch Ingrid had predicted? Lotte wasn't superstitious, didn't believe in witchcraft, but the more time passed, the more she clung to Ingrid's words, wanting them to be true.

The date for their departure to Kleindorf approached and Lotte still didn't have proper papers. Every nerve in her body was strung tight as she observed her family making preparations. She feared she'd have to spend Christmas all be herself in the empty apartment.

"Lotte, why don't you go down and check with the American registration office one more time?" Anna suggested as she prepared to leave for her last day of work before their trip.

"What good will it do? I was there yesterday and Terry will only ask me out again."

Anna gave her a stern glance. "Has it occurred to you that your suitor might be holding back your papers in a desperate attempt to get you to agree to a date?"

"When did you become so shrewd?" Lotte asked her older sister.

"Since I started to work for the master of manipulation."

Lotte's eyes went wide. "Professor Scherer? I thought he was your idol?"

"Was." Anna put on her gloves and coat. "I still admire his brilliant scientific mind, and I can't complain, because he's always looked out for me. But the ways he manipulates people to get what he wants are... outstanding."

"I had no idea..." Lotte said.

"Nobody does. His counterparts don't ever notice, they usually think it was their idea. So, take my advice: put on your best dress, paint your lips red and let Terry know that he'll earn himself your undying gratitude – and a date – if he gets you the papers in time for our trip." Anna glanced at her reflection in the mirror and adjusted her bonnet.

"I don't know if I can do that."

"Think about a Christmas all alone in the empty apartment." Anna blew her an air kiss and rushed out the door. "Good luck! I'm running late."

Lotte left work a few minutes early to pass by the administration office just before it closed. She had abstained from putting on her best dress, but rummaged in her handbag for a lipstick she'd borrowed from Anna and retraced her lips before entering.

As usual, Terry was manning the desk in the office for identification papers and she cast him a bright smile.

"Hello, pretty woman," he said. "Your papers have finally arrived, but the boss is on leave and won't return until after Christmas."

"Oh no! Can't you make an itty-bitty exception and give them to me?"

"I'm not supposed to…" He had an awkward look on his face.

She wanted to scream with despair, but remembered Anna's advice. "My entire family is leaving Berlin for the holidays and I'd be forever indebted to you if I could go with them. Pleeeeaaaaasssse." She threw in a fluttering of her long eyelashes for good measure.

His eyes darted from her to the papers lying in front of him. "I guess… I'm not sure…"

"Do you still want to go out with me?"

"What kind of question is that? Of course, I do!" He looked like Christmas had come early and Lotte felt a bit guilty for using him, because he seemed to be a genuinely nice guy. "I guess I could make an exception."

"You would do that… for me?"

He chuckled. "I know what you're doing, but if you promise to go out with me in the New Year I'll do it."

"It's a deal," Lotte said, feeling immensely lighter. She agreed to see him as soon as she returned from Kleindorf and took her new papers. Then she rushed to the Soviet administration to get her travel permit to transit through their zone.

Three days later Anna, Mutter, Peter, Jan and Lotte boarded the train to Munich. It was an uneventful train ride and in Munich they changed into a regional train to Mindelheim. At their destination Jörg waited for them with an ox-driven cart.

"Jörg? Is that really you? You've grown so much," Mutter said and Lotte rolled her eyes. Did adults always have to say the same things?

"My mom says the same, Aunt Frida," Jörg answered while Peter hefted the suitcases onto the cart. "You must be Jan. You can sit with me on the coach box." The two boys were only one year apart, but the younger Jörg had half a head and two dozen pounds on Jan.

It had started to snow earlier that morning and the ground was covered ankle deep in a blanket of white. The weather made for a magical world with muted sounds. Lotte wrapped herself in the blanket Jörg had provided them and ducked her head between her shoulders, shielding herself from the icy wind.

"We are here." The cart stopped and everyone but Lotte hopped off. She was frozen in place, and the scene unfolding in front of her eyes took her breath away and impeded any movement. Despite the icy cold, sweat broke out on her skin and she felt her face burning up.

"What's happening to your sister?" Peter's voice asked.

"I don't know. She's in a state of shock," Anna answered. "Lotte, darling, can you hear me?"

Lotte shook her head, feelings of unreality overtaking her senses. Anna couldn't be here. Anna was in Berlin.

"I'll carry her inside," a male voice said and she felt herself swept up in a pair of strong arms.

"Let me go! You have no right!" She struggled as hard as she could, but the merciless man only gripped her tighter and threw her over his shoulder. Kicking and screaming she felt the helplessness of her existence invade her soul and the fight left her body. Should he do to her whatever he wished, she was done for.

When Lotte opened her eyes again she lay in bed, staring into the worried eyes of her sister, Anna, who expertly took her pulse and rubbed Lotte's trembling hands.

"What happened?"

"You had a memory lapse and fell into a state of shock. You kicked Peter quite hard when he carried you inside."

"I'm sorry." Confusion colored every thought as she struggled to make sense of the strange room and her sister sitting at her bed. "Where am I?"

"Aunt Lydia's farm."

"I never want to go back." Shudders wracked her entire body and she feared passing out again.

"It's over. Whatever you saw, it happened in the past. The war is over, and you're safe."

Slowly reality returned to Lotte's senses and breathing became easier. "You're right. I was caught in the past, experiencing it all over again."

"Seeing the farm again triggered your subconscious. It does happen. But the good thing is, it probably won't occur again."

"Glad my sister is a medical expert." Lotte tried a small smile.

"Do you feel strong enough to come downstairs and say hello to everyone?"

"I guess I should." Lotte left the bed with wobbly legs and climbed down the stairs with her sister's help. "I want to see my brother."

CHAPTER 27: URSULA

Ursula kneaded her hands, peering out the window at the snowflakes falling on the landscape. The children loved snow, but for her it was only a nuisance – something making her shoes soggy when she had to go to the outhouse.

She turned around to see Richard feeding the tiled stove. It was a majestic piece of artwork, the patterned green tiles telling of better times. Uncle Peter came from a long line of hard-working farmers who'd acquired modest wealth over the centuries. But the war had ripped everything to shreds.

Over the past weeks the children had searched the forests on a daily basis collecting wood for the winter. Felling trees, of course, was strictly forbidden, but lugging away fallen branches usually wasn't prosecuted. At least when a child was the perpetrator.

While the Amis maintained their cool behavior toward adult Germans, they'd considerably warmed up to the children. The younger and cuter they were, the more the Amis liked them. Many mothers in Mindelheim had taken to sending their little ones to the soldiers, begging for food.

Ursula sighed. The rations were scarce and Lydia had to surrender most of her produce to the occupiers. Although, with some ingenuity they had managed to amass a stockpile of preserves from wild berries, dried mushrooms and the odd rabbit caught by the dogs. Compared to townspeople they lived on the farm like a bee in clover.

One of the children came rushing inside, her cheeks red with the cold and excitement. "They are coming! They are coming!"

She walked to the front door, greeting her mother and Jan. Despite never seeing the young boy before, she noted that he looked so much like his father, Peter, there was no doubt who he was. The next moment, Peter pushed past her, a lifeless body thrown across his shoulder.

"What's wrong?" An icy hand closed around her heart as she recognized her sister Lotte's fiery red hair.

"Some kind of shock triggered by a memory," Anna hissed. "Where can I put her?"

"Upstairs in my room. The first on the left."

Richard stepped out, rubbing his sooty hands in the white snow. "What's happening here?"

"Bad memories," Ursula answered, thinking they all had experienced stories that were the stuff of nightmares. It would take a long time to heal. "Let's go inside."

She walked into the sitting room, where unusually emotional scenes were taking place. Even her mother and Lydia were hugging each other as if there were no tomorrow.

Peter was the first one to return downstairs and his

worried expression vanished the moment he saw Katrina carrying a pot of hot soup. As soon as she'd put the pot on the table, he caught her from behind, turned her around and embraced her tight.

Katrina uttered, "Ouch!" But when she recognized the man holding her, tears streamed down her face. "Piotr," she whispered over and over again, showering kisses on his face. "Is it really you? But how? I feared you were dead!"

Ursula stood thunderstruck witnessing the peculiar spectacle. "What's going on here?"

"I don't know," Richard said, his jaw tightening, as if he were about to jump at Peter any moment and rip him limb from limb.

Their mother came over and put a calming hand on Richard's shoulder. "He's Anna's husband, Piotr, but we call him Peter."

"So why's he kissing my woman and not his?" Richard growled and Ursula laughed – almost. It was a bewildering scene to watch.

"Didn't anyone write you?" Mutter said.

"Write what?" Richard and Ursula asked in unison.

"Katrina and Peter are siblings."

Ursula staggered and clasped at Richard's shoulder for balance. After a while a mostly recovered Lotte and Anna joined the family around the table. Everyone talked at once, reveling in the joy of seeing each other again well and alive.

There was just one piece missing for Ursula to be completely happy: Tom. Her thoughts wandered far away to an island she'd never set foot on. Would he be home with his family for Christmas? Would he miss her the same way she missed him?

She ruffled Evie's hair. The girl had inherited her mother's blond hair, but the sparkling green eyes of her father.

Much later, Ursula put the children to bed, crammed into one room to make space for the visitors. Anna sidled up to her, offering to help with the dishes. Ursula knew it was a pretext to get away from the family and talk alone, so she declined Katrina's offer to help. "You stay and spend time with your brother. I'm sure you have lots of catching up to do."

Anna took a pot of boiling water from the stove and poured it into the sink, before she added cold water from the faucet and began scrubbing the dishes. "It's nice to be together at long last."

"It is. We were so worried about you. The news we heard from Berlin ..."

"Don't. I don't want to spoil our stay here by thinking about problems," Anna said and then added, "I haven't seen Mutter so happy in years."

Ursula nodded and murmured, "But she was missing Father today."

Anna apparently had only waited for this opportunity and she put a wet hand on Ursula's shoulder. "What about you? Have you heard from Tom again?"

"No." Ursula pressed her lips together, her eyes filling with tears. "He can't just write me a letter and the only way he can visit me is hitching a flight with his American pilot friend."

"I'm sure he'll find a way to visit again."

Ursula took a wet plate from her sister's hand and rubbed it dry. "I asked to move to Berlin, but the Americans wouldn't allow me."

"What?" A plate slipped from Anna's fingers, making a splash when it entered the dishwater.

"If I'm in Berlin, Tom and I can see each other regularly."

"You have no idea how bad Berlin really is. That supper we had tonight? We'd spread that amount of food out to last for close to a week. We don't have wood or coal to keep us warm, either. And ask Lotte about the kind of work she does. I have to dress the raw skin on her hands every night."

"Talking about me?" Lotte stuck her head inside the kitchen.

"Ursula wants to move to Berlin," Anna said.

"Why on earth would you do that? Kleindorf may be boring, but compared to Berlin it's like paradise." Lotte leaned against the kitchen counter, squinting at Ursula.

"The man she loves is in Berlin," Anna said, as if Ursula weren't even in the room.

Now Lotte turned, looking at Anna. "Who is he? And why doesn't anyone tell me anything in this family?"

Anna laughed, but before she could say a word, Ursula blurted out, "You two are the most annoying sisters—"

"We are your only sisters," Lotte said with a dry laugh.

"Makes you even more annoying. And thank you, I can very well speak for myself."

"Then tell me, who's this mystery man nobody but Anna seems to know about?"

"He's a soldier," Ursula said.

"Well, that is a revelation. Ninety-nine percent of eligible men are soldiers." Lotte pursed her lips, obviously sensing her sisters hadn't told her the complete truth.

"He's a Tommy pilot," Anna added, waving away Ursula's protests. "How long do you want to keep it a secret?"

"Until the day we get married," Ursula hissed, placing the dried bowl in her hand onto the kitchen counter with a thud.

"Married? You are certifiably insane, sister. Haven't you heard about the anti-fraternization rules?" Lotte shook her head in utter disbelief.

"I know all about the rules, but Tom and I love each other and nobody can keep us apart, not even the stupid authorities." Ursula growled, and right now in this instance she'd engage in a fistfight with anyone representing the authorities that hindered her from seeing Tom.

"Oh, Good Lord! Is she serious about this?" Lotte asked.

"I'm afraid so." Anna finished washing the cutlery and cleaned the kitchen counters with the dishwater. "For the past two years she's been pining for him like a love-sick puppy."

"I'm not ...and you'll see... I might not even invite my unsupportive, annoying and obnoxious sisters to my wedding." Ursula pronounced the words with so much passion, her sisters started laughing out loud.

"There's no way I'd miss your wedding, even if I had to swim across the Channel." Anna giggled, before she continued in a serious tone, "I can understand that you want to move to Berlin, but the city is no place for a baby like Evie."

Ursula wasn't about to change her mind and she searched for a way to deflect the attention from herself. "What about you, Lotte? Wouldn't you rather concentrate on your own man?"

"I see Anna has been busy spreading the news," Lotte said in a sad tone. "His name is Johann Hauser. He was captured near Warsaw last January and I haven't heard anything from him since."

"I'm sorry," Ursula said, already regretting her snide remark. Not often had she seen such pain and sorrow on her usually upbeat sister's face.

CHAPTER 28: RICHARD

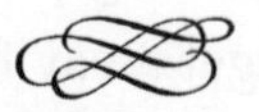

Christmas 1945

Christmas Eve had arrived and while presents were scarce, good humor wasn't. It had been snowing constantly for the past few days and a thick layer of pristine white snow covered the soft hills around the farm.

Richard exchanged a glance with his mother and knew the women wanted to decorate the tree and put the presents – one for each child – under the tree.

"Who wants to go sledding?" Richard yelled and within seconds a bunch of children, including the little ones of the Hansen family living on the farm with them, surrounded him with eager faces.

"I guess I'll sit this one out." Katrina smiled at him. With the baby due within two months, her belly had swollen and she wasn't as agile as she used to be. Richard didn't mind.

His wife's advancing pregnancy had never looked more beautiful to him.

He caressed her baby bump, giddy with anticipation, and kissed her positively glowing cheeks. "Take care, sweetheart." Then he turned around to look at his sisters. Anna and Ursula were busy peeling potatoes, but Lotte eagerly used the opportunity to get away from the dreaded kitchen chores. She threw down the knife and jumped up saying, "I'll go with you."

"Get dressed," he told the children and then asked Lotte to come with him into the cellar, where he grabbed a bunch of empty potato sacks. "We'll have to take turns since there aren't enough for everyone."

"It'll do," Lotte said, taking her share from him. "Do you remember how I used to get into snowball fights on the way home from school?"

"I do. And I always had to come and rescue you from your self-inflicted trouble."

"Not true!" She punched him on the shoulder.

"I'm so glad to have you back," he said, giving her a hug, before they climbed up the stairs again where a bunch of eager children waited for them.

"How many are there?" Lotte asked.

Richard chuckled. "I don't know. I lost count at about a dozen."

"Maybe we should count them before going sledding, just to make sure we bring them all back in the afternoon?"

"Do you really think one of them would want to miss the *Christkind* and its gifts? If anything, we may pick up some children on the way." Lotte laughed and put on a pair of old gloves that belonged to her uncle and would fit two of her hands into one.

"Ready to go?" Richard asked. They all cheered and he led them the way to the hill at the edge of the forest where generations of village youth had been sledding. Lotte made up the rearguard and when he looked back the procession looked like the Pied Piper of Hamelin leading the children away. At the sledding hill they encountered more villagers.

Many hours later they returned with thoroughly tired children who weren't allowed into the sitting room, but had to take a nap or at least rest.

Richard pulled Katrina aside and suggested a short walk through the magical snow-covered landscape.

"Today was nice," Richard told Katrina, holding her gloved hand and loving the rosy glow on her cheeks. "You simply can't take away the cheerfulness of children, even in the most dire situations."

"Children are our future and I believe it will get better over time."

A wave of warmth surged though his body, as he thought of the little bundle of joy that she would soon birth. His child. But his joy was followed by concern and… shame.

"What's wrong?" Katrina asked, perceptive as ever.

"It's just… there's nothing I can give you and the baby except for my name."

"We have everything we need. Food. A roof over our heads. And your love," Katrina reminded him.

"It's not enough. My wife deserves a house of her own."

His inadequacy to provide for his family weighed heavily on his shoulders. "We're living with my aunt because without her, we'd be living in someone's shed just like the Hansen family."

"In time things will get better. You'll see. We can earn money by selling herb potions and…"

Richard nodded and hugged her close for a long moment, pulling away when he felt her shiver. "Cold?"

Katrina nodded. "Getting there."

"Let's return. We don't want to keep the others waiting. I'm sure the children are dying of curiosity."

"Aren't you, too?" She teased him.

They returned to the house just in time to eat a hearty potato soup with thick slices of freshly baked bread.

Richard stole glimpses at his mother and Lotte, who devoured their portions in a blink of the eye. Their emaciated faces reminded him vividly about his own time on the road with little to no food. Yes, conditions had definitely improved. If he worked hard enough, he could one day afford to build a home for Katrina and his children.

After dinner, the children unpacked the presents. Aunt Lydia brought cookies and hot fruit tea – with a shot of rum for the adults. They sang Christmas carols and simply enjoyed being together.

CHAPTER 29: TOM

Gatow Airbase, Berlin

Tom held up his glass in a toast, smiling at the antics of his fellows. Despite being far away from home, everyone was in an overwhelming celebratory mood. The temporary barracks had grown into a permanent home. Some of the married officers had been allowed to bring their wives and children for the holidays – and possibly to stay. The British Army was preparing to stay for a long, long time in Germany.

Despite the jolly mood during the Christmas meal and the dance afterward, Tom couldn't muster up much enthusiasm. He'd rather be with Ursula.

"Westlake, why the sad face? There are plenty of unattached females on their way," Ken called out. The man had been beaming with delight since the moment his wife had arrived two days earlier and seemingly wanted to make sure everyone was as happy as he was.

Tom nodded absent-mindedly. Later he danced with a pretty brunette, but his mind never once let go of Ursula. The woman in his arms soon lost interest and went off to find a more willing man.

He had one week of leave ahead, but Mitch was on back-to-back flights to the Pacific. Therefore, he wouldn't be able to take him to Munich, but Tom didn't dare ask anyone else. He'd considered taking a train, but that notion had quickly been put to rest due to the political tensions with the Soviets. Travel through the Soviet zone had been restricted to official missions, since the high command didn't want to risk their soldiers getting into unnecessary trouble with the former ally.

"Hey, man." One of the aircraft engineers flopped onto the chair beside him. "I'm going to miss this place."

"You transferred home?"

"Nah... they're sending me to Aigen."

"Aigen? Never heard of it. Where's that?"

"In Austria. A forlorn airbase in the middle of nowhere, about eighty miles southeast of Salzburg."

Tom's ears perked up. From Salzburg he could easily catch a train to Munich and on to Mindelheim. "Can't be that bad. I hear the Alps are quite beautiful." Tom had visited Davos and Zermatt in his youth, because his mother had been adamant that any good boy needed to learn how to ski.

The other man scoffed. "Alps. That's nice and fine if you're hot on cows. Because that's all there is."

"Maybe I should spend my leave there. I wouldn't mind

getting away from Berlin and the Soviets for a while."

"Well, if you do, say hello. I'll be there for the next year or two." The man spotted the woman he'd been dancing with returning from the bathroom and rushed off to meet her.

Tom, though, was intrigued. He decided to seize the opportunity and walked over to the base commander, who was standing at the bar. After some small talk, he asked, "Sir, since I'm on leave next week, I was wondering if it would possible to travel to the Aigen airbase?"

"Won't you return to England?"

"No, my parents are with friends in Scotland and I'd rather not spend time with them. Those Scots are peculiar," he lied.

"I can sympathize." The commander guffawed. "But why on earth Aigen?"

"Sounds like a nice quiet place in the Alps. I'd love to do some skiing to recharge the batteries."

"You know how to ski, lad?"

Tom nodded. "I'm by no means an expert, but I manage."

Since the commander was in a Christmassy spirit, he smiled jovially and said, "Well then. Get your travel permits tomorrow in my office."

"Thank you, sir." Tom wanted to leave, but the commander called him back. "Under one condition, Squadron Leader Westlake."

"Yes, sir?" Tom had the annoying feeling that something was off.

"Don't break your neck!" The commander guffawed and emptied his beer, calling out to the bartender, "Another one! And one for this lad!"

CHAPTER 30: URSULA

Work on the farm didn't cease just because of the holidays and twice a day Ursula drudged through the knee-deep snow to the barn to milk the cows. The borrowed wellington boots reached way above her knees, but with that much snow falling every day, they were a blessing.

She finished milking the cows and feeding them for the night and took a moment to take in the soft rolling hills covered in snow. It looked so pristine and peaceful, it was hard to believe that this time last year a war had been raging over much of the land.

Suddenly she heard someone walking down the road. The trampled snow muffled the sounds, and at first she thought it might be a wild animal. But then she saw the silhouette of a human being walking toward the farmhouse. She straightened her back, unsure what to do. It was already dark outside, although the moonlight reflecting on the snow gave the landscape a mysterious glow.

They weren't expecting visitors. None of the neighbors were crazy enough to leave their warm and cozy house this late in the afternoon and venture into the icy cold. Except in an emergency, of course. But this person didn't exhibit any sense of urgency.

He couldn't be an American, either, because they never walked. They always arrived in a crowd, heard from far away in their noisy jeeps. This person might be a refugee on their way home, seeking shelter for the night.

They didn't have any spare space with her family visiting and the Hansen family in the attached servant's house. But if the stranger asked for hospitality, she couldn't well send him on into the cold night.

A more frightening thought occurred to her. What if he was here to steal a cow? The stranger might harm her if she stood in his way. Still pondering whether to hide in the barn, run to the house and alarm the others, or simply wait, she noticed the stranger had a brisk and confident stride. He definitely knew where he was going.

Moments later, she heard him say, "Is that you, Ursula?"

"Tom!" She put down the milk can and rushed toward him. He dropped his duffel in the snow and she jumped into his outstretched arms. "You're here! You should have warned me..." She stopped, laughing at her own silliness. The telephone on the farm still didn't work and sending a letter to her would have been dangerous.

"Believe me, I wanted to." He showered her face with kisses and murmured against her skin, "I missed you so much. Every single day."

"Come to the house. It's cold out here," she said and picked up the milk can.

He took it from her hand. "Let me carry this."

His nearness gave her the strength she knew she'd need when facing her mother in a few moments. Mutter would not be pleased, that much was certain. "Did you fly in with your American friend again?"

"No, he's on leave back home. I asked for a few days of holidays in the Alps and flew into Aigen airfield."

"Aigen? Where's that even?" She scrunched her nose.

"In the middle of nowhere." He chuckled. "About eighty miles southeast of Salzburg."

Ursula nodded. She'd never been to Salzburg, but knew it was a town on the border between Germany and Austria and had a direct train line to Munich. "I'm glad you're here." They reached the back door and she paused, looking into his bright green eyes. "But... my entire family is visiting and my mother... she..."

Tom took her hand and gazed deep into her eyes. "She won't be pleased, right?"

"I'm afraid not." Ursula felt a twinge of guilt.

She was about to open the door, when he said, "Wait. I can't stay for the night. I already arranged for a room in the inn in Mindelheim."

Sadness engulfed her heart. Hiding her love for Tom became harder by the day and she hated the secrecy. It made her feel dirty. Uncertain.

Unwanted.

They stepped into the kitchen where Anna was peeling potatoes for supper. Without looking up she said, "What took you so long, Ursula? I'm waiting for the milk."

"It was my fault," Tom said.

Anna's hand slipped and she cut her finger. "Ouch!" She

sucked the blood from the finger and looked up at them. "How did you even manage to come here in this terrific snow?"

"I have my ways. Are you hurt?"

Anna took her finger from her mouth and looked at it. "Just a tiny cut. Nothing to worry about. But you sure gave me a surprise."

"What…?" The door opened and Peter came inside, alerted by Anna's scream. "You? How did you get here?"

"Why does everyone ask the same question?" Tom shook hands with Peter. "Good to see you again."

"Will you stay for supper?" Anna asked.

Of course, Ursula wanted to say, but then she remembered that her mother still didn't know. "I have to tell Mutter."

"I don't envy you that confession," Anna said and nodded at Peter. "Could you help me with this?"

"Cowardly traitor," Ursula hissed at her sister.

"No, my girl, this is your battle, not mine. You go and tell our mother. Call me when the air's clear, or when a nurse is needed."

Tom looked somewhat confused. His German was very good, but a long way from perfect. "Is someone hurt?"

"No," Ursula assured him. "My obnoxious sister is just trying to be funny. Let's get it over with." She took his hand and pulled him after her into the sitting room, her heart hammering in her throat.

"Mutter, this is—"

Her mother looked up from mending children's clothes and her eyes widened in shock. "What's the foreigner doing here?"

Ursula sighed. "This is Tom Westlake, a British pilot."

"I can see that he's an enemy soldier." Mother pursed her lips into a thin line. "My question was what is he doing here?"

"The war is over. He's not the enemy," Ursula said, squeezing Tom's hand for support.

"That doesn't mean we like *them*." Mutter's voice held the strict tone that could freeze the blood of her children in an instant. Even Aunt Lydia shivered and got up saying, "I'll look after the children." Then she fled the room that had become oppressively small.

"I love him," Ursula said, stubbornly pushing out her lower lip.

Her mother paled, but before she could utter a word, Tom said, "Frau Klausen, please forgive me for not properly announcing my visit. But your daughter is right, we've been in love since we first met years ago."

"Good Lord!" Mutter grabbed for the flask of smelling salts she always carried in the pocked of her apron. "You've been hiding this from me all this time."

"I'm sorry, but I had to." Ursula knew it wasn't Tom's fault, but right now she resented him for having to keep their love hidden like it was something immoral.

Revelation hit her mother's eyes and she sunk back into the oversized armchair and muttered, "By the Blessed Virgin Mary, don't tell me he is..."

"Yes, he is Evie's father, but you can't tell anyone."

Mutter shook her head, glancing at the smelling salts in her hands. "I need something stronger than this." She got up and walked to the door.

"Mutter, please..."

"Not now."

"I'm sorry. That didn't work out very well," Tom said, putting an arm around her shoulders. "Maybe I'd better leave."

"Don't. She'll come around. And you haven't seen Evie yet."

Together they climbed the stairs to the room where the children were playing with their Christmas gifts. Evie had received a hand-me-down doll from one of her older cousins and came running. "Mommy, doll!"

"Do you remember Tom?" Ursula asked her as she picked her up.

Evie nodded and squealed with delight, raising her arms as she requested to be handed over to him.

"Supper is ready," Anna called from downstairs and a stampede of hungry children rushed to the bathroom to wash their hands and then settle around the big kitchen table.

"Will you eat with us? Please?" Ursula begged him and Tom nodded. "I brought food, too, and a Christmas gift for you. It's in my duffel bag."

"You're gift enough." She snuggled up against him with a contented smile. "But all the same I'll unpack your present after supper."

Mother did her best to tolerate Tom and hide her hostile glimpses in his direction, but Ursula wasn't fooled. His presence was a thorn in her mother's side. Much later, when the adults sat chatting in the sitting room, Mutter demonstratively looked at the wooden grandfather clock standing against the wall and said, "Herr Westlake should leave. It's getting late."

Tom got up. "I really should get going, since it's a long way to Mindelheim. Thank you for your hospitality."

"I'll walk you to the main road," Ursula said and followed him into the kitchen where his overcoat and boots were drying near the stove. She hadn't even slipped on the oversized wellington boots when Richard entered the kitchen and said, "Mutter has tasked me with accompanying you to make sure Tom and you won't be tempted to do something improper."

"For God's sake, she can't be serious."

"She is very serious about her unmarried daughter not spending time alone with an equally unmarried foreign soldier." Richard smirked, clearly delighting in Ursula's discomfort.

"You are… insufferable." She punched her brother's shoulder. "So you're our chaperone or what?"

"Looks like it." He grinned and traced his tongue across his teeth, saying, "Although I *might* have something to check up on in the shed by the barn."

Ursula felt her cheeks burning at the memory of what had happened in the barn during Tom's last visit.

"There's a price to it, of course," Richard added.

"A price?" She glared at him. "What do you want?"

"I want to trade rooms with you."

"No way," she said. The attic room was tiny and one had to climb up a wooden ladder to reach it. Tom held the door open for her and she slipped through, taking his hand. The simple touch sent electric shocks through her body and made her want more of him.

"It's getting difficult for Katrina, climbing up, and once

the baby is born, the room will be too small for the three of us." Richard looked at her with pleading eyes.

She bit back a laugh. After what her sister-in-law had done for her, how could she say no? "It's a deal. But I'm doing it for Katrina, not for you."

"Thanks, Ursula." As they reached the barn, Richard said, "Ten minutes," and vanished into the tool shed.

Tom didn't lose time and pulled Ursula into the barn, kicking the door closed with his foot. Then he wrapped her up in his arms and showered her face with kisses. Despite the cold air, she felt like burning up from the inside. She pressed herself against him, reveling in the passion burning through her body.

They were a mass of entangled limbs when a knock sounded on the door and Richard's voice called, "We need to go."

"Coming." Ursula let go of Tom, smoothed down her dress and closed the buttons on her overcoat.

Tom took her face into his hands and said, "I love you. And we have four days to see each other."

"I love you, too."

She looked at him as he walked down the main road and soon disappeared behind a curve.

"We should return to the house or Mutter will question my integrity and accompany you herself the next time," Richard said and laid an arm around her shoulder. "You really do love him, don't you?"

"With all my heart." Ursula sighed. "Believe me, I wished a million times I had fallen for someone else. It was so hard not to know anything. Although now it's even harder to know he's in Germany but I still can't see him."

"You two will find a way, I'm sure."

"Thanks for being on my side."

"Always. You're my sister."

They reached the house and entered through the kitchen door, Mutter already waiting for them with a disapproving stare. "What took you so long?"

"I had to search for this from the tool shed on the way back." Richard held up a pair of pliers and Ursula felt a surge of love for her brother. He really was the best brother she could wish for and she didn't mind at all trading rooms with him. She'd have done it anyway if he'd simply asked her, but she decided to keep quiet about that. Even the best brother in the world didn't have to know everything.

Ursula spent as much time as possible with Tom during the next four blissful days. When the time for his departure neared, she finally breached the topic that had been weighing heavily on her soul.

"I wish to move to Berlin," she said quietly.

"No, Ursula. That's a bad idea. Berlin is a horrible place for you and Evie."

"But I want to be closer to you. We could see each other regularly. You could see Evie." Ursula fought back the tears forming in her eyes.

He clasped her hands between his and locked eyes with her. "But I would worry about you all the time. At least here, I know you're safe and have enough to eat."

"I hate being so far away from you. I can't stand not knowing when I'll see you again. But… the Americans don't want to give me a permit to move to Berlin."

"And with reason. It's not like the city is able to take in any more people."

"Can't you help me to get a permit?" She gave him a pleading look.

"Me? How?"

"There must be a way. It's always the matter of knowing the right people and I'm sure if you talk to the Americans, they'll allow me to move."

Tom shook his head.

"Please. Will you at least try? Don't you want to see me more frequently?"

"Of course I want to see you." He sighed and she sensed she was getting to him.

"Imagine how it would be if we could see each other every week?" She rubbed her body against his, nibbling on his earlobe. He trembled. "We could make love as often as we wanted to," she hissed against his ear, intensifying her nibbling.

"Stop." He pushed her away with a grin. "I know what you're doing. And while I still think Berlin is not a good place for you to be, I also know you'll move heaven and earth to get what you want."

"So you'll help me?" She smiled.

"I'm sorry, but there really isn't anything I can do." He kissed her. "I promise I will return soon, my love."

CHAPTER 31: LOTTE

January 1946

"Pull me next, Lotte," little Maria begged.

Lotte smiled, nodding at her cousin. She'd been outside in the snow playing with the children for most of the afternoon.

"Someone's coming. Do you think it's Aunt Ursula's secret lover again?" Jörg tugged on her coat sleeve.

"Tom's not her secret lover," Lotte chided him.

"What is he then? And why do they always disappear and kiss when they feel unobserved?"

Lotte tried to put on a stern face. "You shouldn't spy on people. It's not nice. And you can't tell anyone, because the Allies don't like us mingling with their men." Her sister really had to do a lot better if she wanted to keep her relationship with Tom hidden from prying eyes.

"I'd never tell," Jörg pushed out his chest. "This is my family and I will protect it."

Lotte hid a laugh and raised her gloved hand to shield her eyes, looking up the road. "Seems to be a woman with a child. What could they want?"

"Let's find out," Jörg said and dashed off.

With a sigh, Lotte told the other children to go inside and get ready for lunch, before she followed him. It would have been wiser to wait, but she couldn't leave her cousin on his own.

"Lotte! Come!" Jörg's high-pitched voice screamed and she darted off, ready to tackle whatever dire straits he'd found himself in. Just when she'd rounded the corner leading to the main road, she stopped dead in her tracks, certain she'd seen a ghost.

Pangs of guilt hammered against her ribs in the same rhythm as her heart did and she blinked several times. This couldn't be true. No way this was happening.

"Lotte," the other woman said with a soft voice, leaving no doubt about her identity. She might be emaciated, her brown hair hanging in straw-like strands from her head, the face disfigured by a long and ugly scar, but her voice was unmistakable.

"Rachel!" Lotte's knees suddenly turned into jelly and she sank against the other woman, tears in her eyes.

"Is it really you, Lotte?" Rachel asked. "The Red Cross told me you'd died in Ravensbrück."

"That's a long story for another time," Lotte said, with a side-glimpse at her cousin Jörg, who still didn't know about her adventures during the past two years. "I'm so sorry."

"It wasn't your fault," Rachel said softly. "You did everything you could to hide us."

"But I failed…" Lotte began sobbing. "I never forgave myself… I thought you were dead for sure… how?" She wanted to raise her hand to touch Rachel's scar, but resisted the urge when she noticed the immeasurable pain in her friend's eyes.

"I really don't want to talk about it."

"That I can understand," Lotte said, gathering her composure. "And this is… your sister?"

"Yes, Mindel."

Jörg cleared his throat. "Where are you going?"

"We… don't know." Rachel whispered. "We passed by our farm and Herr Keller is still there as if he owns it."

Because he does, Lotte thought, her heart filled with hate for the despicable man who'd evaded justice even after the war. "You come with us," she said, with a feeling of déjà vu.

"Are you sure your aunt won't mind?"

"She won't mind," Lotte said, although she wasn't at all sure about that.

The four of them walked back to the house when Rachel said, "Do you know about my brothers?"

Lotte smiled. "They made it to the convent and they're still there. My sister Ursula visited them a few months back."

Rachel halted mid-stride, tears sliding down her cheeks at the same time as her eyes lit up with joy, relief, gratefulness and love. "You truly are our guardian angel."

"I'm no such thing." Lotte writhed with embarrassment. Nobody had ever called her an angel. Usually they used the words troublemaker, nuisance, and rebel when referring to her.

"Why didn't you return earlier? The camps were liberated half a year ago already," Jörg asked.

Lotte glared at him, but Rachel said, "That's true. But so many of us were too weak and ill to leave. Mindel and I had to stay in the hospital for months, before we were considered fit to be released."

"Aunt Lydia, look who has returned!" Lotte stormed into the kitchen where her aunt was cooking soup for lunch.

"Good lord!" Lydia dropped the wooden spoon into the huge pot, thick yellowish drops of soup splattering the kitchen. "Are you the Epstein girls?"

"Yes, Frau Meier," Rachel responded.

"You must be hungry, so please stay for lunch," Lydia said.

"Actually, Aunt Lydia, Rachel and her sister don't have a place to stay so I told her she could stay with us…"

"Here? How do you think…" The house was crammed with people and there simply wasn't enough space to host another two displaced persons. But Aunt Lydia clearly felt guilty about what had happened. She'd had to make a difficult choice back then, one that Lotte's younger self hadn't understood. "…I guess we can have you sleep in the living room until the guests from Berlin have left."

Lotte gave her aunt a grateful smile. As she observed the relief spreading across Rachel's face, something astonishing happened: the load of self-imposed guilt she'd been carrying for so long eased off her shoulders.

It would never completely vanish, but the fact that

Rachel was alive absolved her from any complicity in Rachel's ordeals. The blessed relief was like a refreshing and cleansing bath in the lake. The mud, grime and horror of the past years started to dissolve, leaving Lotte's heart lighter and happier.

CHAPTER 32: RICHARD

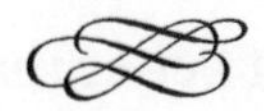

"Will you be alright?" Richard asked his wife.

"Of course I will. The baby isn't due for another six weeks and even if it comes early, what help could you be? Birthing is a woman's job and I'm in the best hands with your mother and your aunt." Katrina gave him a kiss. "You go and see that your sister doesn't get herself into trouble."

"At least that job is familiar," he said on a sigh. He'd had to bail Lotte out of trouble since as long as he could remember. "I really don't know why I was punished with such a sister."

Katrina giggled. "You must have done something really, really bad in your previous life."

Or in this life. The many lives he'd snuffed out on the battlefield still weighed heavily on his conscience. He'd never wanted to become a soldier. But life had decided differently.

"Ready?" Lotte poked her head into the room that had

previously belonged to Ursula and Evie. "How on earth have you convinced Ursula to trade rooms with you and sleep in the attic?"

"Secrets of a genius mind," he grinned.

"Oh... you are... insufferable!" Lotte threw her glove at him, but he caught it in the air with one hand.

"You'll have to do a lot better than that, if you want to hit me, *little* sister."

Lotte glared daggers at him and Katrina said laughing, "Get out of here. The two of you! Take the children for a snowball fight, if you need to get rid of extra energy."

"Your wish is my command, milady." Richard kissed Katrina again and then turned to his sister. "Let's go. I promise I'll lather you up with nice cold snow."

"God, what an empty threat. You're no match for me." Lotte grinned.

That might have been true even four years ago, but since leaving for the front he'd grown at least five inches and put on thirty pounds of muscle. She had no chance against him and she knew it, but she wouldn't be Lotte if she let unimportant facts get in her way.

Almost two hours later Richard, Lotte and Rachel arrived at the town hall in Mindelheim. They entered the registry office where Rachel registered as newly arrived.

The soldier raised a brow when he noticed she was a Jew and asked her whether she had a place to stay.

"In fact, my deceased parents owned a farm not far from here and I wish to return to it," Rachel said.

"You would have to file a claim. Then we'll investigate to find out who's the current owner and whether it was rightfully sold," the GI said, rummaging in one of the drawers until he found the correct form. "Do you know if there's currently someone living on your farm?"

"There is – Herr Keller." Lotte stepped forward.

"Herr Keller? The Mayor?"

Richard was standing two steps behind the women, because he'd wanted to give Rachel some privacy while filling out the registration form. Observing the grim expression on Lotte's face as she nodded, he wondered whether it would have been better to take things into his own hands.

"I'm afraid that will be a problem..."

"Has someone called for me?" Herr Keller stepped into the room, a pleasant smile on his face.

"Sir, in fact, there seems to be a problem." The American soldier, whom Richard recognized as a simple private, looked thoroughly uncomfortable in his situation. "This woman here, Rachel Epstein, claims ownership to your farm."

Herr Keller turned to look at the three of them and only the glint in his eyes revealed his nervousness to Richard. His voice was pleasant and calm as he said, "Oh, that must be a misunderstanding. I bought the farm from her parents before they decided to leave the country—"

"You deported them!" Lotte interrupted him. The rage pouring off her slight form filled the entire office with palpable tension.

"Calm down, Lotte," Richard urged her, placing a warning hand on her forearm.

"Aren't you that spitting mad girl that had to be sent to a

re-education institution?" Herr Keller said, the gleam in his eyes turning from nervousness to hatred.

Richard increased the pressure on Lotte's arm and she murmured. "You can let go of me. I'm fine."

He didn't believe that for a minute but nodded and released her, taking her word. "This woman, Rachel Epstein, claims that the Nazis stole the farm from her parents and I believe there's a process for this kind of issue, isn't there?"

The American soldier nodded, clearly wishing himself anywhere else.

Herr Keller said, "The American administration has installed me as the Mayor and thus I hold the authority to decide upon these cases."

"Perhaps since the Mayor is one of the parties involved it would be wise to include one of your superiors in this case?" Richard gazed at the GI, whose face brightened at the offered way out.

"I'll be right back with Major Chambers," the American said, fleeing from the crowded office.

"How that man isn't in prison is beyond me," Lotte whispered, but thankfully made no move to attack Herr Keller either verbally or physically, for which Richard was grateful. Apparently she'd changed over the course of the war and had managed to get a grip on her flaring temper.

CHAPTER 33: LOTTE

Lotte saw everything through a red haze, but experience had told her that exploding like a barrel of dynamite never amounted to anything good. She deliberately inhaled deeply and pushed the rage from her mind. She released some of the volatile emotions rolling through her body by flexing and straightening her hands several times. By the time the big, awe-inspiring man entered the room, she was as calm as she possibly could muster.

"I hear there's a problem?" Major Chambers asked.

"Sir, yes. My friend, Rachel Epstein, just returned from the Bergen-Belsen concentration camp and finds that this man, Herr Keller, has appropriated the farm of her parents."

"I see," Chambers said. "We do have a process to make these claims and investigate them… although," he gave a short side-glance at Herr Keller, "since the mayor is directly involved, I guess it'll be on me to decide.

"You are the young lady claiming ownership of the farm? Do you have any kind of proof?" he asked Rachel.

Rachel paled. "The entry in the land register should say so. We couldn't take any papers when he," she nodded at Herr Keller, "evicted us."

"Where are your parents?"

"Gassed in Auschwitz," Rachel said.

Lotte felt a cold shiver running down her spine. The American seemed to experience the same feeling, because his jaw tensed for a moment and he took Rachel's registration form to read through it. "You were born in 1926?"

"Yes, sir."

Major Chambers clucked his tongue. "That'll be a problem because you can't legally assume ownership until you have come of age."

"She can't?" Lotte asked, mouth agape.

"Not under the current laws. Fräulein Epstein will need a legal guardian to administer the inheritance for her until her twenty-first birthday." The major looked around the room. "Maybe if Herr Keller agreed to take over guardianship of Fräulein Epstein and her sibling until she comes of age. In the meantime, I'm sure we can come to a solution."

Rachel staggered backward, and it was only Richard's swift reaction that kept her from falling.

"Sir, with all due respect, you can't be serious about this," Lotte said, doing her best to keep calm, although she wanted to scratch out his eyes, or better yet, those of Herr Keller.

"And who are you?" Major Chambers seemed amused by her brash behavior.

"I'm Rachel's friend, Charlotte Klausen. I was the one who hid her before this devious monster found her and took pleasure in sending her to a concentration camp."

The major turned to Herr Keller, his face not giving away the slightest emotion. "Is what this woman says true?"

Herr Keller paled but immediately recovered and shook his head. "No, Major Chambers. I don't even know this woman with the short hair. Look at her. Wearing men's clothing and shearing off all her hair. She can't be a decent person and you shouldn't believe a word she says."

Lotte exploded in anger, and quickly reached for Richard's arm, hissing, "Hold me tight before I strangle that lying bastard with my bare hands." Thankfully, her brother obeyed and took both of her hands into his, clasping them together as if his life depended on it.

"Father, can you—" A lean and tall young man with white-blond hair entered the office, and recoiled when he saw Lotte. "You bitch! You have the guts to return to this place! I thought my father made sure you and your filthy Jewish friend would die in a camp!"

Lotte was grateful for her brother's intervention. Richard wrapped his arms around her, pressing her tight against him. The burning sting of unabashed fury coursed through her veins, and despite her wobbly knees she would have jumped at Herr Keller's son, Hans, to scratch out his eyes.

"That is not true. Hans is inventing a story..." Herr Keller tried to save his neck.

Hans might be a bully, but he didn't have his father's devious trickiness. "But Father... you told me yourself that she'd never forget the lesson you were about to teach her. You even lied to the Gestapo agent—"

"I have heard enough," Major Chambers said and motioned to the soldier standing beside the door. "Take them into two separate cells for interrogation." Then he looked at Lotte, who was still confined in Richard's arms and said with a smile, "You can let her go now. I'm sure she won't pose a danger to me."

Lotte bit back a snide remark. She might be nuts but not suicidal enough to attack an armed officer of the occupying authority. "I won't, sir."

"I'll need to interrogate you, too. Your friends can wait outside."

"Thank you, sir," Lotte said.

The major smiled. "We truly are here to help, even thought it might not seem that way at times."

Lotte nodded, rubbing her upper arms. "You didn't have to grab me so roughly," she whined, pouting at Richard.

He laughed. "I didn't want to risk a distressed lioness charging at whoever was in her way. And the snowball fight this morning showed me just how strongly you can fight if you want to." He turned toward Rachel. "Let's go and wait outside."

CHAPTER 34: URSULA

Ursula moped around. Tom's absence had sucked the joy right out of her bones. What good did it do that he was stationed in Germany, if she still couldn't see him? As far as she was concerned, he could be on the other end of the world.

She balled her hand into a fist and punched it against the wall in despair. It wasn't Tom's fault, but right now she resented him for not standing up for her. He should go to his commanding officers, tell them they loved each other and an exception needed to be granted for them.

"It's hard, isn't it?" Anna had entered the kitchen.

Ursula scoffed. "I'm alternating between wanting to strangle him, his superiors, Churchill himself, or myself."

"Don't do any of this," Anna said, putting a hand on Ursula's arm.

"It's just… I want to see him. No, I must see him. I can't keep living without him. It's as if my heart beats at half-pace when he's not around. I grew so accustomed to having him around these last four days, and now he's gone. Everything's so empty."

"How can a house with twenty-four people be empty?" Anna said, trying to lighten the mood, but it made Ursula sob.

"Because number twenty-five is not here. I miss him so much already, and he has no idea when or if he can return." An overwhelming sense of solitude entered Ursula's heart. She knew it was selfish because so many others, including Aunt Lydia and Mutter, didn't even know whether their husbands were still alive. "I just want what every other woman has: the right to say Tom is my man and I love him."

"I'm so sorry." Anna put an arm around her sister's shoulders and they commiserated several minutes in silence until Anna spoke up again. "I might have an idea."

"You do?" Ursula looked up, a sliver of hope lightening the heavy burden on her shoulders.

"There's no guarantee it'll work."

"I don't care. As long as there's a chance to see Tom..."

"Even when you're in Berlin, you won't be able to officially date him or even see him every day," Anna cautioned her.

"Anything is better than staying here waiting for him until the cows come home. " Ursula sent a pleading look at her sister. "Tell me your idea already."

"Alright. Why don't you return to Berlin with us?"

"Really?" Ursula's entire body filled with giddiness.

"Sure. Getting a temporary travel permit to visit family shouldn't pose a problem. And once you're there, we'll see what we can do."

"Maybe Peter can pull some strings with the British administration where he works?"

Anna frowned. "I doubt he's important enough, but... I could ask Professor Scherer. He's best friends with all the victors except for the Soviets, who still hate his guts for leaving them to work for the Americans."

"Oh, Anna. You're the best sister in the world!" Ursula threw herself at her sister, hugging her tightly.

Late in the afternoon, Lotte, Richard and Rachel returned from their visit to Mindelheim and found Ursula and Katrina in the kitchen preparing the evening meal.

"Did you have any success?" Ursula asked them as she warmed the leftover soup for them.

"In fact, we did." Lotte beamed with pride.

"But there's a small problem," Richard added. "We wanted to talk to Aunt Lydia first."

"She should be here any minute," Ursula answered. Lydia had spent most of the day with Jörg in the utility shed, fixing things.

"I'll go and get my mom," one of the children said and slopped into an oversized pair of boots, not even bothering to put on a coat.

"Hey, wait, it's cold out..." Ursula smoothed a strand of hair behind her ear. "It's no use. These children... it's about as easy as herding cats."

Minutes later Lydia returned with an apprehensive expression on her face. "Helmut said it was an emergency."

"It isn't. No major catastrophe, just a question." Lotte eased her aunt's worries.

"A question from you, Lotte, most of the time is akin to a major catastrophe," Lydia said, sighing. "So what is it?"

Richard cleared his throat and recounted the happenings in the town house.

"So, they locked Herr Keller and Hans up?" Ursula asked, hoping that justice would finally prevail.

"I wish," Lotte sighed.

Richard shook his head. "I don't know what is to become of Herr Keller and his family. But after interrogating everyone, Major Chambers decided they have to leave the Epstein farm by the end of the week."

"Well, that's fantastic news." Ursula beamed, but glancing at the faces of her siblings and Rachel she shrugged and asked, "Or, isn't it?"

Rachel sighed. "I'm not of age yet and can't legally assume ownership of the farm. The major said I'd have to present him with someone, an experienced farmer, who accepts guardianship over me and my siblings. At the same time this person needs to guarantee the farm is tended to properly and keeps up with the food production."

"He said he couldn't risk losing one of the food producers in his area," Lotte added.

Ursula felt sorry for Rachel, because the only farmers she could think of were former Nazis with their only goal to enrich themselves.

"We thought that maybe you could do this, Aunt Lydia," Richard said.

Aunt Lydia shook her head. "What were you thinking? I barely manage to keep my farm afloat, with the labor shortages and everything. I can't be responsible for another farm, or four more people. It's impossible."

Richard sought Katrina's eyes and Ursula witnessed how the two of them exchanged an entire conversation with that one gaze. In the end, Katrina nodded and Richard smiled from ear to ear, leaving Ursula wondering what all of this was about.

"I'll run the farm," Richard said with a loud voice and all heads jerked staring at him. "Katrina and I have been talking about having our own farm one day and this would be a great opportunity to practice. We'll teach Rachel and her siblings everything they need to know about farming and maintaining a house."

"You?" Aunt Lydia said. "You don't even know how to milk a cow."

"But Katrina does. She grew up on a farm. She knows everything there is to know, and we're both not strangers to hard work."

Rachel smiled. Like everyone else she'd come to like Katrina in the short time the two women had known each other. "That would be nice."

"But you're not twenty-one, either," Ursula said. "You can't be the guardian."

"I forgot." Richard's shoulders sagged as he scratched his beard, sad that his brilliant idea wouldn't work out.

"But Aunt Lydia could. Can't you, please?" Lotte pleaded with her aunt. "You'd be the guardian on paper only, but Richard and Katrina would do all the hard work. Wouldn't you be happy to have them out of your hair?"

"Not really," Aunt Lydia laughed. "Both of them have proven to be a great help and I would miss their manpower, but..." She sighed, looking around at the expectant faces. "I guess I can't say no."

"You're the best!" Lotte jumped up to embrace her aunt.

"Impulsive as always. When will you learn to behave like a lady?" Aunt Lydia asked.

"Tomorrow, I promise," Lotte said with a laugh.

"To give her credit, she showed a self-restraint I hadn't thought possible earlier today at the town hall." Richard helped his sister out.

"Well, then it's settled. Rachel and I will visit with Major Chambers tomorrow and deal with the formalities," Aunt Lydia announced.

"I'll go with you," Ursula said, intent on putting Anna's plan in motion. If everything worked out, she'd soon be held in Tom's arms again.

CHAPTER 35: TOM

Berlin, January 1946

Three weeks had passed since he'd last seen Ursula and despite the teasing of his friends, he simply couldn't get her out of his head. Every time they met, the connection between them grew stronger and he loathed the powers that kept them apart. It was such a cruel twist of fate.

One day he ran into Mitch in his favorite bar.

"Hey, mate, I didn't know you were back," Tom said.

"I'm not. Just here for twenty-four hours to grab my stuff. I'm going home." Mitch beamed at him.

"For good?"

"Yep. I've been demobilized and there's a nice quiet job as flight instructor waiting for me."

"Good for you." Tom tried to be happy for his friend, but

he mostly felt sadness that he wouldn't be able to catch a flight to Munich anymore.

"Don't look so miffed. You still thinking about that woman?" Mitch gulped down his beer, ordering another one.

"Always." Tom didn't expect the skirt chaser to understand him, but Mitch was one of the very few people who knew the truth.

"Jesus, you're knee-deep in shit. All this trouble for one woman. Find yourself a warm and willing Fräulein here and get over it. Believe me, they are lining up for the likes of us."

Tom shook his head but Mitch kept talking. "Here's what you do. You buy some chocolates and a box or two of cigarettes… they'll do anything you want."

"What does your girl back home think about this?" Tom couldn't resist the side blow.

"What she doesn't know won't hurt her. I'm like a sailor and I need a warm bed in every port."

Tom shook his head. "That's not for me. I love Ursula and only her."

"Man, she's got her talons into you good. But with the way things are you might start thinking about emigrating to Timbuktu."

"Where?" Tom asked.

"If you ever hope to make things work with this Ursula, you'll need to find a place where nobody has even heard of the war or the Nazis. Antarctica comes to my mind, but Africa is warmer. I personally think you're crazy, but to each his own."

"Things will change."

"Will they? Have you mentioned this girl to your parents or anyone back home yet?"

Tom blanched as he remembered his parents' reaction. The level of hatred they'd shown had caught him unawares. "It might take some time."

Mitch scoffed. "Good luck with that. You and I probably won't be around by then. Heed my advice. Find yourself a nice Englishwoman. If you have to, visit this Ursula every once in a while for a quick boff. It's not like you have to cross the big pond to come here." Mitch tossed some bills on the table and yanked his jacket off the back of the chair. "I need to head out. Have a good life and remember, there are plenty of fish in the sea that are a lot less of a headache."

Tom waved him off, wondering whether he should heed Mitch's advice and forget about Ursula – for the sanity of both of them.

CHAPTER 36: LOTTE

When the family returned to Berlin, Ursula announced that she and Evie were going with them. Mutter, of course, had been adamant that Berlin wasn't a place for a toddler, but much to Lotte's surprise – and admiration – Ursula didn't waver in her determination. That British pilot really had gotten under her sister's skin, which reminded her about Johann.

She thought of him every single day, worrying if he was still alive and under what conditions. Rumors about the deplorable treatment by the Russians ran wild, but Lotte refused to dwell on it, hoping it was just that: rumors.

One day after work she was lying on the sofa listening to a radio program when a knock sounded at the apartment door. Anna and Peter had taken Jan to the motion pictures and neither Ursula nor Mutter were around to answer the door.

With a deep sigh she got up and dragged her tired bones to the door. Her mind was already formulating a snide remark for whoever had forgotten his or her keys and disturbed her well-earned rest. Even after her body had adjusted to the backbreaking work as a *Trümmerfrau,* she still returned home every evening with aching bones and raw hands.

"What...?" She peered at the most haggard, ill-looking man she'd ever seen. There was barely hair on his head and every inch of exposed skin was covered in red dots, some of them oozing pus.

His hollow eyes focused on her with some difficulty and he said, "I'm looking for Alexandra Wagner."

The words were a punch to her stomach and she gasped for breath. "Who are you?"

"A comrade of Johann."

Her heart melted and she gave the man a once-over. It wasn't the wisest thing to do, inviting a bedraggled stranger into her home when she was alone. But despite his dreadful appearance, she was certain he wouldn't pose a threat to her.

"I'm Alexandra. Would you like to come inside?" she asked, only to wish she hadn't as an appalling stench wafted into her nostrils when he agreed. Forcing down the vomit coming up her throat she led him into the kitchen.

"Please have a seat. Do you want a glass of water?" He greedily nodded and she added, "And something to eat?"

"That would be grand." His smile bared a row of black and broken teeth.

Lotte turned her head away at the foul stench leaving his mouth. She walked to the kitchen and filled a glass with water, before she rummaged through the pantry to find a piece of bread and some cheese.

"Here you go." She sat across the table, a safe distance from him, trying not to stare at the oozing dots on his face, neck and hands.

"Thank you." He emptied the glass of water and then began talking. "I'm Karsten. Your fiancé Leutnant Johann Hauser and I were together in a Russian POW camp in Voronezh."

Lotte hissed and thousands of questions attacked her, but she didn't interrupt his laborious speech, which was only interrupted by careful chewing of the bread she'd given him.

"They let me go, because," he scoffed and gestured to his body, "as you can see, I'm no use to them anymore. I'm too sick to work. Johann gave me a letter for you, but it was confiscated by the bloody Soviets before I crossed the border. So I can only give you this." He took a tiny piece of wood from his pocket. "He made this for you, so you have something to remember him by."

A wave of emotions washed over her and she had to will away the tears forming in her eyes as she took the wood and looked at it. It had the form of a body and traces of a face, and with much imagination she recognized it was indeed a doll resembling Johann.

"Thank you," she said, her voice trembling. "Is he... well?"

"Well is a word I wouldn't use to describe any of my comrades, but he's alive and in a much better condition than I am. Although it was only my deplorable condition that caused them to send me home." He stared at her. "You are exactly like he described. Beautiful. He said to let you know he loves you very much and only the thought of returning to you makes him stay strong day after day."

Tears ran unchecked down Lotte's cheeks and she squeezed the wooden doll in her hand. "Thank you so much for going to the trouble to come here and find me. You can't imagine how much this news means to me."

"Anything for a dear comrade like Johann. I hope he and the others will return soon."

"Can I do something else for you?"

"No, thanks. I need to catch my train to Oldenburg and see if I can find my family," he said, rising.

"God bless you." Lotte cut another piece of bread, fully aware that she'd go without dinner tonight if she gave it to him. "Here, take this for the journey. I'm sorry, but I don't have more."

"That is a lot, actually." He bared his rotten teeth again in something that probably was meant as a smile and then left the apartment.

"Who was that man?" Ursula entered the apartment with a concerned look on her face that shifted into full-blown panic when she saw the traces of tears on her sister's face. "What did he do to you?"

"Nothing." Lotte bawled, holding out her hand with the wooden doll. "He's… a… friend of Johann."

"That's good news, isn't it?" Ursula's question came out hesitant.

"I guess. This man, he was a prisoner in the same camp with Johann."

"That means Johann is still alive, and that is a good thing." Ursula sat on the sofa beside Lotte and put an arm around her shoulders.

"They confiscated the letter Johann sent me. Why would they even do that?" Lotte wiped the tears from her face.

"I don't know. Maybe he wrote something the censors didn't like?"

Another round of sobs shook Lotte's body. "So we're back to having censors again? Wasn't that supposed to end with the Nazi reign?"

"It was, but since Johann is still a prisoner I guess they still censor the letters."

Lotte looked at her sister, not knowing whether she should be happy or sad. Her darling was still alive, but after she'd seen the deplorable state Karsten was in she wasn't sure that was a good thing. Another thought tormented her mind and she blurted out, "I don't even know where Voronezh is!"

"Me, neither." Ursula glanced around the living room. "If Richard was here, we could ask him."

"Or look it up in his school atlas." Lotte felt a surge of energy. "I'll go to the public library tomorrow and find out where Voronezh is. And now I'll write a letter to Johann." She got up, leaving a perplexed Ursula on the sofa.

On the next day before work, she went to the Red Cross office to send a letter to *Leutnant Johann Hauser, POW Camp, Voronezh, Russia.*

The friendly woman at the reception couldn't promise the letter would reach its recipient. The Red Cross had some difficulties getting the Russian authorities to actually distribute the stacks of mail received. But she encouraged Lotte to return every month with a new letter, because a letter not sent never had a chance to be delivered.

Lotte glanced at her wristwatch. She wouldn't be able to

make it to the library before work, so that had to wait until the afternoon.

The only library she knew of that was sure to be open was at the Berlin University. It had only recently started lectures again, having been closed down after the capitulation.

She waited her turn at the information desk.

"How can I help you?" the older woman behind the counter asked.

"Do you have an atlas I could borrow?" Lotte inquired.

"Certainly. Right over there. They can't be checked out, but you can use it here in the library."

"Thank you." Lotte crossed the huge library, which still showed traces of destruction, despite the efforts undertaken to reconstruct it. She found an atlas and searched the index in the back for a place called Voronezh.

With trembling hands she opened the huge book on the indicated page and reverently ran her finger across the thick paper. At last she found Voronezh in the European part of Russia, about the same longitude as Moscow, but considerably further south.

On paper, it didn't seem that far away. Especially not compared to places further east like Novosibirsk or Vladivostok on the Pacific Coast. For a moment she felt hope, but that was shattered when she made the calculations and found out it was almost two thousand miles east from Berlin to Voronezh. Not that she had hoped to be able to visit him, but two thousand miles?

No wonder letters didn't go back and forth. All the hope faded from her heart. She clapped the atlas shut and returned it to its place on the bookshelf. On her way out, she passed a poster announcing the Berlin University was open for degrees in medicine, philosophy, theology and law.

Lotte gazed at the poster for long moments, remembering the moment in Denmark when she'd promised herself to fight for justice and become a lawyer. She returned to the information desk and asked the friendly lady, "Ma'am, what do I need to matriculate in law?"

"Your identification, permission of your parent if you're underage and your high school diploma."

"I don't..." Lotte looked down at her clasped hands. Due to schools' being shut down during the war, she'd never had the chance to finish high school and take the final exam.

"Not to worry, Fräulein, you're not the only one who doesn't have *Abitur.* In fact most of our would-be students don't have it; that's why the university offers a semester-long preparation course. It will enable you to take the *Abitur* exam at the end and enroll for the course of study of your choice in the following semester."

"Really? I could do that?"

"Of course. As long as you meet the other two requirements. Here's the form to fill out. Come back anytime before the end of this month to start this semester."

"Thank you, ma'am." Lotte put the sheet of paper into her bag and walked home more upbeat than she'd been in quite a while.

Her parents hadn't allowed Anna to enroll in university to study biology, but that had been before the war. Times had changed, and Lotte was confident her mother couldn't withhold her permission, not with Anna and Ursula on her side.

CHAPTER 37: URSULA

"When are you returning to Kleindorf?" Mutter asked.

"I'm not." Ursula braced herself for the inevitable argument.

"What do you mean? Your travel permit expires tomorrow."

"I'm not returning before I have seen Tom."

"You can't defy the authorities just because of this man." Mutter sighed, unpacking the groceries. It had seemed like a lot in her shopping bag, but now, neatly positioned in the pantry, the items looked forlorn.

How anyone was supposed to feed five adults, one growing youth and a toddler with this for an entire week was beyond Ursula. It was only thanks to the huge amounts of food Aunt Lydia had given them upon their departure that they wouldn't be hungry for another month or so.

But still, Ursula had no intentions of returning to Kleindorf.

"I'll go and ask for an extension tomorrow," Ursula said, although she had different plans.

Mutter furrowed her brows. "Why don't I believe you? This *foreigner* has messed with your head." Her mother still refused to call Tom by his name. She was indignant that Ursula had disgraced the family by not only falling for one of the enemies but also having a child out of wedlock with him.

"Don't worry about me, Mutter." Ursula wrapped a shawl around her shoulders and put on her gloves, ready to go out.

"Where are you going?"

"Out. Don't wait for me." Ursula didn't want to lie to her mother, but she couldn't well tell her that she was about to – finally – see Tom. He'd been in England since she'd arrived in Berlin, but according to one of his comrades at the base he'd been scheduled to return that morning.

"What about Evie?" Mutter asked with a disapproving gaze.

"Lotte is outside with her and she promised to take care of her until I return. Bye, Mutter." Ursula escaped from the apartment, afraid her mother would start a full-blown interrogation.

She took the tram to Gatow airbase and approached the sentry with a thumping heart. In her finest English she said, "Excuse me, may I talk to Squadron Leader Westlake, please?"

"What's your concern?"

She had planned for the question. "I work for the bakery down the road and he wanted to talk to my boss about making a birthday cake for some friend."

She waited with bated breath while the sentry used the telephone to call Tom's quarters. "Wait here. He'll be down in a moment."

It didn't take long until Tom approached the gate with a long stride. He looked dashing in his blue uniform and love poured from her heart, warming her entire body.

"There's a Fräulein from the bakery waiting for you," the sentry told him and pointed his thumb in Ursula's direction.

She saw how Tom's eyes turned wide like saucers, but apart from that he kept a motionless face and said, "Thanks, I'll talk to her."

When his face was out of the sight of the sentry, a huge smile appeared on Tom's face and he hissed, "A Fräulein from the bakery?"

"Yes, sir, you wanted to talk to my boss about a cake. Would you be kind enough to accompany me?"

Tom squinted his eyes, but turned around and told the sentry, "I'll be back in an hour or so if anybody asks."

They walked down the street and Ursula could barely wait until they turned a corner into a small alley. Once out of sight, Tom looked around frantically and finding no one, he grabbed her face with both hands, devouring her mouth with a passionate kiss.

"You almost gave me a heart attack," he said after coming up for air.

"I'm sorry, but I couldn't let you know." She pressed herself against his body, basking in the glorious feeling of his presence. Hand in hand, they walked down the alley, until they reached a park, where they found an empty bench.

"Where's Evie?" he asked.

"With Lotte." She looked up, noticing that he understood. It was less suspicious if she came without his daughter.

"How did you even get here?"

Ursula looked at their intertwined hands. "I came for a visit when my family returned to Berlin after the holidays."

He took her chin into his hand, forcing her to look at him. "How long is your travel permit valid?"

She squirmed under his stare. "Until today."

He sucked in a breath, then squinted his eyes. "So when are you planning to return to Kleindorf?"

Ursula bit on her lower lip, returning his stare. "Never."

"You can't be serious!"

"I am. I waited such a long time for you, I'm not going to Kleindorf where I won't be able to see you."

"But you can't stay here illegally. They'll take your ration cards away and what will you live on?"

"I'll find a way. And I still have you." She stubbornly pushed out a lip. She hadn't expected him to take her mother's stance on this issue. "I thought you'd be delighted to see me."

"I am delighted. Very much so, but at least one of us has to be sensible here."

She gave a dramatic sigh and snuggled up tighter against him, her hand wandering across his muscled stomach. "Can't you stop being sensible for at least a little while?"

The spark of passion darkened his eyes and he groaned. "It's too cold out here – come with me."

CHAPTER 38: TOM

Tom uttered a muffled curse. He desperately wanted Ursula. Of course it was strictly forbidden to bring a German into the barracks, but he knew there were ways – others had done it before him.

Weighing guilt about breaking the rules against the throbbing need to make love to Ursula, he did exactly what she'd asked him to. He stopped being sensible, just for a little while.

"Come with me, but you can't be seen," he said and then led her back to the barracks. There was a small hole in the fence next to one of the barracks, a place that had been used countless times for nightly visits. It was already getting dark when he showed her the clandestine entrance and how to get to his barracks unseen. There, he would wait for her and let her inside through the window.

The excitement and nerves reddened her cheeks and for a short moment he wanted to cancel the whole thing. It was wrong. Sneaking her into his quarters like a harlot wasn't how he wanted things to be. Ursula was the mother of his child, for Christ's sake.

But when she pressed a kiss on his lips, those thoughts flew away. "I have to return through the main gate. Knock at my window in about twenty minutes."

"I will."

Tom fought against the urge to run to his quarters. Instead he kept up appearances and behaved the way he did every other day, including a short chat with the sentry.

Once in his quarters, he locked the door and switched on the light, counted to five and switched it off again. A minute later he heard a knock and opened the window, carefully scanning left and right. When the coast was clear, he held out a hand to help Ursula climb in through the window.

"So this is your place," she said, inspecting the drab room while he closed the window, drew the curtains and switched on the small nightlight.

The awkwardness lasted only a couple of seconds, before his passion, heightened by the sense of danger, took over. He pressed her against the wall, tracing heated kisses down her neck. When she moaned, he put his hand over her mouth and whispered into her ear, "You can't make a sound."

Ursula nodded, her eyes wide with lust as she helped him divest themselves of their clothing.

"You're so beautiful," he said, sweeping her into his arms and carrying her over to his bed. There, he ravaged her body with the urgent need of weeks of separation and then continued to make sweet love to her for many hours. When they lay finally sated in each other's arms they talked about their uncertain future.

"You can't stay in Berlin. Have you thought about what happens when you get caught violating the restrictions on moving about?" He traced a finger down the silky skin on her shoulders.

"No, I haven't. Anna said, her boss, Professor Scherer, might be able to pull some strings. I'll meet with him tomorrow."

He cast her a doubtful glance, but couldn't go through with crashing her hopes, so he asked, "Who's this Professor Scherer?"

"A famous medicine and human biology professor whom apparently the Americans hold in high esteem. They wooed him away from the Charité hospital to work for them. The Soviets were furious to say the least."

"Seems like the kind of shenanigans the Yanks would pull." Tom chuckled.

Ursula laughed and caught his hand moving down to her breast. "Not only the Yanks, as you call them, but your lot as well. According to Anna they outbid each other to get him to work for them. I have no idea how he does it… the Nazis, the Soviets, … everyone seems to love him."

"I hate to break it to you." Tom used the small distraction to free his hand and move it down her stomach. "But the rich and powerful always come out unscathed while the little people are the ones paying the price."

"Don't tell that to my sister, Lotte. She enrolled at the Berlin University for a law degree, driven by a need to avenge those who were harmed."

His hand moved lower, but she caught it again. With a

mischievous glint in her eyes, she said, "Squadron Leader Westlake, if you want more of this, you need to feed me first." As if to emphasize her words, her stomach grumbled and a pang of guilt stabbed him.

"I'm sorry, sweetheart. I was so hungry for you, I completely forgot that most humans don't exist on air and love alone." He got up and pulled some cookies and apples from a drawer. "Here. Do you want me to go to the mess and see if I can bring you more food?"

"No." She shook her head, gobbling up the cookies. "But next time, you'd better be prepared."

"Next time? There won't be a next time."

She batted her eyelashes at him, and bit heartily into the apple instead of giving an answer. Why did he have to fall for the most stubborn woman on earth? But it had been her spunk that had saved his life back then, so who was he to complain?

After Ursula finished eating they made love again, and again, and again until they fell asleep in each other's arms. Tom woke with a start, something pressing heavily on him. It took him a moment to remember it was Ursula, but he was terrified all the same. Turning around he switched on the night lamp and checked his wristwatch lying on the nightstand – four a.m.

In an hour the base would come to life, and the risk of her being seen became greater by the minute. He roused her and whispered urgently, "You have to leave before morning breaks."

Shame flushed her cheeks and he knew she hated the hiding, lying and secrecy as much as he did. But right now there was no time to dwell on embarrassment. He helped her find her clothes and then opened the window for her to jump out. But first he pressed a last kiss on her lips, with a whispered promise to meet the next day.

Tom returned to his bed, hoping to catch another hour of shuteye, when an insistent knock on the door woke him and he opened it. Two MPs burst into his room and demanded he get up and come with them.

"What's this about?" he asked, but didn't receive an answer.

CHAPTER 39: URSULA

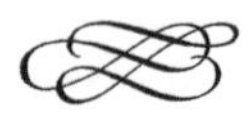

Ursula slipped out of the window and walked along the wall in the shadow of darkness. She had to cross an open space to the next barracks and from there it was only a few steps to the hole in the fence.

She glowed inside from the lovemaking with Tom and had to bite down on her lips in order not to hum a happy tune. The compound still slept, but on the far side she saw light in one of the barracks. Her mouth watered at the unmistakable sound of kettles being put on the stove as the kitchen staff prepared breakfast.

A wistful longing came over her. It would be so nice if she could just walk into the mess and have a hearty break-fast. She turned around the corner and bumped into another person.

"Well, well, well. What have we here?" the soldier said.

Ursula couldn't see his face in the darkness, but his creepy demeanor sent a shiver of fear up her spine. She glimpsed the fence less than ten yards away and pondered whether she should make a run for it. Tom had assured her that most of his comrades ignored the non-fraternization policy and most superiors turned a blind eye to nightly visits.

But this man smelled like trouble.

Before she could come to a decision, he grabbed her wrist and said, "I saw you climb out of Westlake's window and I know what you've been doing with him." He leered at her. "It would be a shame if someone told on you. Or on him..."

"Please let me pass," Ursula asked him quietly, her heart thumping hard against her ribs.

"I don't think so. In fact, I have a better idea. My room's right here and we'll call it even, if you come with me and give me a sample of the skills you applied to Westlake. How does that sound?"

Ursula shook her head in horror and jerked her arm from his grip, running back the direction she'd come from. In her haste to get away from him, she lost her orientation and kept running straight ahead, with no idea where she was going.

Suddenly she stared into the stern faces of two MPs pointing their rifles at her. It occurred to her that running like a mad hen through a military compound was the worst thing she could have done. She came to a skidding halt in front of them, stitches making her breathing labored, and slowly raised her hands.

"Where do you think you're going?" one of them asked her. Or he could have said something entirely different, because she was too terrified to make sense of his English words.

"Come with us," the short, burly one said, not entirely unfriendly. She guessed him to be in his late twenties.

She nodded and followed them into one of the barracks where they led her into a room that seemed to be some kind of office. Ursula frantically tried to come up with an excuse, since she didn't want to expose Tom and risk him being discharged from service.

"What are you doing here? Don't you know Gatow airbase is off-limits to Germans?"

"Isn't it clear what she's been doing here?" the other one said with a salacious click of his tongue. "I wouldn't kick her out of my bed."

Ursula's face blazed fire, because that's exactly what she'd been doing. But they didn't understand. Tom and she were deeply in love and she wasn't some tart who came here for nylons and chocolate. "I'm sorry. It seems I got lost. I have no idea how I ended up in here."

"Why did you run away?" the burly soldier said, trying to hide a smirk at her obviously fabricated lie. People didn't simply stumble into a heavily guarded, fenced-off military compound.

But despite his attempt at an intimidating stance, she wasn't afraid of him. Not like the one who'd confronted her at the barracks and had given her some awfully creepy feelings.

"I heard a strange sound and got scared," Ursula said.

"Show me your papers," he demanded.

Ursula handed him her identification card that had *Mindelheim* and *American sector* printed on it.

He squinted his eyes. "You don't even live in Berlin? You know it's illegal to leave your occupation zone, right?"

"I have a travel permit. I came here to visit my mother," Ursula quickly explained and withdrew from her pocket the permit issued by the Americans and stamped by the Soviets.

The MP scrutinized the paper. As soon as he set his jaw into a hard line, she knew she was busted. "That travel permit was valid until," he looked at his wristwatch, "four hours ago. You're an illegal in Berlin."

"But I have all of today to return..." she protested.

The dark-haired MP joined the interrogation. "Which no doubt you won't be able to make, because you'll spend some time in one of our cells. Because I'll tell you why you're here, and it's not because you're *lost*. You're here to spy for the Soviets."

The mounting tension between the Soviet Union and the Western Allies was a constant companion in the lives of every Berliner. Tom had told her that the Russian *accidentally* showed up near the airbase on a regular basis. Their barely concealed animosity annoyed the hell out of the British crew.

"I'm not a spy, and definitely not for the Russians. I hate them as much as you do."

"Then tell us what you were doing on the base!"

Ursula remained silent. She'd rather suffer punishment herself than get Tom in trouble.

"Now? Do you want us to throw you into prison?"

"No, please..." The memory of her last stay inside a cell was still fresh and she couldn't bear the thought of not seeing Evie for days, weeks, or even months. "...You're right. I sneaked in here to see one of the soldiers."

"Aha..." The short one seemed content with this answer and said to his partner, "She clearly isn't a spy, just a frightened and stupid girl. We would have a lot to do if we arrested every peachy Fräulein serving bed duty with the servicemen. So what do you want to do with her?"

Ursula didn't know whether to protest the classification as a whore or sag in relief. Finally, she decided anything was better than being accused of spying for the Russians and gave them a tentative smile. "Please, I have a baby daughter waiting for me. May I go home?"

She saw the expression of the man in charge soften and already wanted to cry victory when a knock on the door interrupted them. The other man went to answer it and came inside with the soldier who'd accosted her earlier. Her toes curled at the sight of him.

"It's her!" the newcomer shouted out. "This is the woman I saw climbing out of Westlake's window."

Ursula wrapped her arms around herself, afraid of what would come next. Because after such a dramatic entrance, it was clear, the MPs couldn't just let her go, even if they'd been inclined to do so mere minutes before.

"Is this true?" the MP in charge asked her.

"I don't know who Westlake is." She made a desperate attempt to protect Tom.

"She's lying." A sly smile crossed her accoster's face. "She even attacked me when I confronted her and then ran away. That's not how an innocent person reacts. I'll bet she's a spy. I'll bet she and Westlake are in cahoots together passing along information to the Soviets."

Ursula balled her hands into fists. These soldiers had watched too many spy movies. Sure, everyone was neurotic about the Soviets wanting to squeeze the other Allies out of Berlin, but that was no reason to automatically assume everyone was a spy.

"That's a serious accusation, Bronson. Do you have any evidence to prove it?"

"I've been suspecting Westlake for quite a while, Blake," Bronson said, the wheels in his brain visibly turning, as he glowered at Ursula. "Doesn't it strike you as peculiar that Westlake was never seen with a woman before?"

"There's a first time for everyone." Blake laughed.

"Not when he's known to be queer."

Ursula sucked in a breath, not exactly sure she understood the correct meaning of Bronson's words, because he couldn't possibly be insinuating that Tom… no… no… or?

"Oh, come on, weren't you the one who invented that unfounded rumor?" Blake said.

"Rumor or not," Bronson said. "I'm here to file an official complaint against this German tart and Tom Westlake. You'd better go and investigate him or I'll have to file a complaint against you as well."

Ursula saw the vein at Blake's temple pulsating, but he managed to keep his voice amazingly calm when he answered, "Of course, we will investigate. Come with me, Johnson. We'll question Westlake right away."

"You'd better stay here, if you don't want to dig yourself deeper," the man called Johnson said before the three men left the office.

She overheard them sending Bronson to his barracks and then Johnson saying, "Bronson is a veritable pain in the arse."

"You can say that again. Thanks to him we now have to

go on a wild goose chase because of a woman. As if we didn't have more serious problems."

"What an arsehole!"

CHAPTER 40: TOM

"What's the matter, Ken?" Tom asked. He'd glanced at the MPs face only once and it had been sufficient to realize Tom was in big trouble. The vein in Ken's temple pulsated, and if that wasn't enough evidence of his wrath, the unusually rough treatment said the rest.

"Shut up until you're asked."

And then Tom saw Bronson lingering in front of the administration building with a dirty smirk on his face. It was like a punch to his gut. Whatever was going on, it had something to do with his nemesis. That was a bad sign. A very bad sign, indeed.

"We have received a serious accusation that you're involved in spying for the Russians." Johnson said as they reached an interrogation room

"That's complete bullshit!" Tom exploded. They could as well accuse him of being friends with the Nazis. "You chaps know me; you can't possibly believe this shit."

"Calm down," Johnson said.

"Squadron Leader Bronson saw a woman climb out of your window," Ken added.

"He must need glasses." Tom did his best to keep his rage under control and maintain an easygoing friendly rapport, while his mind tried to make sense of the accusations. Why all the fuss? Having a female visitor on base was strictly forbidden, but it was hardly the crime of the century. Usually the pilots got away with a slap on the wrist and some nasty maintenance duty. Nobody had ever gotten accused of spying because of it.

"Good man, tell us the truth and nobody gets hurt," Ken said.

The smirk on Bronson's face, though, had alerted Tom that something was seriously wrong. What kind of lies had the bastard spun this time? Tom worried about Ursula, despite the fact he'd seen her slink away behind the barracks closest to the secret exit in the fence. That had been almost one hour ago and she was probably home with Evie and her family by now. Yet, he worried.

"There's nothing to tell. This accusation is outrageous." Tom had to keep Ursula out of this at all costs. If they found her, they'd inevitably notice that her permit for Berlin had expired and she was here illegally. He didn't know what punishment that entailed, but he sure as hell didn't want to find out. *I should have insisted she leave Berlin immediately. She should never have come here in the first place.*

"Tom? Have you had a German woman in your quarters?" Ken prodded him.

"I have no idea what you're talking about." Tom ran a hand through his hair. Denying would be the best course of action, since nobody could prove that she'd in fact been in his quarters.

"We're going to find out the truth anyway, and since Bronson filed an official complaint, you'd better start talking right now."

"So that sleazy snake accused me of another crime I haven't committed. Doesn't he shrink back from anything to ruin my career?"

"You're right. This may well ruin your career and even get you court-martialed, if you don't start talking. An accusation of spying for the Soviets is not something anyone can and will overlook, unlike other minor offences. Just give us the name of the woman," Ken said.

Tom understood the unspoken message. If he confessed, they'd let him go with a slap on the wrist, but if he didn't, they'd investigate him for espionage. It was a tempting bridge that Ken was building for him, but he couldn't cross it. Not if Ursula would have to pay the price.

"I have nothing to say." Tom lowered his head, because he'd just sent his entire military career down the drain.

"I'm really sorry about this, but I have to arrest you, Westlake. I hope she was worth it."

She definitely is worth it. He'd do anything to protect her.

CHAPTER 41: RICHARD

Kleindorf, February 1946

At the Epstein farm, they had a lot more space than in the crowded farmhouse at Aunt Lydia's. Ricahrd and Rachel had traveled to the convent in Kaufbeuren to fetch her brothers Aaron and Israel several weeks ago. It had been a very moving reunion and Richard had surreptitiously blinked away a few tears.

Israel was thirteen years old and Aaron ten. They were easy enough to handle, because the nuns had done stellar work in teaching them manners and obedience. At the moment, they were a bit too soft for his liking, but he was certain he – or better Katrina once she had the baby and was on her feet again – could teach them everything there was to know about running a farm. At least the older boy would be of great help.

Right now, as snow still kept the farmer's hands idle, he'd taken to teaching them mathematics, literature, geography and anything else he could think of. He found the nuns had done a stellar job on their education too and the boys were exceptionally well versed in reading, writing and most of the other subjects.

What he worried about, though, was their Jewish heritage. Richard had no idea about Jewish culture or traditions and he feared he'd fail the children in this respect.

"Richard, you don't have to shoulder all the burden. This is something Rachel can do. She's their sister and she knows all about Jewish traditions," Katrina said, intent on soothing his worries.

"But the boys need an older male to look up to for guidance. And I might teach them things the wrong way, because I don't know how it's different in their religion."

Katrina laughed. "Aaron and Israel have withstood three years of living in a Catholic convent, run by nuns."

"Exactly!" A shudder ran down his spine. One of his mother's favorite threats had been, "If you don't behave, I'll send you to a convent." Any child knew it wasn't fun to be raised by nuns.

"Darling," she put a hand on his shoulder, "you worry too much. You're doing a great job and those boys adore you."

"It's just so hard. When I signed up to run this farm, I had no idea what I was in for. The responsibility for five people now rests on my shoulders. I'm already feeling overwhelmed and we're still in winter and..." He didn't say that the nearer the due date for their baby came, the more inadequate he felt. If they'd been back in Aunt Lydia's house, he could rely on Lydia and Frau Hansen to support Katrina with the new baby. But now, she would have only Rachel to help. And in addition to not having children of her own, Rachel was still incredibly frail. "You should move in with Aunt Lydia, at least for the first weeks after the baby is born."

"You'll be a great father and I will be alright here with you," Katrina insisted.

"But what if something goes wrong?" Awful images crossed his mind.

"I can always send you for your aunt, it's less than fifteen minutes—ouch." Katrina doubled over in pain.

"What's wrong, sweetheart?" One look at her distorted face and he thought the worst.

"Nothing." She breathed heavily and then said, "The baby is coming."

"What? Now?" Panic roared through him and he hastily glanced in all directions, unable to move or think a clear thought.

Katrina, though, seemed to have recovered quickly and she smiled at him. "Go and get the midwife."

"But what if the baby is born while I'm away?" Richard was out of his mind. The midwife lived halfway to Mindelheim and it would take him at least an hour to walk there and back.

"Nothing will happen. The first baby usually takes twelve or even more hours to come out. Now go."

Richard paled. "Twelve hours? Oh my God. I'd better go."

He put on his coat and his boots, which were strangely uncomfortable today. He didn't have the time or inclination to give it further thought, not until Katrina called him, "Richard. You put your boots on the wrong feet."

He glanced down. She was right.

"Look, darling, there's no need to worry. Promise." She observed how he changed the boots onto the correct feet.

"I still don't feel good leaving you alone in the house." Rachel and her siblings had walked into town that morning to file some paperwork.

"If it makes you feel better, why don't you run over to Aunt Lydia first and tell her to visit with me before you get the midwife?"

"That's a great idea. I will do that." He pressed a kiss on her lips, but even as she was in his arms, she recoiled again. "Oh no. Oh no. What is it this time?"

"Just another contraction. You go and get me the midwife and then you disappear from my sight until the baby is born or you'll make everyone crazy with your worry." She laughed and sent him away.

Richard, though, couldn't understand her cavalier attitude and trudged through the snow as fast as his legs would carry him. He reached Aunt Lydia's house in record time and barged into the kitchen yelling, "Aunt Lydia! Aunt Lydia!"

His aunt came rushing and at the sight of his reddened, heated face filled with panic she asked, "What happened?"

"The baby is coming!" he pressed out between frantic breaths.

"Just this morning I thought it was about time," Lydia answered. "What did the midwife say?"

"Nothing! I'm on my way to get her. I came here first, because Katrina is alone in the house and she's in pain."

Lydia, who'd borne nine children in her life, cast an indulgent gaze at this aggravated first-time father. "I'll go right away to see her, but you stop worrying and leave this job to us women."

Richard nodded, feeling slightly better now that his aunt was taking control into her hands and he was just a runner tasked with getting the midwife.

CHAPTER 42: URSULA

"Tom Westlake denied everything," Blake told Ursula when he and his partner returned about an hour later. Meanwhile it was approaching 6 a.m. and soon her mother would get up and notice that Ursula hadn't returned home last night. She didn't know what was a more frightening prospect: arrest by the British military or the wrath of her mother.

Her face must have shown her fear, because Blake motioned for his partner to leave the room. He settled on the chair beside her and said, "If you think you're protecting Tom, you're not. Since there is a witness who saw you climb out of his window, he'll be tried for lying, breaking base rules and possibly treason."

"Oh, no." She hid her face in her hands, guilt sweeping over her. It was her fault, and hers alone, that he was in this situation. She should have been more careful when making her exit, shouldn't have run away like a headless chicken, shouldn't have fallen asleep – shouldn't have agreed to come with him in the first place. It was only her unfulfilled wanton to have privacy with him that had caused this entire mess. What kind of awful woman was she?

She should forget about him, for the sake of everyone involved. Hadn't even the wise Confucius said, "If you love somebody, let them go free"? Tom would soon forget about her, find himself a swell Englishwoman, one he could present in public, and he'd live happily ever after. But the mere thought of him in the arms of another woman burned like fire in her gut.

"Look, Tom's a friend and I'd hate to see him discharged dishonorably or worse."

Ursula glanced up, a sliver of hope entering her. "I'll do anything to exonerate him. This entire situation is completely my fault."

"So you did climb out of his window."

"Yes." She cast her eyes downward, too embarrassed to look at him because she knew what he was thinking now. A tart. Selling her body for amenities. "It's all my fault. I should never have come here."

"Why did you?"

"I can't tell you," she whispered. "But Tom is lying to protect me. He probably assumes I'm home already."

"Why would he want to protect you?"

Ursula fought an inner war whether to expose their big secret or not. She didn't want to aggravate Tom's situation any further. "Sir, would… I mean, will you promise not to tell anyone else if I tell you?"

Blake furrowed his brows. "I can't really promise this, because if it's a crime then I have to prosecute—"

"No! No!" Her hand flew to her heart. "It's nothing bad. I mean, maybe it's kind of bad." She observed his frown deepening and hurried to explain, "At least not worse than me staying in his quarters." A heated flush burned her cheeks. "It's actually the very reason why I was even there."

Blake relaxed. "Just tell me and I will keep quiet if at all possible."

"Tom and I have been in love since we first met years ago."

"Wow! So that's the reason..." Blake obviously hadn't expected her answer, because he leaned back, looking at her with wide-open eyes.

"Reason for what?"

"That he's never shacked up with one of the Fräuleins." He cocked his head and said, "If you really love him, you have to convince him to admit to inviting you to his quarters."

She could feel her flush intensifying. The entire base would know that she had spent the night with Tom. But she courageously nodded. Whatever it took to get him out of the mess she had created.

"I have to warn you, though, it might not be pleasant. You might be questioned about... about what you were doing in his quarters. And you'll definitely have to answer about your expired stay permit."

"I don't care. I'll do anything. Can I talk to him?"

"Not now." He glanced at his wristwatch. "My shift ends at 6 a.m. Return here at noon and ask for me at the gate. Corporal Ken Blake."

"Thank you, Corporal. So..." She looked around unsure whether she should get up. "You're letting me go?"

He chuckled. "Yes. I'm not in the business of arresting beautiful young women in love."

"Won't you get into trouble for this?" she asked.

"Let that be my problem. I'll take you to the gate."

CHAPTER 43: ANNA

At least the buses are running again, Anna thought as she stepped onto the bus taking her home after another night shift at the American hospital. The bus was filled with people heading for work and she had to walk all the way to the last row until she found an empty seat. She flopped onto the seat with a sigh and then almost jumped up again.

"Ursula, what are you doing here?" Her sister had the crumpled appearance of someone who'd spent most of the night awake.

"Me?" Ursula's eyes widened in shock and she bit on her lower lip.

"Where's Evie? And where have you been? You look awful."

"Is that an official interrogation?"

"Well, since you choose not to answer, I'm getting my own ideas and they involve a certain man…" Anna couldn't believe her sister had been reckless enough to spend a night with Tom.

"Shush." Ursula glowered at her. "I'll tell you alright, but not on the bus."

"Good gracious! That sounds bad."

"It is. Kind of."

Anna was dying to hear the news, but she had to wait until the excruciatingly slow bus finally approached the stop nearest to their home and they got off.

"Tell me!" she demanded.

"I went to see Tom, and he smuggled me into his quarters."

"Goodness! How could you? Illegally entering a British airbase. What kind of crazy woman are you?" Anna couldn't believe her own ears. Her sister Ursula, the obedient girl who'd never done anything forbidden and never once gotten into trouble during their childhood. That same person had sneaked onto a highly guarded military airbase. Anna shuddered at the thought of what might have happened had someone seen her on site. "At least you didn't get caught."

"Actually, I did."

Anna stopped in her tracks and jerked her head around, her jaw hanging agape. "You… what? You got caught? And they let you go?"

"Yes, and can you please hear me out without interrupting me every five seconds?" Ursula had an annoyed expression on her face.

Spunk, Anna thought. When and where had her sister developed that unwavering determination, that steely courage to defy anyone and everything that stood in her way? "Sure."

"When climbing out of Tom's window someone saw me

and confronted me. I panicked, ran, got held up by two MPs and was arrested." They had reached their apartment building.

"Want to walk around the block while you keep talking?" Anna asked.

Ursula nodded and continued walking. "So they found out my stay permit has expired..."

I have good news for you on that front. Anna kept the thought to herself and instead listened to her sister recounting the events of the night.

"... the soldier who confronted me seems to have a personal vendetta against Tom and he insisted I'm a Soviet spy."

Anna felt like someone pulled the rug out from under her feet. If Ursula continued to pile worse on bad, she'd start screaming. "So why did they let you go?"

"It seems this Corporal Blake, the MP, he's a friend of Tom's and wants to help him."

"Him? What's with Tom?"

Ursula scrunched her nose. "Didn't I tell you? This other guy, Bronson, the one who hates Tom, he reported him for espionage, treason and whatnot. So they had to arrest him."

"Tom's been arrested?" A dizzy spell attacked Anna. She would have expected this kind of irresponsible shenanigans from their younger sister Lotte, but not from Ursula.

"I should have had Peter throw you over his shoulder and carry you to the train back to Aunt Lydia's."

Ursula laughed. "I would have jumped off the first chance I got. There's nothing that can keep me away from Tom."

"Not even prison walls?"

"Well now, here's the thing. This Ken Blake, he asked me to return at noon and ask for him. Then I can see Tom and convince him to confess."

Anna groaned. They had reached their apartment building. "Is there more or can we go inside?"

"That's it. I'll know more in the afternoon."

"Oh, I totally forgot," Anna said as they climbed the stairs. "I have good news for you."

"I could definitely use some good news." Ursula smiled, reinforcing the bond between the sisters.

"Professor Scherer has managed to get you a permanent permit for Berlin."

"Oh! Wow!" Ursula hugged and kissed her sister. "That's fantastic."

"Under one condition." Anna knew her sister would hate the condition.

"What is it?"

"You'll have to work at the hospital."

Ursula gulped and turned greenish-pale around the nose. She had an irrational fear of blood, needles and all things hospital. Even the distinctive smell made her skin crawl. Her voice was but a whisper, "Does he expect me to become a nurse?"

"God forbid! We don't need fainting nurses." Anna giggled. "In fact, it was his first suggestion, but I managed to convince him that it wasn't in the best interest of our patients. But since you've been practicing your English all this time, I told him you'd be a good secretary who can deal with the American bosses."

"Oh, Anna, I love you!" Ursula hugged her sister again and they stumbled against the apartment door. Just as they had found their footing again, the door opened and a scowling Peter peeked his head out.

"What on earth... Anna... Ursula? Why are you putting up such a fuss?" He glanced suspiciously at the crumpled but positively glowing Ursula and asked, "Are you drunk?"

"No!" Ursula hugged her brother-in-law, dancing him around and said, "I got a stay permit. I got a stay permit."

Peter shook his head at his wife and retreated into the apartment, the singing and dancing Ursula still in his arms. Inside, he extricated himself from her embrace and took cover behind the sofa. Anna followed him and fell into his arms.

"Are you tired?"

"Yes, but I need to talk to you first. You still have half an hour before you need to leave for work, right?"

Peter kissed her and watched as Ursula disappeared into the bathroom. "Let's go into the kitchen. I have the water boiling for coffee."

He poured her coffee and handed her some hard and dry biscuits. By the look of his ice-blue eyes boring into her Anna knew he had picked up on her disturbed mood.

"You're late," he said.

"Ursula and I walked around the block."

"A romantic sisterly walk at dawn after a grueling night of work?" He teased her.

Anna got up and closed the kitchen door. "She spent the night with Tom on base and they both got arrested. Tom is accused of espionage and waiting for who knows what."

"That is indeed a reason to go for a walk." He flopped into the chair beside her, sipping on his steaming hot coffee.

They sat in silence for a while, his arm around her

shoulder giving her the comfort she craved so much. Coming home to his side every morning or every night was what kept her grounded, sane, and optimistic in a bleak world. She wouldn't survive if he left her… a fear squeezed down on her, pressing the air from her lungs.

"What else has you tied in knots?" he asked, pulling her closer.

She'd been holding Professor Scherer's offer a secret for fear Peter would feel inferior and leave her. He'd joined the Polish army at eighteen and being a soldier was everything he'd ever learned.

"Professor Scherer thinks I should continue my biology studies."

"Really? That's good, right?" Peter asked.

"Very."

"Can you do this while working as a nurse?"

Naturally he was worried about food rations. The winter had been harsh and many people in Germany had starved to death. Her job at the American hospital came with perks: food on site. Her meager outside rations supported the family, especially Jan, who seemed to be always hungry.

Anna kissed him on the cheek and laid her head on his shoulder. "The professor offered to move me to the biology department once again, where I can combine my work and my studies."

"So where's the problem?" He took her face into his hands and locked eyes with her.

"It's just…" She shrugged. "This is just the first step. Professor Scherer is convinced I can make it big in the world of science. If I accept his offer, he'll show me off to his colleagues. I'll be working long hours on prestigious projects and he even plans to make me head of a department as soon as I finish my studies."

"And now you're worried you're leaving me and Jan behind?"

She nodded, afraid that he would agree with her assumption.

"Oh, sweet Anna. I love you for everything you are and I fought for the longest time with my feelings of not deserving such a spectacular woman as yourself. I never felt worthy of your love. Not until you taught me I could still be a man and protector even if you are more intelligent and earn more than I do. I will always love you and I will proudly be the man behind the famous human biologist you're bound to become."

Tears spilled down her cheeks. "You're not angry?"

"Of course not. If anything, I'm proud of you. Professor Scherer may have malleable morals but he has an uncanny eye for talent."

"I love you, Peter."

"I love you too, Anna."

CHAPTER 44: TOM

Sleep proved elusive. Despite being tired to the bone, Tom worried incessantly. It had been an irresponsible, reckless, and outright stupid move to smuggle Ursula into his quarters.

He shook his head at his own antics. He hadn't survived the Luftwaffe lads wanting to shoot him down and the Gestapo by being reckless. Ken had seemed outright furious and Bronson… Bronson had laughed all the way back to his barracks over his lucky day.

Thinking things over with a clear mind, one thing was certain. They wouldn't let him stay in Berlin. If they sent him back to England, he might never see Ursula again. That thought weighed heavily on his heart, but at the same time a doubt entered his mind.

She would be better off without him. She'd soon find herself a nice German man, marry, have more children and live happily ever after. His stomach churned at the thought of Ursula in the arms of another man, but he ignored it. He would sacrifice himself so that she could live a happy life without the challenges of loving a British serviceman.

When he finally fell into a fitful sleep, he had nightmares of another German prison in another time. Just as the Gestapo agent beat down on him with a lead pipe he raised his hands to protect his head and woke drenched in cold sweat. Sunlight streamed into his cell, moving his mind forward into the present. He pulled his knees up to his chest and concentrated on slowing his breathing down.

He'd been incredibly naïve where Ursula was concerned. Consumed with missing her, he'd never given a thought to how their relationship should work after the war. In his dreams, he'd find her, marry her and start a family. He hadn't even considered the little detail of where they should live. Germany, England, in his dreams location didn't matter. Neither did fraternization rules, hostilities or the shocked reactions of his parents.

In his dreams everything had been so easy. Inconsequential.

At noon someone entered the cell. It was Ken Blake. "I know you're protecting this woman."

"I have no idea what you're talking about."

"Will you please stop being a blockheaded bull and talk? Or do you want Bronson to get away with his baseless accusation?"

Tom shook his head. Should they court-martial him and send him behind bars for the rest of his life, it was for the best. As long as Ursula and Evie were kept out of this.

"Stubborn as a mule," Ken mumbled and then said, "You have a visitor."

"Me?" Tom expected Bronson to strut into the cell,

basking in the glory of his victory. Maybe he'd at least find out why Bronson disliked him so much. But the small, blonde person stepping inside flipped his heart over.

"Ursula?" Tom completely forgot Ken's presence and jumped up, hugging, kissing and caressing her. When he finally came to his senses, he took her shoulders and held her at arm's length. "You shouldn't have come here. I don't want you to get into trouble."

She smiled. "*You* are my trouble. If I didn't love you so, everything would be so much easier."

"You have to leave and forget about me. Return to Kleindorf and find yourself a nice man to help you raise Evie."

Her eyes glazed over with tears and she whispered, "Don't you love me anymore?"

"Of course, I love you. From the first moment I saw your blue eyes looking at me in that little cave in the wall I couldn't get you out of my head. Our souls connected in that moment and that gave me the courage to return to you for help. Because I knew you had sensed the same thing."

"Then, how can you want me to forget you?" A single tear slipped down her cheek, but he resisted the urge to kiss it away.

His voice dropped to the lowest of whispers. "It's for the best. Believe me. We can never marry and have a family together. I'll always have to hide you and Evie. Even if you think you are fine with being my mistress, think about how Evie would suffer if anyone knew she was mine. Don't do this to her."

"Things will change with time," she said.

"Maybe not in our lifetimes."

"I don't care!" She pushed out her lower lip, expressing

the unwavering determination he loved so much about her. He couldn't bring himself to tell her to give up hope, slashing her heart the same way her tears had slashed his.

"Please, sweetheart—"

She put a finger to his lips. "I came here to convince you to tell them the truth about last night. Please don't keep trying to protect me. I couldn't live with the fact that you lost your military career because of me."

"But—"

"No buts." She looked around the cell, a teasing smile tugging at the corners of her mouth. "You really need a new hobby. It's a very bad habit you're developing of being accused of espionage."

It wasn't until someone cleared his throat that Tom remembered Ken's presence.

"You've been arrested for spying before?" Ken asked, clutching his gun tighter.

Tom gave a dry laugh. "Courtesy of the Gestapo, who didn't believe I was a simple downed airman, but that I was a spy for the British."

"The Gestapo arrested you? How did you get out?" There was a trace of reverence in Ken's voice.

"That's a long story, but I was lucky and then Ursula hid me and smuggled me out of Germany."

"You did that for him?" Ken asked and when she nodded, he looked utterly baffled, his entire belief system of good guys and bad guys being shattered to pieces. "I'll be back in a few minutes."

Tom watched the door close and heard the key turn in the lock, then he pulled Ursula back into his arms. "I think he left us on purpose."

"Corporal Blake is definitely a romantic," Ursula said. "When I told him yesterday that we've loved each other for years, his eyes got a wistful expression."

"He misses his wife and two daughters very much. But I never tagged him for playing Cupid." Tom wasted no more time with words and ravaged Ursula's mouth. He poured all his love, passion, desperation, need, worry, sorrow and relief into the kiss.

Metal clanged on metal – very loudly – and Tom ended the kiss just in time before the door opened and Ken stepped inside with his superior in tow. Ken grinned at the sight of the pink blush on Ursula's cheeks and winked at Tom.

Ken's boss said, "Squadron Leader Westlake, I'm sorry for the inconvenience caused. All charges have been dismissed, since it seems this was nothing but a misunderstanding. Please sign your release forms."

Tom kept a straight face and answered, "Thank you, sir. I do understand that we have to be aware at all times and the threat of the Soviet Union can never be underestimated."

"As for you, young lady," the officer said. "I understand that you've been helping Corporal Blake to solve this case, therefore I won't turn you over to the civilian authorities for infringing on residence law. But you need to leave Berlin and return to the American sector within twenty-four hours."

"Thank you, sir."

The officer left and Ken accompanied them to the gate, impressing upon them that Ursula was never to return to the base or even near the gate.

Tom asked for permission to escort her to the next bus

stop and while they were waiting for the bus to arrive, he asked, "Where do we stand now?"

"At the bus stop." Ursula giggled.

He playfully slapped her behind. "Cheeky woman! I meant when do we see each other again?"

"Tomorrow?"

Her joyful smile didn't quite match his feelings of goodbye, and he gave her a suspicious glance. "You're not genuinely planning to stay here as an illegal?"

"I'm not." She burst out laughing and squeezed his hand. "Anna's boss, Professor Scherer, has arranged a job for me as secretary at the American hospital in Berlin. As soon as I sign the papers this afternoon, I'll receive my residence permit for Berlin."

"This is wonderful!" Tom itched to swoop her into his arms, kiss her senseless and whirl her around until they both fell to the ground, breathless. But he resisted indulging in such a spectacle and squeezed her hand.

Just as the bus rolled toward the stop, they made plans to meet in front of the citadel in Spandau. It lay halfway between RAF Gatow and her building – and was a favorite place for lovers seeking an undisturbed spot on the bank of the Havel River.

CHAPTER 45: RICHARD

Kleindorf, April 1946

His son was already two months old. They had named him Jarek after Katrina's brother who'd died at the hand of the Nazis. Little Jarek had inherited his mother's soft brown eyes and his father's light blond hair.

After such a short time on earth, he'd already won over the hearts of the extended family and he was the only person who could make Rachel smile. After her return to the farm, she'd been sinking deeper and deeper into depression, the memory of the awful experiences preventing her from finding joy in her life. Richard was more than a little worried about her.

She needs some time to adapt, Aunt Lydia liked to say. Katrina reassured him, *Wait until spring comes with more sunshine. This weather is tearing down everyone.* But spring had come and with it sunshine, blossoming flowers and longer days. Everyone in Kleindorf had lost the grayish tone of their skin and looked more alive, better fed, and healthier.

Except for Rachel. She sulked in misery, unable to fight her way out. As soon as the first leaves of rose of Sharon had sprouted in Aunt Lydia's herb garden, Katrina had made a potion for Rachel. But even this had only shown negligible effects.

Richard was at his wit's end. He walked over to Aunt Lydia, hoping to get some wisdom from her, but she only shrugged, saying, "Some can forget and others can't. We don't really know why or how. The only thing we can do is wait and hope. But since you're here, let's go to the shed. I have a few things that you can take to the Epstein farm. They'll come in handy now that sowing and planting season has started."

He nodded, relegating worries about Rachel to the back of his mind as he focused on the task at hand. When he looked up much later, he saw a ragged looking old man stumbling up the driveway toward the house. The stranger stepped into the yard, aiming for the back door.

"There's a man walking through the yard. Should I have a look?" he said to Aunt Lydia, who was still in the shed, setting aside tools she could give to Richard.

"Probably a refugee looking for food or work."

Richard put the wrench on the ground and walked over to see what the man could want, but Sandra, his six-year-old cousin, beat him to it. She sprinted to the yard, put her hands on her hips the way she'd seen her mother do countless times and accosted the stranger. "What do you want here?"

Richard couldn't hear his answer, but whatever it was, it

must have impressed Sandra, because moments later she came dashing toward the shed. The stranger looked oddly familiar, though not enough to trigger Richard's brain to come up with the name. His eyes were drawn to the man, because of the peculiar grayness. Not only the hair and stubble were gray, but also the hollow eyes, the skin and even his clothes. He seemed to have walked straight out of a cloud of gray dust.

"Mama, Mama, there's a man who says he's my father," Sandra shouted even as she ran toward them. "But I told him to leave, since my father is a soldier."

Lydia dropped the saw she was holding and clasped her hands together, before she gathered her skirt and ran off to meet the man in the yard.

Sandra looked at Richard with a foolhardy expression on her little face. "I don't need no father; we're fine as we are."

Richard's heart broke for the little girl who'd seen her father only a few times in her life. Obviously she didn't have any idea what to make out of his existence. Lydia, though, beamed with delight as she hugged and kissed the man.

"Good lord, Peter. Where have you been? I never received notice. I'm just so glad you're here..." Emotions overwhelmed Lydia and her voice broke.

Richard took Sandra's hand and approached the couple. "Uncle Peter, I'm Richard."

"The last time I saw you, you were but a boy." Uncle Peter's voice was coarse and he seemed to have difficulties standing upright.

Since his aunt had stopped thinking clearly and did

nothing but fuss over her husband, Richard took the initiative and said, "Let's go inside. You must be hungry."

"Oh, how could I forget?" Lydia rushed away, no doubt with the intent of heating up soup.

"I'm sorry," Richard said. "She is quite overwhelmed by your return. It has been tough on her, too."

Uncle Peter nodded, his eyes telling stories about the atrocities of war – the same things Richard had seen during his time in the Wehrmacht.

"So they let you go?"

Richard shook his head, suddenly ashamed. "I evaded capture in Poland and walked all the way here."

"Better choice," Uncle Peter said with a voice as hollow as his eyes and Richard couldn't decipher whether this was meant as a compliment or mockery. They reached the house and Richard helped his uncle get out of his greatcoat and boots – both torn and mended many times.

Seeing Aunt Lydia's emotion laden face, Richard decided to give them some privacy and turned around, bumping into Sandra, who held an almost belligerent stance. "Does he stay here?"

"Yes, since this is his home."

"This is my home! And we don't need him here."

"Look, sweetie, he's your father. And while he's been away for many years, now he has returned to live with your mother. To have a father is a happy thing," Richard answered, not sure how to explain matters of life to a six-year-old.

She didn't seem convinced. "Does this mean I have to do what he says now?"

"Well yes, that is what your mother expects of you."

"Then I want him gone." She glared at Richard and ran away. Following an impulse he went after her, but stopped the pursuit a few steps later. Sandra, and the other children, would need some time to adapt to the new reality of their lives.

Later, during supper, which should have been a happy celebration of reunion, a tense atmosphere hovered over the table. Sandra barely cast a glance at her father, and the younger children didn't understand what was happening. Only the three oldest seemed to be glad that their father had returned from the war alive.

Lydia was too absorbed in her husband to notice anything. But, as always, Katrina picked up on the mood of those surrounding her and offered to put the children to bed.

Aunt Lydia thanked her with a glowing smile and quickly disappeared with her husband into their bedroom.

"I have no doubt that the two of them will be making the next baby tonight," Richard said and added with an appreciative glance at Katrina with little Jarek strapped to her front, "Which I think is a great idea, and we should be doing the same once we return to our farm and Jarek's asleep."

Katrina blushed furiously and slapped his chest. "Hush, the children might hear you."

He bent over to kiss her and whispered into her ear, "You'd better put those children to bed fast, because I'm starving for you."

CHAPTER 46: URSULA

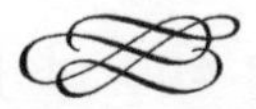

Berlin, July 1946

Summer had arrived with scorching heat and Ursula spent most of her leisure time with Evie and her nephew Jan at one of the lakes in Berlin. It was nice and tranquil out there, quite the change from the still depressing sight of a city in rubble.

She and Tom managed to see each other once or twice a week in public places. Sometimes he even surprised her with a clandestine overnight stay in a hotel that didn't ask questions. It was the nearest they could have to a normal family life.

Evie didn't seem to miss him when he wasn't around, but squealed in delight whenever he accompanied them on one of their walks. They had decided not to tell her that he was her father for now. Not until either things changed or she was a schoolgirl and wouldn't accidentally let the truth slip out. For her he was just Tom.

While Ursula looked forward to seeing Tom every time, she also hated skulking around like their love was a dirty thing. But whenever she complained to Tom about it, he told her to be patient.

One day, toward the end of July, Tom visited her at work, which he'd never done before.

"What are you doing here?"

"Can you take your lunch break now?" he asked instead of giving an answer. His nervous smile gave her a sense of foreboding and she glanced at the clock in her office. "Give me five minutes. I'll meet you outside."

She went to the adjacent office with the doctor on duty and informed him that she'd be taking her lunch hour a few minutes early today. Grabbing her handbag, she walked out the main entrance, all while she worried herself sick about the reason he'd come to see her at work.

When she saw him standing beside the only remaining tree in the hospital front garden, her heart leaped the same way it always did. Whatever bad news he'd come to tell her, as long as they still loved each other there wasn't a thing she couldn't bear.

She walked over to kiss him, but he was unusually tense and pushed her away, saying, "I need to ask you something."

The queasiness in her stomach intensified, but she put on a brave face and nodded.

Much to her surprise he went down on one knee and looked up at her with his amazing green eyes. Before she comprehended what was happening, he took her hand and asked, "Ursula, my love, will you marry me?"

She shrugged, slightly embarrassed at the spectacle of Tom proposing marriage where onlookers could see. "Of course, I'll marry you… one day." It was her fondest wish to become his wife, but there was a ban on marriage between German women and Allied servicemen.

"What about right now?" The nervous tension had left his body and a boisterously happy smile appeared on his face as he got up to kiss her.

Ursula still thought he was pulling her leg. "What's gotten into you, Tom? We both know it can't happen."

"It can. And it will." He pulled a pamphlet from his pocket and handed it to her.

She could only decipher the title, before tears streamed down her face and the letters swam before her eyes. *The conditions under which British Service men may marry German women in the British Zone of Germany.*

"What's wrong, Ursula?" Tom asked with worry. "I thought you'd be happy."

"I am. Terribly happy. Is this real?"

"Yes, it's real." He wrapped his arms around her and continued in a soothing tone, "It's a lengthy process, and there are conditions. But we can apply right now, if you want."

"Yes, I want. You can't imagine how much I want to be your wife." She dabbed the tears from her eyes and cheeks. "What do we have to do?"

"I can file the application for us tonight on the base, but shouldn't we first tell your family?"

"Oh… I totally forgot." Ursula's brain was mushy with the news and she was going to let him handle everything.

"I'll pick you up after work and bring you home. Then

we can tell your family." Tom beamed with joy and gave her a kiss on her lips – in public no less – before he left her at the main entrance to the hospital.

In the evening he held her hand as they climbed the stairs to her apartment. Her heart thumped so loudly in her chest, it drowned out her footsteps and she was sure her nosy neighbor, Frau Weber, must certainly hear it. Any moment the vile gossip would swoop out of her door like a looming dragon and tell her *such a thing* would not happen in this decent building.

But nothing happened and they reached their landing without incident. Ursula fumbled with the key in her trembling hands until Tom took it from her and said, "Calm down, sweetheart. It's just your family."

Just my family. My mother will not be amused.

Her mother shouted from the kitchen, "You're late, Ursula. Dinner is ready."

She took a courageous step into the lion's den, Tom's comforting presence right behind her. The entire family was assembled around the kitchen table about to have dinner.

"Mutter, I have—" All heads jerked around, gaping openmouthed at Tom, who looked quite dashing in his dress uniform. Ursula's voice creaked off and refused further service. Thankfully, Tom came to her aid.

"Frau Klausen, please forgive this unannounced visit, but we came to tell you that your daughter has graciously agreed to marry me."

"I thought that wasn't allowed?" Jan blurted out, which earned him a glower from his grandmother.

"In fact, it wasn't until today." Tom beamed at the family

and Ursula saw that all of them sat thunderstruck, unable to move.

"I heard there are rather stiff requirements to getting an intermarriage application approved," Peter finally said.

"There are," Tom answered. "But they're not really that hard to fulfill. Apart from a security and background check, a medical certificate, and a certificate of good character signed by a relevant official for the prospective wife, the hardest thing will be that we have to wait at least six months from the date of application, during which I'll have to return to England for at least three weeks."

Ursula leaned against him. Three weeks without him? He hadn't mentioned that part to her.

"Well then, congratulations!" Peter said and stood to slap Tom on his shoulder and hug the future bride. Evie beamed at Tom, Anna and Jan were genuinely happy for them and even Mutter managed to smile and mumble something similar to congratulations.

Lotte was the only one who couldn't hide the sadness in her eyes, as she must be thinking of her boyfriend Johann, who was suffering somewhere in a POW camp in Russia.

"He'll come back to you soon, you'll see." Ursula tried to cheer up her sister, because she couldn't stand anyone being sad on this happy day.

CHAPTER 47: LOTTE

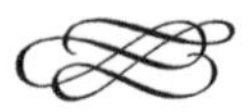

Berlin, October 1946

Lotte watched enviously how Ursula and Tom fell deeper in love with every passing day. Since they had officially applied for an intermarriage license, Mutter had grudgingly agreed that Tom was allowed to spend time in the apartment – although never the night. Lotte laughed at her mother's bigotry. The two of them already had a child together, for God's sake.

Thankfully, she herself was too busy with her studies at the university and her part-time job to dwell much on missing and worrying about Johann. She wrote him a letter every month and delivered it to the Red Cross office, although she never received anything in return.

By now the older woman there knew Lotte well and only shook her head slightly when she saw her again. Lotte wasn't the only one. There were tens of thousands of women like her clinging to the hope that their men would one day return from captivity.

The Western Allies – except for the French – had released big batches of POWs already, but from the Soviet Union, only a few had returned. In general, those who had were more dead than alive, unable to work and thus of no use to the Soviets.

She sat on the sofa, hanging after her thoughts of the few happy weeks she'd had with Johann. Perhaps her fellow students were right and she should move on. It wasn't as if she and Johann were married or even promised to each other.

A deep sigh escaped her and she turned her attention again to the law text lying on her lap. Some time later she heard a soft knock on the door. Her first thought was that Jan had forgotten his keys again, but then she shook her head. Her nephew's knock was loud and blustery.

She put the law text aside, glad for the distraction from the dry subject and opened the door. It was like déjà vu and she stumbled backward from the impact. The emaciated man standing in front of her had the same bedraggled appearance as Karsten, who'd brought her news about Johann's whereabouts in the beginning of this year. But this man was much older – and – it wasn't until he raised his voice and all but fell into her arms that she recognized him.

"Oh my God, Father. What did they do to you?"

"Lotte. Look at you. You've become a woman." Tears sprung from his eyes and he stumbled. She caught him in her arms. Her strong father, who used to dwarf his daughter, now felt light as a feather. She might as well have carried him to the sofa as if he were her child and not the other way round.

"Sit. I can't believe you're here." Her own eyes filled with tears. "Mutter will be overjoyed. She never gave up hope that you'd return."

"Frida… where is she?"

"Queuing up for food." Lotte patted her father's shoulder, feeling the bones protruding from the leathery skin, and said, "Speaking of food. Are you hungry?"

"Very." He closed his eyes, seemingly exhausted by the few words they'd exchanged.

Lotte got up to bring him a glass of water and a big chunk of bread with the rest of their cheese. Everyone else would have to go hungry tonight.

He was still chewing on the bread when the door opened and Mutter came in with Jan in tow. She looked at the stinking, dirty, bedraggled man on her immaculate sofa for an instant, dropped the grocery bags, rushed over and fell on her knees in front of him.

"Georg. You're back. You're back. You made it. You're really here with me. Is this a dream?" she murmured again and again.

Lotte decided to give them some privacy. She picked up the dropped groceries and then nodded at Jan to follow her into the kitchen where she closed the door behind them.

"Who is that?" Jan asked.

"My father."

"He looks really bad. Even worse than my own father when he was liberated."

Lotte busied her hands with putting away the groceries. Her nephew had not yet learned to conceal his thoughts behind polite remarks. "That's because he was in Russian captivity for five years."

"Five years?" Jan whistled through his teeth. "Nobody survives five years in a Russian camp. Your father is a hero."

It was meant as a compliment, but Lotte's heart froze with the icy chill his words brought with them. Johann had already spent one and a half years in Russian captivity. And she had no way of knowing whether he was still alive. Except for the stubborn voice inside her saying that he couldn't be dead, couldn't fail in his promise to return to her.

One day.

Father was much too frail, sick and weak to contribute to the household. Mutter cared for him almost around the clock, with short reprieves when their daughters, and especially trained nurse Anna, pitched in.

But winter was approaching soon and it was foreseeable that rations would be reduced again, because there simply wasn't enough food to go around. According to the farming association, this year's harvest had been the worst in over a hundred years. Naturally, the war they'd endured was to blame for a great portion of that with devastated landscapes and lack of farm workers. But the unbearably hot summer with little rain aggravated the situation even further.

Peter had alerted the family to start scouting for coal, wood, or anything at all, to heat the apartment during the cold winter months. And since heating material was so hard to come by – even with Tom's help – he'd also declared that from now on they couldn't use the kitchen stove for cooking, except on the weekends.

The living room was the only place they were allowed to heat. Lotte despised her brother-in-law every morning for these tyrannical rules when she had to get up before dusk in the chilly apartment. But the year progressed and winter arrived with exceptional brutality, making it one of the coldest winters of the past one hundred years.

As early as November the thermometer fell below freezing temperatures and many families had used up their coal by mid-December and froze in the cold houses. Hundreds of Berliners died daily from what they called the *White Death*, the merciless cold taking the lives of those who were too weakened to resist.

By that time, Lotte was immensely grateful for Peter's foresight that gave them at least one moderately warm room. The entire family of eight had moved their bedding into the living room and slept there, huddled together. Her father, though, had caught a bad case of pneumonia and, after him being hospitalized for weeks, they had to make a decision.

"He won't survive the winter in Berlin. You should send him to the country," Anna said, her fists on her hips.

"I won't let him leave again," Mutter said.

The two of them had argued at length over the topic when Ursula chimed in with a sensible solution. "Look, Mutter. Why don't you call Aunt Lydia and ask her if the two of you can live with her?"

"I can't possibly impose on my sister like this," Mutter said, too proud to ask her sister for help.

"At least for a while," Lotte pleaded.

"She doesn't have room. Since Ursula and Richard moved out, the Amis have ordered her to take one displaced soldier and one refugee couple." There was a short silence in the room.

"What about Richard?" Lotte suddenly asked.

"What about him? He's fine." Mother looked at Lotte with confusion.

Ursula, though, understood Lotte's way of thinking and came to her aid. "I'm sure he'd be delighted to have you live with him."

Lotte thought that was a stark exaggeration and he'd in fact make his sisters pay for the grandiose idea of having his parents move in with him. But sometimes sacrifices had to be made.

"It's, in fact, the perfect solution." Anna's eyes lit up. She and Peter had been sharing their room with Jan since Father had returned and she yearned to have some privacy with her husband again. "I'm sure he and Katrina will love to have help with little Jarek and you can finally get to know your grandson."

Mutter smiled at the mention of Jarek. "Well, yes. We shall go to live with Richard, but only until the winter is over."

"And who's going to tell him?" Lotte whispered to Ursula.

"Mutter, of course. Since it was her idea."

Lotte turned to look at her sister. "Since when have you become such a scheming woman?"

"Since Tom and I had to hide from the world."

CHAPTER 48: TOM

Northolt, January 1947

Tom returned to England for his leave. His application to marry a German woman had made the rounds on his home base and he dreaded the saucy jokes his comrades would crack.

Willie caught up to him the moment he left his aircraft. "Hey, Tom. How's life in Berlin?"

"Good, old chap. Very good." Tom grinned at his friend and former superior. "How about you?"

"Same old same old. I have to warn you, news about your imminent marriage shocked the hell out of the chaps. I mean, it's not every day one of us wants to marry an enemy national."

"Ex-enemy national," Tom corrected him.

"Still, a gutsy move. When will I finally get to meet her?" Willie asked.

"About that…" Tom hesitated for a moment. Willie was

his best friend, but he was still nervous to ask. "... will you be my best man?"

"Me?" The question knocked the breath from Willie's lungs.

"Yes, you? Or do you see anyone else standing around?"

"Wow... well... wow... I mean... sure. I'd love to. So you're going to tie the knot over here?"

"Hmmm... no. Ursula won't get a visa to come here, at least not until we're married."

"So, you want me to go to Berlin? How? When?" Willie seemed overwhelmed with the news.

Tom chuckled. "You climbed so far up the ladder you've forgotten how to fly a kite?"

Willie punched him in the chest. "Of course not, but I can't just use our craft for personal purposes."

"Since you're the boss around here, you can easily assign yourself one of the missions to Berlin." Tom grinned. "Or you could ask one of your minions to give you a ride on the jump seat. I'm sure the lads would like that, having the boss looking over their shoulder."

"They would fight for the honor..." Willie laughed. "I'll find a way; just tell me the exact date at least two weeks in advance. By the way, will your parents attend?"

Tom's face fell. "I haven't exactly told them."

"You... haven't told them... what?"

"That I'm going to marry Ursula. The last time I mentioned her, they were less than amused."

"I can imagine." Willie leaned against the wall, studying his friend's face. "I don't even want to imagine your mother's face when you present her with a fait accompli."

"Me, neither." Tom shrugged, pushing the anxiety away

that crept into his bones. For God's sake, he was twenty-eight years old, had served years in the Royal Air Force, survived hundreds of sorties during the war, and braved the Gestapo. He shouldn't be afraid of his own mother.

But he was.

He knew she wouldn't like his news one bit. He came from an affluent family with a long history of both military and political service to their country. None of his family members harbored any sympathy for the Germans.

"I'm leaving to spend my leave with them as we speak."

"Good luck. You'll need it." Willie grinned. "If things get really bad, give me a call and I can assemble a rescue mission."

"Thanks, mate!" Tom bid his goodbyes, thinking that Willie was the best friend he could ask for. That daredevil would even be willing to face Tom's mother and tear him from her clutches.

Tom caught a bus to his parents' house in London, giving the housekeeper a warm greeting when she let him into the foyer.

"It's good to have you home, sir."

"It's good to be back on English soil, Teresa. Are the parents around?"

"They are in the library having their afternoon tea. Would you like me to bring some for you?"

Tom nodded. "Thanks. I'll run my bags up to my room first and get changed. I'm off base for the next week and it will be a pleasure to wear something other than my uniform."

"I understand; however, you do look rather dashing in it."

"Thank you," Tom told her with a wink. He headed up the stairs to his room and made short work of unpacking his belongings and changing into a pair of trousers and a plain button-down shirt. He headed for the library, pushing the doors open just as Teresa finished setting up another cup and saucer. "Thank you."

"Of course."

"Mother. Sir." He greeted his mother with a kiss on each cheek and then shook his father's hand.

"Welcome home, son. Did you have a good flight?"

"Just like normal. Anything new been going on around here?"

"Not really. It's cold. It's damp. It's drizzling outside. It's January in London."

"Point taken." Tom chuckled. "The weather in Berlin hasn't been much better. They say it's been one of the coldest winters in a century."

His parents didn't seem to be too interested in talking about Berlin so he spent a few minutes asking about their various hobbies and interests. When their tea was almost over, he decided there was no time like the present to tell them about his upcoming marriage.

"The rules over in Germany have been changing," he started out the conversation.

"How so?" his father asked, giving him a lead-in.

"Well, the fraternization rules started changing more than a year ago, allowing British servicemen to interact with Germans in public places."

"From what I hear there are numerous of your peers who are interacting with German women in very non-public places," his mother said in derision.

"That's true. I personally find the practice appalling. Some of the men I know who have wives and fiancées back here also have two or three mistresses scattered around Berlin and Germany."

"They should be ashamed of themselves. No English lady would ever act so brazenly or with such a lack of modesty," his mother said, sipping more of her tea.

"Not all German women are hussies and not all English women have obeyed the polite rules of society." Tom tried to find a way to return to his plan instead of discussing the virtues of English women over German women.

"Those rules are there to help distinguish the British from Johnny foreigner who knows no better," his mother informed him.

"I assume you consider all Germans in that class?"

"Of course. What do they know of polite Society, or how to conduct themselves in a variety of circumstances?"

"Mother, they are not uncouth Neanderthals. The Germans actually date back before the English as far as customs and protocol go."

"An English lady knows her place. She tends to the children, her home, her gardens, and her clubs. She is generous with her praise and looks for ways to bless those less fortunate with whom she comes into contact."

Tom looked at his mother with disbelief on his face. "Are you listening to yourself? There are so many things wrong with what you just said."

"Tom," his father cautioned him.

"No, this needs to be said. You didn't tend to your children, you hired a nanny, tutors, and a cook to do so. Neither did you tend to your home. Teresa did that, along with the maids she directed before the war. We used to have gardeners who tended to the grounds. You do attend your clubs, but I'm not sure anything productive ever comes out of those meetings."

"What on earth..." His mother's expression would be almost comical if it weren't blazing red with anger.

He held up a hand between them. "As for being generous with your praise, I've never witnessed you praise the household staff." Tom knew he should keep his mouth shut, but his mother's snobbish opinions irked him.

"The way to get better service is to let those in your employ know the areas where they can improve," his mother said.

"So, no one has ever done something in a manner that deserved a compliment? As for blessing those that are less fortunate than yourself, you and father do a remarkable job of being altruistic, but always through father's solicitors."

His father put in, "We have been blessed with enough money and resources to provide jobs for all the things you just mentioned. Don't fault your mother or me for that."

Tom sighed. "I don't. I was just trying to make a point that the British aren't the only people on the planet who can be considered good people."

His father observed him and Tom met his gaze. "I've asked Ursula to marry me."

"No!" His mother gasped, covering her mouth with her hands. His father's jaw clenched tight. "Don't ruin your life, Tom!"

"I love her. We've already applied for approval of an intermarriage, and should be granted the permission within a month."

"I forbid it," his father told him in a stern voice.

"Tom, you can't be serious. You'd embarrass us this way?"

"If you knew her, you'd see she's not in the least bit embarrassing."

His father shook his head, regret coloring his expression. "See what you're saying, son? You haven't even introduced her to your parents."

"They aren't exactly handing out travel passes to Germans these days. But I invite you to visit Berlin and get to know her."

"Over my dead body will I set foot in Germany." His mother turned away, indicating the conversation was over.

"I was hoping you could support me in my choice of a wife," Tom said to his father.

"Son, you have a responsibility to this family…"

"And what is that? I've done my bit. I have defended my country with a lot of personal sacrifice, if I may say so myself. We won the war, now it's time to move forward into a better future. A future filled with peace, friendship and understanding."

"There can never be friendship with the Germans." His mother glowered at Tom before she turned toward her husband. "Thomas, would you please accompany me to your study?"

Tom stared at their backs. This hadn't gone over the way he'd wished it would. It tore his heart apart, but he was going to marry Ursula, whether his parents approved or not.

CHAPTER 49: URSULA

Berlin, March 1947

The small, relatively new and plain church had weathered the war without much damage, except for the broken stained glass windows that had been replaced with simple transparent ones. The outside had been painted in hundreds of hours of work with white color during the last year, and it shone in the spring sun.

Ursula grabbed the hand of Anna, her bridesmaid, as she knocked on the door of the attached rectory and waited for the priest to open it. Pfarrer Bernau wasn't any more, but his successor was progressive enough to marry a Catholic woman to an Anglican man. It wasn't officially condoned by the Vatican, but the pope was far away.

She fondly thought about Pfarrer Bernau, who'd helped her through difficult times of inner torment when she hadn't known what was right and what was wrong. During the Nazi era, morals had been swept upside down and she had struggled with what she did best: follow the law and obey like any good citizen.

The door opened, and the young priest asked her inside. Just as he was about to close the door behind the two sisters, Lotte dashed across the lawn.

"Glad you could make it." Ursula smiled. Nothing would dampen her mood today, not even her tardy sister.

"Sorry, I'm late, but Evie and I had to…" Lotte caught her breath and jumped up the stairs with the broadest grin. "It's a surprise, actually."

Inside they went through the instructions one last time and then the priest left them alone to change into his sacramental vestments.

Suddenly the air in the room cooled off and a shudder racked her body and she asked her sister, "What if he changes his mind?"

"The priest? He's just going to change," Lotte said, still catching her breath.

"No, Tom."

"Tom?" Anna shook her head. "After waiting for you four years and jumping through a thousand hoops? Why on earth would he change his mind just when you're finally about to walk down the aisle?"

"You have nothing to worry about. That man is so head over heels in love with you, he'll never change his mind," Lotte added.

Ursula knew they were right, but after all the hardships, the red tape, the waiting, the fighting, the enmities, the shaming, the despair… she simply was at the end of her strength and wouldn't be able to survive another setback.

"By the way, neither of you can change your minds at

this point. We just came from the registry office where you signed your legal vows. This here..." Lotte pointed at the door leading into the church. "...this is only the romantic add-on."

Anna laughed, but Ursula felt the uncertainty rising in her heart and shook her head. "The registry office, that was only some piece of paper. Something for the government. But this here feels like the real wedding...Do you think I'm doing the right thing?" she asked, thinking of the many judgmental looks and remarks she'd had to endure from compatriots. The shameful names strangers had showered her and Evie with. The open hostility on the streets. The way the neighbors looked away when they saw her.

"Are you having second thoughts?" Lotte gasped.

"She's just nervous," Anna said. "Every bride is nervous at her wedding."

"No. Yes. Maybe. I mean, I do love him with every fiber of my soul, but I hate to be the cause of wagging tongues."

"They'll get over it. It's not like you're the only one to fall in love with a British soldier," Anna said.

"In ten years nobody will care two hoots about it," Lotte added.

"In ten years?" Ursula almost broke out in tears, unsure whether she could withstand the constant broadsides for that long.

Anna stared at Lotte and took Ursula's hand. "It'll change once you get to live with Tom."

Ursula nodded. She was eagerly looking forward to that bit. Living together like a real family, eating meals together, saying goodbye with a kiss in the morning, waiting for Tom to return after work. Cooking his meals. Seeing him read a book to Evie before bedtime. Sharing the bed every night and waking up in each other's arms every morning. That's what she'd been dreaming about for such a long time.

Happiness hovered just at the end of her fingertips. She simply had to gather her courage around her like a cloak and take it.

"Come on. You don't want to keep your groom waiting," Anna said and helped her to drape the hat with the veil across her hair and face.

There wasn't a mirror in the anteroom to check her appearance one last time, but both her sisters assured her that she looked amazing in the smart cream business costume. She'd chosen it with the notion that she'd be able to wear it as a Sunday dress after the wedding.

Anna had tortured her with rollers and the curling iron for hours to put Ursula's golden hair into an elegant updo hairstyle with single corkscrew curls hanging down from her temples. She'd even *found* a brand new nacre-colored eye shadow and matching lipstick.

"You look amazing," Lotte said and handed her the long cream gloves, the only piece of extravagance in the bride's outfit. The three sisters left the rectory to enter the church through the main door.

Mutter was already waiting for them with Evie holding her hand. Evie looked adorable in her new dress, embellished with light blue ribbons made from pieces of parachute silk Tom had brought them. Her golden hair shone like a halo as the sunlight hit it.

"Everyone is already inside, and Richard is waiting for you," Mutter said. "I wish your father could be here with us." Her father had been too fragile to make the long journey to

Berlin, but Mutter, Richard and Katrina plus their two children had arrived yesterday. In the absence of her father, it would be Richard's privilege to giver her away to her new husband.

"Are you ready?" Mutter asked, apparently quite nervous herself.

"I am." Ursula turned to walk toward Richard, but her mother held her back.

"I…it was hard for me to understand how you could fall in love with one of *them*." Mutter looked up at the sky that had been filled with deadly bombers for so many years. "But all I want is for you to be happy. And Tom seems like a decent man."

"Thank you, Mutter." A burden lifted from Ursula's heart. While her mother had made her peace with Tom, she'd never actually said anything nice about him before. So far, her acceptance of him had been rooted in the fact that having an English son-in-law was the lesser evil to having a single mother for a daughter.

Lotte took Evie by the hand and walked away. Ursula's eyes followed her daughter and she noticed the basket swinging in her hand. A smile crossed her lips. So that was the big surprise and the reason why Lotte had been late.

Anna and Ursula approached Richard, who looked quite smart in the black suit he'd borrowed from his father. It brought memories of old times when they'd still been children.

"Ready, sister?" Richard grinned as he held out his arm for her.

First were Lotte and Evie. Evie's eyes danced with

excitement as her tiny hands scattered the wild flowers she and Lotte had picked earlier with great diligence.

Next came Ursula on Richard's arm, followed by Anna. When the door to the church opened and she stepped inside, she involuntarily gasped.

Apart from her family – Tom's parents had refused to travel to Berlin – the church was filled not only with friends, but also with a huge number of British soldiers who looked quite dashing in their dress uniforms.

For a moment she went dizzy, but only until she caught Tom's eye; he was waiting for her in front of the altar, accompanied by his best man, William Huntley.

Tom was by far the most handsome of all the good-looking men in the church. His eyes never wavered from his bride and the love she saw shining in his eyes whisked all her doubts and sorrows away. As long as he loved her, she'd overcome all the harassment and struggle thrown her way.

She reached Tom and he took her hand, giving it a good squeeze and whispering, "You look gorgeous."

Ursula blinked. She wouldn't succumb to tears, not even happy ones, because she feared for her makeup.

The priest began the ceremony and she focused her attention on him, blocking out the muffled noises of crying in the first rows. Why did everyone cry at a wedding?

"Will you, Tom Westlake, take this woman, Ursula Hermann, to be your lawful wife? Will you love, cherish and protect her, from this day forward, in good times and in bad times, in sickness and health, until death do you part?"

Tom's gaze took her breath away and she barely heard his answer "I will" through the rushing in her ears. He slipped a golden wedding band with a tiny diamond ring on her ring finger, and suddenly all her nerves were gone. This was the culmination of a love story that should never have happened, but persisted through all odds, hardships and obstacles.

"Will you, Ursula Hermann, take this man, Tom Westlake to be your lawful husband? Will you love, cherish and care for him, from this day forward, in good times and in bad times, in sickness and health, until death do you part?"

"I will." She put the simple golden wedding band on his ring finger.

"Hereby I declare you wife and husband in the name of God. May your marriage be prosperous, fruitful and full of joy," the priest said and then added with a smile, "You may now kiss the bride."

Tom pressed a sweet kiss against her lips and murmured, "You'll get the real one once we're alone."

Ursula's cheeks heated and she hoped that the onlookers assumed it was because of the excitement of the wedding ceremony. Together they walked out of the church, an unprecedented lightness making her hover a few inches above the floor.

The couple received congratulations from every guest. Ursula did her best to remember the names of Tom's comrades, until she widened her eyes in shock at the sight of a familiar face.

He must have noticed her reaction, because he said with a grin, "Not to worry, I'm not here to arrest you."

"Hey, Ken, don't scare my wife." Tom shook hands with the MP who'd arrested them both more than a year ago. "If it weren't for you, we probably wouldn't be here."

It was true. Ursula didn't even want to imagine what

would have happened if he hadn't been so exceptionally understanding and kind.

"Thank you," she told him. "We will always be indebted to you. How can we ever return the favor?"

"Come and visit us when you're in London," Ken said.

"You leaving us?" Tom asked.

"Yes. I'm finally going home. Can't wait to see my darlings every day." Ken beamed with delight and Ursula certainly could relate to the feeling. She leaned against Tom for a moment, relishing the fact that she was now his wife. Finally.

CHAPTER 50: TOM

London, June 1948

Exactly one year after their wedding ceremony, Tom's beautiful wife had given birth to a baby boy. They'd named him Thomas after his father, in the hopes his parents would reconcile with the fact that he'd married a German woman.

He'd visited them twice in the past year when he'd been on overnight missions to Northolt. His mother, though, remained adamant that she didn't want to know anything of his "other family" as she liked to call Ursula and their children. She wouldn't even let him rave about Evie.

As the tensions in Berlin between the former ally Stalin and the Western victorious powers ratcheted up, Tom decided it was high time his parents came to terms with their daughter-in-law. If the Cold War escalated, the British might have to evacuate Berlin and he and his mates might be sent home to England. If that happened, he wanted to know Ursula had a family she could count on; otherwise she'd be alone in a foreign country.

The birth of little Thomas was the perfect reason to coerce his parents into finally getting to know Ursula and Evie.

"What will your parents say?" Ursula asked once more as the cab drove them from the base airport to his parents' estate.

"Well, they weren't at all happy when I told them we wanted to come to visit. But the fact that they agreed is a good sign." He banked on his mother going soft over her two grandchildren the way all grandmothers in the world did. "Mother is eager to get to know her grandchildren."

"What if she doesn't like them?"

"Don't worry," Tom told her, reaching across to take her hand. "Who could resist our children? Thomas is such a cute baby and as for Evie, you'll see my parents won't have a prayer."

Ursula looked at their daughter. Evie was full of questions about anything and everything. She had adapted well to life as a family and adored her baby brother. But his family suffered from the cold treatment the English wives living on the base gave them.

Despite finally being Mrs. Westlake, Ursula's life definitely wasn't full of roses – and he felt guilty for it. As the cab took the long way to the Westlake estate Tom worried about Ursula's fear about the upcoming meeting with his parents.

"They will come around, eventually," he said after

another gaze at her tense facial expression. He faked a confidence he didn't possess. His mother held rigid opinions. The car drove up to his parents' house and he helped Ursula with the baby in her arms, while Evie jumped from the car all by herself. She'd been cooped up on first a plane, and then a car, and needed some time to stretch her legs.

"Tom?" He heard his mother's voice coming from the front doors.

He waved saying, "Hello, Mother." He reached for Ursula's hand and walked toward his parents. "Mother. Sir. I'd like to introduce you to Ursula, my wife. And this is Thomas, your grandson."

His mother's lips broke into a smile at the sight of her grandson and she murmured, "Isn't he a precious little darling."

"It's nice to meet you, Mrs. Westlake," Ursula said.

Ursula's English had improved in the last year while living on the military base, but she still had that godawful German accent that betrayed her with every word. Evie, though, who had turned four this month, spoke English like a native and even corrected her mother at times.

"Yes, well… come inside." His mother started to turn her back but then Evie poked her head out from behind Tom's knees.

"Oh, you must be Eveline?" Mrs. Westlake glanced at her son and asked, "Does she at least speak English?"

Evie giggled and made something that looked like a curtsy, "Yes, Grandmother, my dad speaks only English with me. My mother, she manages the language too, but sometimes she makes mistakes."

Tom saw that his mother had to struggle not to laugh.

Evie really was a precocious little girl. In this instant he knew that no matter how much of a fuss Mother and Father might put up, they wouldn't be able to resist the little sprite of a girl.

"We call her Evie." Tom looked down and watched Evie charm his mother with her impish smile and bright-eyed wonder.

There was a pause and then Tom's mother smiled. "Do you like sweets?"

"I love sweets. But my mother says it's not good for my teeth."

"Well," Tom's mother cast a glance at her daughter-in-law and smiled, "Don't tell your mother, but in my house, you're allowed to eat sweets. Do you want to come with me into the kitchen?"

Evie jumped with joy and Tom whispered into Ursula's ear, "See, I told you."

Over the next days, his mother completely fell in love with Evie and Thomas. She even softened up to Ursula, who did her best to impress a positive image on her.

"How do you like living on the base?" his mother asked.

Tom had a moment of worry that Ursula would start complaining, but instead, she smiled and talked about how nice the accommodations were and how pleasant the other women were. Which they were, to each other. Not to Ursula, though, and neither to Evie.

But rather than disparage them, Ursula actually found a way to speak kindly about them to his parents, and for that, he loved her even more.

When his mother offered to take a stroll through the

gardens with Ursula, Tom smiled, confident the women in his life would learn to like each other.

His father approached him as the women left the room. "I'm still not convinced that you wouldn't have fared better with an Englishwoman, but as it is... it's plain to see that you love her, and she loves you. And your Evie is such a well-behaved child, she'll blend in perfectly."

"Thanks, Dad. That means a lot. About..." Tom wanted to sound out whether his father was open to the idea of supporting Ursula and their children if anything awful happened in Berlin.

His father though had already noticed that something was wrong and said, "Now that we're alone, tell me what is really going on with Ursula and the other women. Your mother may have bought that drivel she was spouting but the smile on her lips never reached her eyes."

Tom lost his bravado and he shook his head. "They hate her. Because she's German." *Just like you did.* "They won't talk to her. They don't include Evie in any of the activities. I'm gone so much that she's alone most of the time. They don't even give her a chance to get to know her..."

His father frowned. "I'm afraid we did the same and I'm not very proud of that. But maybe it's time to leave the hurts of the past behind and start a better future. A future of understanding, if not between our nations as a whole, then at least on a personal level." He paused and looked at his son. "I haven't talked to your mother about this. But both of us wish to be closer to our grandchildren. And if your wife agrees, she and the children are welcome to stay with us."

"You would do that?" Tom almost toppled over at his

father's words. Not in his wildest dreams had he imagined his father would offer that.

"Don't look so surprised. I'm sure you came here counting on the charms of your offspring to wrap your mother around their little fingers. It worked. Evie has not only your mother, but also me and Teresa, under her spell. And baby Thomas...what woman can resist a baby drooling saliva all over her?"

"Indeed, I wanted to mend the rift. I thought when you found out just how happy Ursula makes me, you'd give her a chance."

"So will you ask her? She can live in the guest house so she has her own space. And you've been flying in and out enough that you might ask to spend your leave days over here instead of in Berlin."

"Thank you for the generous offer. I'll speak with her about it..."

"Speak with whom about what?" his mother asked, stepping back into the library.

Tom hid his smirk, as his mother's question had been far from the proper behavior of an Englishwoman. "I was sharing with father how difficult living on base is for Ursula and the children. He suggested they stay here in the guest house."

She sent her husband a scolding stare, but Tom knew his mother well enough to know that she was trying to keep up appearances. In fact, both of her grandchildren and even Ursula had won over her heart during the past days.

The discussion was tabled for the moment, but several days later, Tom found an unexpected ally in the least probable person alive: Josef Stalin.

He received a telephone call from the base in Northolt that his leave had been canceled and he was to return to Berlin immediately. The day before, Stalin had ordered electricity cut off to the Western part of Berlin. Furthermore, all land and water connections for transporting goods and persons between Berlin and the Western sectors were severed.

General Lucius D. Clay, in charge of the U.S. Occupation Zone in Germany, had come to an agreement with his British counterpart General Sir Brian Robertson. It was a daring undertaking, but they would embark on a joint airlift to provide the people in Berlin with the food, medicine, coal, and petrol required for survival. Every available pilot was ordered to report for duty immediately.

Even Tom's mother agreed that she could not let Ursula and the children return to a Berlin cut off from the rest of the world – and possibly fall under the Soviet thumb. Thus, it was decided that Ursula would stay with Tom's parents in England and he would use any time off to visit them.

He just hoped Ursula would have an easier life here with his parents' connections shielding her from the hate and harassment she'd endured at RAF Gatow.

EPILOGUE

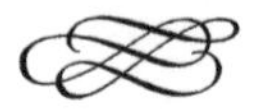

Boston, Summer 1950

"Anna, Anna, they are coming!" Jan pointed with excitement at the group of people disembarking from the ocean liner.

Peter and Anna stood side by side with Peter's adult son and their two young children. As they waited for their relatives to pass immigration, her mind turned to the past.

Two years prior, just as Anna had finished her doctorate at the Berlin University, her mentor, Professor Scherer, had been offered a professorship at the prestigious Harvard University in America. When he'd asked her to come with him as his right hand, she'd jumped at the opportunity. Professor Scherer had passed away of a heart attack recently and Harvard University had offered Anna his position.

Leaving a Germany in ruins hadn't exactly been hard, but not seeing her sisters had been. Letters and the rare – expensive – telephone calls couldn't make up for the loss of familial intimacy.

Peter, though, had been nothing but delighted to leave the country he'd never really liked and escape to America. There, nothing reminded him of the Nazis and the hardships he'd had to endure at their hands. He supported Anna every step of the way, which wasn't natural or even expected. For a while she'd been the sole breadwinner of their family and he'd even stayed at home to raise their two common children. That alone made her love him even more.

Just before they had set foot on the ocean liner bringing them to Boston, her brother Richard had called in with surprising news. Rachel Epstein had applied – and been granted – an immigration visa to Israel and in fall 1948 she and her three younger siblings had left Kleindorf.

The months leading up to that date had been full of activities for Richard and his family, because Rachel had offered to sell her farm to him. Richard had scrambled for money to conclude the transaction. With the goodwill of so many people including family, relatives and friends, he'd finally been able to gather enough of a down payment to secure a loan from the bank. He had paid Rachel what the farm was worth and taken her to the train leaving for the harbor in Genoa. It had been a bittersweet farewell, because they most probably wouldn't see Rachel again.

Anna's little sticking-his-nose-in-a-book brother had officially become a farmer.

Times surely had changed. Even her spunky, impulsive

sister, Lotte, had settled down and worked for a well-known law firm after graduating from law school with honors. Her employer specialized in human rights, fighting to return property and belongings to the victims of the Nazis.

Lotte a lawyer. Anna shook her head. She wouldn't have believed it, if anyone had told her five years ago.

But the best news was that Peter's brother, Stan, his wife, Agnieska, and their three children were coming to America as well – for good. The more the communists transformed Poland into a puppet state behind the Iron Curtain, the more discontented Stan had grown. Despite Agnieska's efforts to rein in his temper, he'd been constantly in trouble with the authorities. It would only be a matter of time until they sent him to a Siberian Gulag, even with one leg.

Peter and Stan had sent letters back and forth and diligently worked with the authorities both in America and in Poland to finally make the impossible happen.

Tomorrow the family reunion would be complete when Ursula and Tom arrived with their two children on an airplane from London. Ursula had adapted well to the life in England and had even become friends with her mother-in-law.

Anna looked forward to meeting her again and seeing little Evie, who had just turned six years old. How fast the time had flown in the past years.

She wished her parents had been able to make the journey. But her father's health had never truly recovered from his ordeal in Russian captivity and her mother refused to leave him alone for such a long time. They lived in a small house in Mindelheim and often visited with Richard or

Aunt Lydia, who'd birthed another three children, raising the number to nine.

It seemed everyone in the family had picked up the pieces after the war, snapping them together to create a new and happy life. Except for Lotte, who still waited for Johann to return from captivity in Russia.

Johann's experiences in Russian captivity feature in the next book. Order Endless Ordeal: https://kummerow.info/book/endless-ordeal

AUTHOR'S NOTES

Dear Reader,

Thank you so much for reading Together at Last.

War Girl Ursula was the first book in my War Girl series. Since then many of you have asked me for a happy end for Ursula and Tom. So here it is.

Sorry, to have kept you (and them) waiting for such a long time, but I couldn't bring them together before the end of the war.

The difficult times didn't miraculously stop with the German surrender. All of Europe continued to be in dire straits with famines, destroyed living spaces, lack of heating material during an exceptionally harsh winter, and millions of displaced people. Animosities between nations that had been cultivated for more than a decade were still running high.

There are countless stories of women all over Europe who fell in love with a man from another nation. Many times they were shamed, ridiculed, and even punished for collaboration.

For many reasons the Western Allies were adamant in keeping their soldiers apart from the German population, which was quite difficult as you can imagine. The soldiers were mostly young men, away from home for the first time, and intent on having a good time after the cruel fighting.

On the other hand, there were young women who'd lost everything and fought for raw survival. A comparatively wealthy and well-fed Allied soldier could provide food and many other things. Oftentimes the relationships of necessity turned into true love.

In the movie *A Foreign Affair* by Billie Wilder, Marlene Dietrich summarizes the situation of the German Fräuleins quite well. She and an American congresswoman are competing for the same American officer and she lays a trap for the other woman, but first apologizes to her. She says something along these lines: *It's a ghastly thing to do, but you must understand what happened to us.*

As always, I want to give thanks to everyone who helped make this book a reality. Daniela Colleo from stunningbookcovers.com made another fantastic cover for me. My editors Tami Stark and Martin O'Hearn polished the manuscript to shine.

But my special thanks go to my English beta readers Shanti Mercer and Rachel Zaouche. They have helped me to make Tom act and sound like a Brit and not like an American.

Lyn Alexander's expertise as a former member of the Royal Canadian Air Force was invaluable. She was stationed in Germany in the 1950s and I couldn't have written a realistic scene of Tom hitching a flight with Mitch without her advice.

More thanks go to David Huntley who was crucial in finding answers to the question whether Ursula could actually have climbed into Tom's quarters. Apparently, yes. Nobody admitted to having done such a thing, but several descendants of WWII Veterans said they'd heard about similar incidents. So, there you go.

Thank you, my reader, so much for keeping me company on this exciting journey!

If you liked Together at Last (or even if you didn't) I would appreciate an honest review on the retailer of your choice.

Marion Kummerow

ALSO BY MARION KUMMEROW

Love and Resistance in WW2 Germany

Unrelenting

Unyielding

Unwavering

Turning Point (Spin-off)

War Girl Series

Downed over Germany (Prequel)

War Girl Ursula (Book 1)

War Girl Lotte (Book 2)

War Girl Anna (Book 3)

Reluctant Informer (Book 4)

Trouble Brewing (Book 5)

Fatal Encounter (Book 6)

Uncommon Sacrifice (Book 7)

Bitter Tears (Book 8)

Secrets Revealed (Book 9)

Together at Last (Book 10)

Endless Ordeal (Book 11)

Not Without My Sister (Spin-off)

Berlin Fractured

From the Ashes (Book 1)

On the Brink (Book 2)

In the Skies (Book 3)

Historical Romance

Second Chance at First Love

Find all my books here:

http://www.kummerow.info

CONTACT ME

I truly appreciate you taking the time to read (and enjoy) my books. And I'd be thrilled to hear from you!
If you'd like to get in touch with me you can do so via

Twitter:
http://twitter.com/MarionKummerow

Facebook:
http://www.facebook.com/AutorinKummerow

Website
http://www.kummerow.info

Milton Keynes UK
Ingram Content Group UK Ltd.
UKHW011829300823
427775UK00001B/141

9 783948 865078